MOURNINGTIDE
The Second Book
of The Memphis Cycle

By D M Wilder

A broken heart is a terrible burden…
Even for the most powerful man in the world.

Prologue

Eighteen years have passed since Seti commanded the Royal Army in The City of Refuge. Now he rules Egypt as King.

While Seti is far away to the south, his eldest son is ambushed and killed through a tragic mistake. His family sends word to him, but it is never delivered, and Seti returns to the news that his son is dead and sealed away in a tomb. With sorrow weighing heavily upon his heart, and yet constantly under his subjects' gaze, Seti's grief threatens to tear him apart.

He seeks anonymity in a small village of workmen near the Valley of the Kings, only to learn that marauders from the western deserts have been attacking the town, which is helpless to resist them. During that summer, the greatest warrior-king of that dynasty teaches the villagers the art of battle.

CONTENTS

List of Characters

Djedi..................Painter at Deir el Medineh
Henetre..............Head Woman at Deir el Medineh
Hori ....Seti's oldest grandson
Intef..................Vizier of Southern Egypt
Iset....................Eldest child of Seti
Kenamun...........Senior Foreman at Deir el Medineh
Khonsu..............Admiral of the Memphis fleet
Nakhtamun........Eldest son of Seti
Nebamun...........High Priest of Ptah
Nefer ....Woman at Deir el Medineh
Neferhotep........Junior Foreman at Deir el Medineh
Nesuptah ....Governor of Memphis
Pasenhor...........Vizier of Northern Egypt
Ptahemhat..........Commander of the Memphis Army
Ramesses...........Second son of Seti
Senwadjet..........General commanding in Canaan
Seti ....King of Egypt
Sokhari..............Guardsman in Ramesses' service
Tia ....Younger daughter of Seti
Tiyah ....Husband of Tia

I
Canaan, Reign of Seti I, Year 3

The rider drew rein at the crest of the hill and frowned down at the encampment below him. The early morning stillness magnified the neighing of horses, laughter, the throb of a drum, the clang of metal. He sat forward on his saddle pad. He could catch the spicy scent or grilling fish overlying the tang of cooking fires. ...And could he smell hot gruel?

Motion to the left-one of the large tents collapsing in a billow of stripes. He grimaced. *Breaking camp.* It was a good thing he had not spared his horse after receiving his General's summons. A hot breakfast would sit well after two days of cold porridge and onions.

A line of chariots was moving toward the gateway, the lead team, with gold-mounted harness, driven by a taller man wearing a gold circlet. The messenger grimaced again. He was just in time to make his report to Pharaoh's eldest son Nakhtamun, The Co-Regent, trying his strength in the field for the first time while his warrior father traveled to Nubia. The rider nudged his mount forward toward the gate guards.

**   **   **

Nakhtamun smoothed the reins and looped them through the chariot's rail. The sun's warmth on his shoulders provided a pleasant counterpoint to the brisk wind blowing down from the highlands. He frowned toward the west, narrowing his eyes in the light. "All right, then, General," he told the man beside him. "We can send point patrols north, since you say we will be seeing some movement in the hills now we're approaching Megiddo..." He nodded to the distant bulk of a structure just visible to the northeast. "That looks promising," he said. "A good size, I'd think. What of it?"

"That's the first of a string of fortresses stretching into Palestine," General Senwadjet said. "They border the coast. In past times they controlled the trade routes under Thutmose the Great and his heirs." The man's eyes narrowed as though he were looking into the past. "Until the Heretic and his father turned their attention elsewhere. They are all falling into ruin now."

Nakhtamun nodded. "But they may be brought back to strength without much effort. It is worth investigating." He lifted his face into the wind. *Fortresses, old wars...*

[9]

He caught a tang of salt from the ocean, west of his force. He gazed into the distance, seeing billows of dark water... He had traveled on 'The Great Green' once, when his father was Vizier of the North, sailing from Pelusium to Byblos on the Mediterranean coast.

He still thought of the journey, the sea streaming past the bow of the ship, the dance of the dolphins escorting them. He could feel the plunge and rear of *Prince of the Winds* as she surged across the waves, her sails bellying in the wind, all oars shipped. He remembered shaking his head and laughing aloud at the wind's cold, vigorous tug in his hair, feeling, just for that moment, that he belonged there, that was what he had been born to do.

He blinked at the memory and realized that it had underlain the fabric of his soul for years, lending a touch of mystery, a sweetness, never lost. Could it be recaptured? He was Co-regent; could he command Egypt's fleet? He raised his dazzled eyes to the horizon. Or perhaps he might lead an expedition of discovery deep into the south, as did the great explorers all those centuries ago. To see new sights, to bend his mind to puzzles and new information.

The elation faded and he sighed. ...Or, most likely, he would be trapped, in a lifetime of courtiers, ritual, procedure, things to do and ways to do them, to be the focus of all reverent eyes, the ornament of Egypt. Pharaoh.

He straightened and gathered the reins in his hand with a sigh. *Pharaoh. How to escape that fate?*

"Majesty!"

He blinked and looked up.

Senwadjet was approaching him, his straight brows drawn together. Was the man *never* enthusiastic about anything? "Our point riders have seen the fort, Sire. They went inside. It is open and abandoned now, but commanding the countryside."

"Does it seem like a good possibility?"

"Definitely, Sire. It's sturdy, in a good location..."

"Something to remember," Nakhtamun said. "I will include it in this evening's dispatch. Continue your sweep and report back this evening. Send some scouts to see what they can find. Bring in some of the local citizens. We can question them."

II

Nakhtamun turned to look back at the force fanning out behind him. The Company of Ptah was cresting the rise to the east, their standard flashing in the afternoon sun, leading the river of heads moving up the grassy incline. They were singing a Memphis ballad. He paused to listen and then grinned. Not the commonly known words! In fact, the verse had something to do with the lavish charms of a woman who lived beside the Nile.

His grin widened: the descriptions were very specific, and he knew the brothel that was named in the song. He shook his head, laughing. Soldiers! Storehouses of lewd information, with hearts as soft as bowls of gruel. He might be tempted, he thought, to investigate the truth of the song when he returned to Memphis.

...Or he could ask his younger brother to look into it for him. He wondered what Ramesses was doing at that moment. Hearing an embassage? Holding a child on his knee? His amusement faded to warmth. Whatever was occupying Ramessu at the moment, he was probably smiling and at ease, even as he ruled the country. *That* had come at the end of a week's worth of strong argument. Pulling rank was a dirty trick, perhaps, but it worked. Ramesses would be fine as regent, with Lord Nebamun beside him.

The land rose before him. The swell of hills reminded him of the seas on the way to Byblos.

Byblos... He raised his head to the wind, his mind back at the ocean, remembering, longing... He frowned and turned his thoughts aside. Was he truly unhappy? Or was it his trick of inserting emotions into everything?

'You should be a poet, Nakhti,' his father had said once when he had let his speech soar into emotion. *'You can imagine yourself into any situation and suffer with the sufferers, be they however far removed by time and distance!'* They had both laughed, but it was true.

"Bah!"

"Majesty?"

The voice made him start. Suti, his driver, was back from his circuit with General Senwadjet beside him.

His grin altered to a wry smile. "What did you find?" he asked.

[11]

Senwadjet was frowning. The expression eased after a moment. "Another Migdol. Deserted now, some parts crumbling..."

"Did you go inside?"

"Yes, Majesty. I took a company. We found signs of occupation within the past few months, but no later. Ashes from fires, rubbish—these Canaanites are pigs!—nothing recent. The walls are still strong, the place can be refurbished."

Nakhtamun nodded slowly. "Send my scribe to me. I will want to report to His Majesty."

** ** **

"Do you have all that?" Nakhtamun asked. He shifted in the shade of the sycamore tree and sipped from his flask of water. The senior Army Scribe, was cross-legged before him, frowning down at the papyrus stretched across his lap. He raised his head. "All of it, Sire."

"Seal it, then, and send it off. His Majesty will be interested in reading it. We need to extend our presence here." He saw that the man was hesitating, eyeing the sheet of papyrus and then frowning at his brush. "What is it, Per-Hor?" he asked.

"There's better than half a sheet left, Sire. Do you wish to say anything else?"

Nakhtamun took another sip of water and corked the flask, frowning. "Set it aside. Senwadjet is bringing in some local folk for questioning. I can include that in the report."

** ** **

The three tribesmen stared at him across the campfire that evening. Senwadjet had brought them in without undue courtesy, though he had ordered a supper for them. Nakhtamun had waited until they finished the beans and roasted meat before questioning them.

Their answers had been easy and general, though Senwadjet was frowning at some of them. Nakhtamun continued. "That fortress, now, who is occupying it?"

The tribesmen traded glances and then bowed to the ground. "There is no one there, My Lord," said the oldest, a hawk-faced man with keen eyes set into a network of fine lines. "It has been abandoned for years, with shepherds corralling their sheep there from time to time."

"Hm. Is it wrecked, then?"

"There is shelter, Majesty. The wind does not enter. the roof is not destroyed, and it has a well."

The answer made Senwadjet fold his arms.

Nakhtamun ignored him. "A well, you say? With sweet water?"

"Oh yes, Majesty. I have drunk from it many times. The roof is sound, the stones still in place. It is a fine shelter."

"I see. Interesting." Nakhtamun turned to the Sergeant at arms. "Take them away. Give them food to take with them and send them forth."

Senwadjet moved. "Did you order that we let them go, Sire?"

"They have given me the information I need." Looks exchanged; he could almost hear the man's thoughts. "Well?"

Senwadjet's eyes were fixed on the three. "We can take them with us on the march and send them on when we reach the fortress. They will serve as our guides. Once we are there and inside it, with them accompanying us, we can release them with, perhaps, some payment." His gaze had become an intense stare.

One of the prisoners took a half-step backward. "I must go home tonight!" he exclaimed in a thick patois. "The baby is coming!"

Nakhtamun considered this as the tribesmen and his staff watched him. Ramesses had a pregnant wife, and while he pretended to be confident and happy, Nakhtamun had caught an undertone of worry. He shook his head finally. "Let them go."

Senwadjet's brows drove together in an incredulous frown. "But Sir! We will house them in comfort. We can take them with us and let them depart once we are at the fortress. They can accompany us inside."

"This man says his wife needs him. We come peaceably and I have no wish to cause any hardship."

"If Your Majesty is kind enough to hear his servant," Senwadjet said with a thin smile to the three men, "I suggest we send an armed escort with this fellow to bring his wife back here. Your Majesty's private surgeon can tend her. I suspect she would get better care with him than in her own home."

"If she is pregnant," Nakhtamun said, "It would be dangerous to move her."

[13]

"If Your Majesty will deign to hear his servant," Senwadjet said, speaking with slow clarity, "This man has spoken of a pregnant wife. He is greatly troubled by worries for her safety, and yet he has abandoned her while he goes far from family and herdbeasts in order to watch us. *And,* let me add, we knew nothing of this woman's existence until perhaps ten heartbeats ago."

The older man straightened. Senwadjet looked at him.

Nakhtamun frowned. "No livestock?"

"No goats, sheep, cattle, horses. Nothing."

Nakhtamun turned away from the leader to look over his shoulder at Senwadjet. "Are you saying, General, that these three are lying?"

"I am saying, Sire, that we know nothing of these people aside from what they have told us. I am reminding Your Majesty that it was very easy for our outriders to capture them. Much of what they have told you is incorrect based on what I know personally. And I am suggesting that having this fellow pass a night away from his wife, who is obviously not in labor at the moment, else he would not have been able to tear himself from her side, will not harm anyone. They can escort us to this fortress and return to their people once we have given them leave to go."

Nakhtamun raised his head to stare at Senwadjet, who returned the gaze without any hesitation. He drew his brush through his fingers and frowned at the three tribesmen. The younger man's eyes were wide and pleading.

"Let them go."

"Sire—"

"Do as I tell you! You keep warning me of dangers that all have come to naught. We will be going with our full force, and they will regret any treachery. Go. You are dismissed."

He watched them leave and then turned back to his writing. He finished his report, including a note for Ramesses:

> *I have been thinking, Ramessu, how you would enjoy traveling here and governing these people. You have an instinct for diplomacy, odd though it seems, little brother. I would think you would thrive here, and you would have plenty of scope for rebuilding.*
>
> *I will be inspecting a fortress on the morrow. One of those built by Thutmose the Great at the*

height of his reign. I will be looking it over carefully, but the chain of fortresses, of which this is one, will be a powerful network of defenses once they are repaired. It is something to consider; I will mention it to His Majesty when I return.

I have enjoyed this time of exploration, though there have been annoyances with my staff. Time and again they have warned me of problems that subsequently did not arise.

He lowered his brush and slumped where he sat. The past two weeks had been busy, strenuous, and wonderful. But the work had exhausted him. How long had it been since he had accompanied his father on campaign? More than two years, certainly. He folded his arms and sat back, closing his eyes. His surroundings seemed to blur. The wind pushed into his tent...

He is astride a great, star-flecked horse, riding across the night sky, following the glittering 'Trail of the Crocodile' to the great beast itself. He urges the horse into a circle as he nocks an arrow. The Crocodile lunges toward him, roaring, jaws open wide, teeth glinting in the moonlight while the horse squeals and rears. He dismounts, draws the bow as the Crocodile looms above him...

He jerked awake, his heart pounding. It had been so real for a moment. He shook his head and frowned down at the papyrus, then took up his brush again.

Tomorrow should be eventful. I will inspect the fortifications and decide whether it will be worth our time to bring the fortress back to strength or to raze and rebuild it. Its location is perfect, and I hope that it is repairable. A garrison there, with access to our headquarters at Gaza, would be useful, and serve as a base to extend our holdings. I will let you know my conclusions when I write to you this evening.

Give my most respectful greetings to His Holiness and to your ladies. Count Pasenhor

*will be getting a separate letter from me since I
need to deal with some things before my return.*
*Behave yourself, little brother... until we
meet again.*

He set the papyrus aside with a smile. Ramesses would
have some things to say, no doubt. And they would be
interesting.

III

Riding along in the wind and the sun the next morning, Nakhtamun found his thoughts circling around Ramesses. Court life did not suit him, but Ramesses, though younger than him by more than a decade, thrived on it. Could he, Nakhtamun, appoint Ramesses to serve as his deputy, or viceroy? It was worth considering. The press of government was weariness to him. He preferred to be out and doing rather than conducting ceremonious business, important though it was.

Would it be possible? He frowned and considered. It was asking much of his brother's honor and courage. Perhaps they could be co-regents, Ramesses performing the tasks of Kingship that lay within his strengths, and he following his own abilities?

But what *were* his abilities? He was a competent fighter, but others had formed strategy. He was a meticulous observer of things that interested him... He faltered. What *could* he do?

The moment's doubt passed. The brothers Kamose and Ahmose had had such an arrangement at the start of the previous dynasty, didn't they? He would speak with his father.

His smile grew crooked at the thought of His Majesty's reaction. It would be wiser to wait. It might be a long time before he was sole King, and arrangements could be made then, without fear of his father's devastatingly pointed method of dealing with what he judged to be arrant stupidity.

He drew in his team to await his outriders circling back toward him with Senwadjet at their lead.

"Well?"

"It seems to be intact, Sire."

Nakhtamun set the notion of co-regency aside. "Excellent. The less rebuilding we must do, the more quickly the fortress can be put into service. Let's look it over."

Senwadjet watched him gather his reins. "I will select a squadron to escort us, Sire."

Nakhtamun frowned as he adjusted the tension. "Don't be a fool. They'd have to march on the double and they would not thank me for ordering it without need. The fort is obviously deserted."

Senwadjet lowered his head and spoke over him. "If it please Your Majesty: we followed your orders and did not enter the structure, nor did we approach it closely. We do not know whether it is deserted. At this moment we know nothing of it apart from its outward appearance."

Nakhtamun stared for the time it took to check the arrow-filled quiver to his right. "We can verify that ourselves," he said.

Senwadjet raised his head. "Sire, I beg you. If I have done anything that has pleased you in the time you have been with me: we should have our foot soldiers and scouts supporting us. It will be slower, but we can face and fight any resistance we may encounter."

"No!"

Senwadjet continued doggedly. "But, Sire, if they are dealing treacherously—"

"The place is deserted! I can see it, myself! There is nothing there. The troops will follow us as they can."

"But Majesty!"

"Don't try my patience, General! If they have betrayed us, you have my leave to put them all to the sword!" And he urged his horses to a canter before Senwadjet could protest any further.

**   **   **

Magnificent! The sun-bleached stones of the fortress seemed set within a frame of mountains rising almost purple to either side. The brightness echoed the lightness in Nakhtamun's heart. He would speak with his father and with Ramesses.

He eased his hold on the reins and his team quickened its pace. The canter became a gallop until they were in the shadow of the fortress' square gatehouse. He drew up, then, smiling at the tower, picturing it stuccoed and painted, peopled with soldiers and traders, as it had been in the great times. His horses felt the tension on the reins and shook their heads, their feathered headdresses tossing in the wind.

He turned to Senwadjet, who was beside him. "They spoke truth," he said. "It's in fine shape, from this vantage! We will see how it seems from inside!"

His horses stiffened their necks, snorting as he shook the reins. "What's *this?*" he demanded. He loosed the lash of his short driving whip and cracked it over their heads. The team lurched forward and then steadied, though their ears flicked back and forth. "*That's* it, my beauties!" he said.

He swept through the gatehouse, Senwadjet's panicked shout ringing in his ears behind him. A twang from the right, then a heavy thud as a long black shaft seemed to bloom in his breast. The horses screamed and reared. He heard the whine of a bowstring and looked down, choking, as another arrow appeared beside the first.

The back of his throat was filling with blood. His hands were losing their strength as he fell forward against the chariot rail.

Screaming– shapes circling him– the ring of bronze– a horse shrieking– He could feel arms around him and Senwadjet's voice saying his name as the blue sky turned black and all sound faded into murmurs and then silence.

Father... he whispered in the moment before he was gone.

**   **   **

The wind blew south from Joppa, channeling through the Nubian hills, throwing a glittering net of sunlight upon the blue waters of the Nile. Low hills rose to either side of the river, their shoulders half-hiding the expanse of grasslands beyond them. The man turned his face into the wind, tasting the scent of the veldt.

He turned to the man standing beside him with his arms folded on the ramparts of the fortress. "Another splendid day drawing to a close. We can start for Uronarti in the next two days. The soldiers are ready."

No answer: his friend was staring north and east, his clear features somehow frozen. As the other watched him, his brows came slowly together in a puzzled frown.

The man hesitated, eyeing the stiffness of his friend's stance. "What is wrong, Seti?"

Seti, King of Egypt, turned, still frowning. "We must start back," he said.

Intef, Vizier of Upper Egypt, nodded. "We can certainly do so if you wish," he said. His voice was calm. "When do you want to leave?"

"Quickly," Seti said. "Can we sail tomorrow?"

"We can if you command it," Intef replied.

Pharaoh looked down at his hands, gripped together on the battlements. "I command it."

"What is it?"

Seti's dark eyes raised to meet Intef's. "I need to return to Memphis. As soon as I can. Nakhtamun was...troubled when I left. I thought he would settle in, since Nebamun's at his shoulder... But..."

Intef pushed away from the battlement. He knew that expression. "A feeling?" he asked.

Seti folded his arms and frowned down at his feet, a stance Intef remembered from their campaigning days. The frown had eased when he looked up. "Something is terribly wrong. I must get back at once."

Intef nodded, his broad face expressionless. "I will order a galley. We will have the current and the oars working for us."

IV

Memphis

Senwadjet watched the blue river unwind from the stern of his boat, as they moved between hills of sun-gilded stone, bordered by sweet-scented acacias. The wind sent the feathered tops of the tall papyrus stalks dancing and cooled his face as he turned to gaze upriver. The ship was far behind him now, lumbering in the boat's wake somewhere north of Giza. The scent of death had begun to fade when they left Joppa, but it still lingered, and he was glad to be away from it.

He set his loosely clasped hands on the top rail and frowned south at the faint haze that would soon resolve itself into the city of Memphis. The wind strengthened; he turned his back to it and thought that he would prefer being on that ship, death and all, to bringing news of a death to a great lord.

He covered his face and was once again in the heat and noise as he held Nakhtamun and watched his life fade. He felt the moment when, kneeling in the shadows of the gatehouse, he had looked up at the officer before him, heard that the army had arrived and awaited his orders, and said, "Kill them all. No prisoners."

He frowned and opened his eyes to the western hills. Course upon course of white glinted in the sun. Imhotep's masterpiece, the Pyramid of Djoser, seemed to rise to the west. They were entering the slow eastward curve that would bring them to the docks.

He straightened. The tall pylons of the Temple of Ptah rose above the eastern shore of the river. He caught the spark of gold, brilliant color upon white. He raised his head and watched them as his boat approached, his gaze lifting as they drew near, until he had to look away and down to the docks to port.

Shouts from the shore, a rope snaking through the air, caught and looped about a piling... The boat made fast. He closed his eyes, opened them, and drew a long breath, as the harbor master approached, alerted by the royal emblem on the sail. He stepped forward...

**   **   **

"He is here, General." The young officer escorting Senwadjet paused to stand to the side, giving a clear view of the throng.

The throne room of the Memphis Royal Palace was large and long with a course of six pillars to either side. The dais was at the end of a walkway frescoed with depictions of bound captive figures symbolizing the enemies of Egypt. Golden winged disks, representing the god Horus, surmounted the doors leading to the rooms at the rear and sides, containing Pharaoh's private chambers.

A gilded throne dominated the dais; a lesser seat, also gilded, sat to its right, and a plain chair of ebony to the left and a little behind it. A young man occupied the smaller throne. An older man with the look of a soldier stood beside him.

Senwadjet hesitated. Nakhtamun had told him that Prince Ramesses had three children, and he had imagined him to be in his late twenties. While the man seated in the lesser throne was composed and calm, he could not yet have reached his twentieth year. Senwadjet judged him too young to receive this shock in public.

He set a quiet hand on his escort's shoulder. "No. I must send a note to His Highness. Bring me writing materials."

When the papyrus and ink came, he wrote quickly, folded the message, and handed it to the officer. "Take this to His Highness. Tell him I beg private speech with him on an urgent matter."

The officer moved down the walkway. The older man watched him approaching with slightly raised eyebrows and then turned his gaze to Senwadjet. From the leopard skin tied across his chest and the gold fillet on his brow, he was a priest of considerable seniority. Senwadjet bowed. The man smiled and returned the salute.

Prince Ramesses had the message. He opened it, read, and looked up at the older man, who bent over him to listen. A quiet murmur of words... The priest descended the three steps and went to Senwadjet.

"His Highness will meet you in the garden, General," the man said. "From your note it is bad news, and he judges it best to be private. I will escort you there."

They moved silently along a hallway paved with tiles the color of lapis, which opened into a garden filled with the scent of roses and acacia. A small, tile-bordered pond reflecting the blue sky with a light pavilion beside it, two chairs. The serenity of the setting seemed to somehow highlight the pain that Senwadjet knew he was bringing.

The priest paused beside the water. "Wait here, General. His Highness will be out directly." He added, "I will send food and drink to you. Are others following you that we must make provision for?"

"Yes, Lord. A ship should be arriving well before dusk."

The priest raised his eyebrows. "A ship?"

"Yes, Lord," Senwadjet said. "I left it behind north of Giza." He watched the man straighten and made a quick decision. "It is very bad news, Lord."

The priest frowned down at his hands and then directed a straight gaze at Senwadjet. "His Highness must hear the tidings first, as is proper. But if this word is what I fear it may be, I will wish to speak further with you this evening. My name is Nebamun."

He turned as the thud of the door broke the quiet behind them.

Prince Ramesses strode toward them, Senwadjet's message in his hand.

Senwadjet had met King Seti when he was still Vizier of the North and General of the Armies under his father, whom Horemheb had just named Crown Prince. Aside from his impressive height, Prince Ramesses was a younger version of his father, with the same eyes and classically balanced features.

The dark eyes lowered to the message. They raised and fixed on Senwadjet. "I regret that I could not speak with you at once, General. I can do so now. I know your rank. Who are you?"

"I am Senwadjet, Highness," he replied. "Commander of One Thousand in the Royal Army at Gaza. I served most recently as His Majesty's second."

"I greet you, then, Senwadjet," Ramesses said. "You seem exhausted. Please sit down. Have you eaten?"

"I will ask that food and drink be brought here, Highness," Nebamun said.

Ramesses watched him leave and then turned his gaze back to Senwadjet.

"Highness," Senwadjet's voice shook.

Ramesses' smile faded.

"I..." Senwadjet collected himself and offered his report. "I grieve to bear bad tidings."

Ramesses frowned. "Bad tidings?"

"The worst, Highness. King Nakhtamun was killed in battle, in Palestine."

Prince Ramesses opened the message and read. He looked up, his eyes somehow blind, shook the note, read again and then lowered it. "Nakhtamun..."

"I am sorry, Highness."

Ramesses smoothed the note with hands that did not seem to work properly. "Tell me," he said.

"Enemy forces set a trap in an abandoned fortress along the Ways of Horus, not far from Joppa. His Majesty, wishing to inspect the structure, to see if it could be brought to a livable state, drove into the ambush and was killed in the fighting."

Ramesses looked at the message and then folded it with shaking hands. "Thank you," he said. His voice was very low. "Was... was the ambush unexpected? No. Of course it was unexpected. One doesn't expect an ambush, does one?"

"It was a surprise, Highness," Senwadjet said. "He was not expecting it."

"But you were, I think."

Senwadjet looked down.

Ramesses blinked back tears. His voice was level when he spoke again. "You must have been with him. That is why you came personally. Were you close to him when he died?"

"Yes, Highness. I was by his side."

"Was there much pain at the end?"

Senwadjet thought back to the sunlit streamers of dust, the smell of blood, the whine and thud of arrows. The din and confusion as he cut his way through with the rest of Nakhtamun's staff behind him, then kneeling with his dying King in his arms as the rest of the force arrived. And then he remembered the smile.

"No, Highness. I held him safe. He was smiling, and his last words were of his family."

Prince Ramesses covered his face. "Dear God!" he breathed. "Had you not been there..." He straightened with an effort and clapped his hands for a servant. He said to the man who entered. "Send a messenger to the Vizier at his villa. Ask him to wait upon me at..." he hesitated, gnawing his lip. He drew a deep breath, expelled it in a sigh. "I will receive him here. Tell him the matter is urgent, and I beg his haste." He paused. "And Lord Nebamun was with me until a few moments ago. Find him, if you would. I need him."

[24]

He turned to Senwadjet, who had been watching him with growing admiration. "And you, General," he said. "I will order rooms to be prepared for you and your force."

Senwadjet set the cup down. "Highness, you cannot know how desperately I regret bringing this news to you."

"You did well," Ramesses said. "It is for me to do as well, now." He pulled off his ring, frowning at it before handing it to Senwadjet. "If you left the ship behind you at Giza, it is most likely approaching now. Take this and ask one of the guards outside to bring you to the Harbor Master. I will be there when the ship arrives with my brother's body."

V

Count Pasenhor, Vizier of Northern Egypt, had been interrupted at his noon meal with his family. He showed signs of having donned his court finery in a hurry; his wig was crooked, and his sash twisted as he hurried forward, skirting the pond. "I received your summons, Highness."

Prince Ramesses had been sitting with his hands folded in his lap, his wide eyes fixed on a point in the air before him. He straightened as the Vizier entered the garden and brought his expression into calmness. "Thank you for coming, Count," he said. "We have received...received news."

Pasenhor looked from Nebamun to Ramesses. "I was dining with guests," he said. I was told it was urgent." A stare from Nebamun silenced him.

Ramesses drew a shaken breath. "I have received news that my brother was killed in an ambush. The ship bearing his body will be arriving shortly."

"This is terrible!" the Vizier exclaimed.

Nebamun lifted an eyebrow. "We thought so, My Lord."

Pasenhor blinked at the unmistakable rebuke. "I await Your Highness' orders."

Ramesses moistened his lips and squared his shoulders. "My father must be told at once. I think one of the fleet should be provisioned and sent to Kush with word for him." He raised his eyes to the winged sun disk by the door. "My brother's ship is coming here in all haste. It has been three weeks ..." He stopped and looked at his hands and then at Nebamun.

"His Holiness and I have discussed this. I wish I could go to my father and tell him, myself. He needs to know the truth from a son, not from a stranger who bows and calls him 'living god', but I must remain here to perform the duties set upon me by Nakhtamun when he left."

He pushed himself to his feet and paced to the pond. "And regarding my brother's burial, Lord Nebamun and I believe it is best to send Nakhtamun to the embalmers now. We cannot wait until His Majesty returns. My father had a tomb constructed near Thebes...not large. I remember it was when he had been Vizier for a time. He commissioned it, but when Grandsire was named Crown Prince there seemed no reason to—to finish it. He and Nakhtamun saw it when they were in Thebes, I know. The two of them went there some time ago, and they were laughing about it when they came back..." He hesitated and added, "My wife was in her confinement, and I couldn't leave."

Nebamun watched Ramesses' expression. He spoke quietly, "He will be in the fields of the Gods, Ramessu. In the land where there is no strife, where all is clean and strong, where joy flows like a river."

Ramesses had been looking down. "I thank Your Holiness," he said. "I will go to Thebes with … With Nakhtamun's body." He added, "General Senwadjet tells me that they will be bringing him ashore when the ship docks." He looked up. "I remember Father commissioned a statue of Nakhti when he became King. He wanted one done of each of us… I did see this, and it is well done. It could be placed in the tomb."

A fist thudded on the door.

Ramesses looked up. "Yes?"

"Highness, the ship is docking!"

Ramesses drew a slow breath and rose. "I will go to the quay," he said.

VI

The soft plash of water against the oars seemed somehow loud along the hushed quay. The nearly constant breeze had stilled; Ramesses could hear the chuckle of the water against the ship's hull as it glided toward the dock.

Ramesses looked around at the bystanders, citizens who had come to the dock to greet a "great ship." and were silent with the realization of the magnitude of this ship's mission.

Peru-Nefer, Ramesses thought. *It means 'Fair arrival'. Is this a 'fair arrival'? The ship coming to the dock, the silent oarsmen... The cargo...*

Lord Nebamun was standing calmly as the ship was made fast to the dock. Perineb, his second, stood beside him, watching without expression as the gangplank was lowered to the dock and the bier carried ashore.

Oh, Nakhti... he thought, wrinkling his nose at the throat-clogging smell of decay. *This should not be happening.*

His anguished gaze caught Nebamun, who reached out and gripped his shoulder. "If it *must* be done, Ramessu," he said, "then it *can* be done." He nodded to Perineb. "The two of you, go prepare yourselves. I wish to speak with General Senwadjet and inspect the body, myself, before you come to wash and compose it."

Ramesses hesitated.

Nebamun smiled at him. "Go ahead, lad," he said. "I've been on many a battlefield and seen the results. And I loved him, too. But I need to learn some things." He nodded to Perineb. "The answers will be useful this evening as we make preparations. And His Majesty will be glad of them when he returns."

**　**　**　**

Ramesses gathered the reins in his hands and shook them. The near horse jibbed at the bit and backed the light chariot several paces before he was brought to a halt. Another command given, they sprang forward, their feet thudding on the packed dirt.

The land blurred before him. He raised his head, his eyes narrowed against the sand-laden wind of his passing, fixed on the gleam of white in the distance. The Pyramid of Zoser. He could see it rearing above the necropolis of Saqqara, fabulously ancient, pure in its symmetry of form, steps leading up into the sky glinting in the sun.

He urged the horses to a gallop, reveling in the feeling of freedom after the past day of grief and indecision. The scattered stubby outlines of ancient tombs streamed past him in a blur, as he kept his eyes fixed on the pyramid that loomed before him, the vast, pillared complex commemorating a King whose history was lost somewhere in the past.

He reached the processional way and turned the chariot, rumbling down the wide, limestone-paved road, the high walls rising to either side. It was along here that the sledge bearing the King's sarcophagus had been brought. He could see it in his mind's eye, impossibly small when viewed through the passage of time. The sweating bearers, the billows of incense, the priests moving in stately ceremony. Mourners wailing.

Looking behind him, he could almost see a shadow approaching, vast, ponderous, punctuated by the creak of rope as the sledge was drawn to its resting place in the tomb. Faint skeins of incense, the soft sound of chanting... It loomed over him; for a moment it enveloped him, and then, as he watched, it vanished into the distance.

His heart thundered within his chest; the vision was so clear. He still seemed to see one man standing apart from the others, looking up at the stepped structure and nodding. Imhotep?

He blinked and decided that the strain of the past day had made him fanciful. He turned his horses to follow the pillared wall of the Heb-Sed court before drawing them to a halt and stepping down. He hobbled them and turned toward the great complex that opened before him through a doorway into dimness and the echo of incense.

He was in an entry hall, columns rising up about him like a thicket of papyrus stalks. He could feel the weight of the ceiling pressing against the upward thrust of the pillars.

He turned and moved into the large courtyard with its carvings commemorating the ceremonies of rejuvenation. He could see the pyramid beyond it through a procession of doorways. He sighed and dropped to his knees to watch it glinting in the thick light of the lowering sun. He had so many things to consider, and the grateful memory of a fear brought to nothing.

He remembered the previous day. The terrible news, the time spent dreading the moment when he would see Nakhtamun's body, handle it, prepare it…

The ship had docked, and Nebamun had sent him and Perineb away, saying that he needed to question the escort and would send for them when all was in readiness. He was startled to see the brief look of relief in Perineb's eyes as they turned and left the dock. They returned together that evening, silent…

Why had he been so terrified? What had he expected to find?

Nakhtamun's body had been presentable. He could see that nature was taking its toll, but his brother had died smiling. Perhaps the most stunning realization of that day had been that the thing presented for his view and ministrations had not been his brother. Nakhtamun was gone, and while it was his duty as the next of kin to prepare his body for its embalming, the movements had been simply movements, a nod to tradition, care given to a tool no longer needed. Nakhtamun had moved beyond this world.

But the rest of those he loved had not. And Ramesses had serious questions to ponder.

Should he go to Thebes to oversee Nakhtamun's interment? Travel to Kush and bring the terrible word to his father? What was best?"

He settled himself more comfortably, his eyes fixed on the sides of the pyramid.

He was acting for Pharaoh and governing Egypt at that moment. He could not remove himself for the time it would take to travel to Kush. He needed to send a deputy. Whom should he send?

He sat back on his heels and considered.

VII

Lord Nebamun took the cup of wine offered by the slave and smiled his thanks. He raised it to his lips; the sunset glow of the sky seemed to dance on the surface of the wine, mingling with the rich scent of the vintage.

"Is it to your taste, Holiness?" Prince Ramesses asked.

Nebamun had just arrived from the archery courses on the outskirts of the Temple of Ptah. He nodded to Nesuptah, the Governor of the powerful first Nome, or Province, of Lower Egypt, and Count Pasenhor, slid the quiver from his shoulder and set it against the low wall beside the bow. The lowering sun, now behind Djoser's pyramid, bathed his shoulders with warm red-gold light.

The High Priest sipped and set the cup down. "It is very good, Highness," he replied, adding with the hint of a smile. "As you know. What do you want of me?"

Ramesses sat back, avoiding His Holiness' amused hazel gaze. He was delaying and he knew it. It was one thing to reach a decision; it was another to propose it to counselors who were far older than him, and one of whom was twice as intelligent as anyone in his family.

Nebamun had always told him to 'spit it out'. Ramesses drew a long breath and did so. "I wish to discuss sending word to my father without delay."

Nebamun lifted his cup again and smiled at him. "What do you propose, Highness?"

"It has been nearly a moon since my brother was..." Ramesses hesitated, and then pushed on. "Since my brother was killed. I am sending his body to Thebes escorted by an honor guard and a corps of priests as we discussed."

Nebamun nodded. "I agree," he said.

Ramesses lifted his cup and frowned unseeingly at its elegantly molded form. "We know that His Majesty is somewhere south of Buhen."

Pasenhor had been staring at his feet. "We can send a messenger. With a fair wind it might take a fortnight for the man to reach His Majesty."

"I want my father to receive the news gently," Ramesses said.

Nebamun nodded. "He needs to be told by someone who loves him. I will travel to him and bring him back."

"Your Holiness is well-stricken in years!" Pasenhor exclaimed. He stopped as Nebamun eyed his midriff and reflected on the unfairness of a man of His Holiness' years having the form and health of a much younger man.

Nesuptah smiled to himself. "His Lordship's concern has some validity, My Father. It will be a difficult journey, and you are needed here."

Nebamun lowered his eyes for a considering moment and directed his gaze to his son-in-law. "Perhaps so, Nesu..." he said. He turned to Pasenhor. "You have a point, My Lord Vizier. This is a matter of the utmost gravity. Prince Ramesses must go to Thebes to oversee the entombment. It is best, though he can remain here until matters are ready for his departure, and Pharaoh may arrive between times. This brings us to the question of the person to go to His Majesty.

"Being one with a foot in the tomb, myself, as you have so kindly pointed out, I concede that another should be given the task. As Vizier—"

Pasenhor drew a deep breath and squared his shoulders. "I agree. As Vizier to my King, I should be the one to bring the news."

"I was thinking of Intef..." Nebamun said.

Pasenhor stared. "The Vizier of *Upper* Egypt?"

Nebamun folded his arms. "He is in Nubia with His Majesty. They are old comrades and good friends. They fought shoulder to shoulder in many battles under Horemheb. We can send to him."

"I insist on going!" Pasenhor exclaimed. He halted in the face of Nebamun's stare.

Ramesses' expression had eased somewhat. "Intef is with my father now. Could we get the word to him, do you think?"

Pasenhor spoke with more force. "I will bring the message to His Majesty. It is fitting that I do so, as Vizier to my King. We need not trouble Intef with it. I will leave at once."

The Governor traded startled looks with his father-in-law. "But, Pasenhor—"

Nebamun spoke over him. "Don't you think, Pasenhor, that it would be a waste of your time to carry a message that would as well be entrusted to a courier who could travel swiftly?" he asked. "Would it not be better for you to remain here and deal capably with affairs of state while His Highness ensures his brother's proper interment?"

"I would be bringing the message to my King."

"...Who would be just as well-served to receive it from Intef, who has been properly prepared with the news, a good friend who could travel with His Majesty and give him comfort during a time when it is needed."

"I resent that remark!" Pasenhor exclaimed.

"Why? It is nothing but the truth!"

"Do you say that His Majesty does not value me?"

"I say that His Majesty has never fought shoulder to shoulder with you, traded war stories, split a jar of beer or laughed at crude jokes with you. I say that he would be appalled to find that he had to camp with you for any length of time. Bluntly, two weeks confined on a boat with you would drive His Majesty mad."

Pasenhor drew himself up, his hands clenched. Nebamun's cool gaze had not shifted.

Nesuptah gripped his father-in-law's arm. "My Father, I could go in your place."

Nebamun's scornful stare had altered slightly. "My Lord Vizier, you said that you have guests. We can continue this discussion later if you wish to return to them. We have noted your objections and will take them into account."

Ramesses was frowning as he spoke. "Yes. We shall."

Pasenhor smiled at them both and bowed. "Until tomorrow," he said.

Once he was gone Nebamun sat back with a thoughtful frown. "Count Pasenhor gives His majesty the fidgets," he said.

The Governor nodded. "He irritates me, as well, my father."

"If he goes, it will be with orders to give the letter to Intef and then sit silently," Ramesses suggested.

Nesuptah frowned. "He should remain here as Vizier. Are you afraid of a tantrum if you force him to stay?"

Ramesses scowled, an unaccustomed expression for him. "He would be in my hair, and it would annoy me."

"In your hair?" Nebamun repeated.

"I need you here," Ramesses said. "I will write a letter to my father. He will receive the word from me. And he will have Intef and Pasenhor."

Nebamun nodded after a long, frowning pause. "Very well, lad. Pasenhor will take the message as we discussed, and give it to Intef, who will know what to say. I will make sure *Sceptre of Ptah* is ready to sail at dawn."

VIII

Ramesses walked to the harbor at Peru-Nefer just as the eastern sky blushed rose with the approaching sunrise, edging the cedar planks of the Temple's flagship with red-gold fire. Nebamun was there before him, frowning up at the bow of the ship, almost as though he were trading stares with the painted prow. He saw Ramesses and bowed. "I am willing to go, Sesse," he said quietly. "And you know that I can stand the journey."

Ramesses took his hand and held it. "No. This will do. Intef will be there, and I need you."

Nebamun nodded after a moment. "Very well, lad." He looked along the dock. "Here is Nesu."

The Governor stepped down from his chair as the bearers set it on the dock. "I came as quickly as I could." He bowed to his father-in-law and then more deeply to Ramesses.

Ramesses turned to gaze along the dock. "Count Pasenhor is coming," he said.

The Vizier was smiling, genial, striding along in the quiet breeze from the river. He had received the message from Nebamun the night before and sent his acceptance back. It appeared that he had curtailed his drinking somewhat. He bowed to Ramesses, who did not forestall him, and then to Nebamun. "A splendid morning!" he said. "Boding well for a fine journey." He drew a deep breath, expelled it, and looked at the sky again. "An auspicious journey and a fair wind to guide me."

Nebamun's frown deepened. "'Auspicious'," he repeated.

"We will have the wind behind us!" Pasenhor said.

Nebamun directed a narrow stare at the Vizier. "If he stands behind the sail and continues prattling," he said to the Governor, "he will make twice the time, having twice the wind!"

Nebamun looked up at the captain of the ship, caught the man's nod, and turned to Pasenhor. "It's ready to sail," he said.

Ramesses nodded, cleared his throat. He offered a tied, sealed packet of papyrus. "Count," he said. He closed his eyes, opened them. "I am sure you loved your father, Count. Please. Give this to Intef and be there when my father comes to you and Intef. It is a very hard blow, and while he is Pharaoh he is also a father, and this will devastate him. Intef and you will be a comfort to him."

Pasenhor took the package. "I will give this to Intef as you direct, Highness. And afterward, when His Majesty has been told, I will be there."

"I rely upon your kindness," Ramesses said. He waited as Pasenhor ascended the ramp to the ship but turned and left as the ship cast off.

**   **   **

Nesuptah watched the ship draw away. "He may do well, My Father," he said.

Nebamun was scowling after the ship. "I should have gone."

"Ramesses needs you," Nesuptah said.

"He would do better with Perineb."

"But Pasenhor will hand over the message to Intef and accompany His Majesty here."

Nebamun transferred his scowl to his son-in-law. "Do you think so? I've never known an ass to do anything but bray." He squared his shoulders and suddenly smiled.

"What is it, My Father?"

Nebamun nodded slowly. "Yes..."

"What?"

"I will send a special messenger south by galley with orders to make all speed to Semna. That jackass may or may not deliver the message; His Majesty will certainly get it from me."

IX

The archer settled the bow's grip into the V formed by the notch between his thumb and his palm. He reached behind him and brought an arrow hissing from the quiver at his back. The shaft settled on the bowstring, captured between the archer's fingers as the arc of the bow grew tighter, drawing the arrow back and back until its fletching brushed the man's cheek. A pause, hazel eyes looking straight along the shaft. The almost imperceptible relaxing of the fingers holding the bowstring, sending the arrow singing into the sunrise to bury itself in the target of mounded straw beneath a sheet of leather.

Another arrow followed the first. The archer lowered the bow and turned to the man waiting quietly beside him. "There, Perineb," he said, pulling a cloth from his belt and polishing the bow's grip. "I'm finished. I apologize for keeping you waiting. What did you want me to see?"

Perineb, the second ranking priest of the cult of Ptah, shook his head. "It is always a pleasure to watch a master at his craft," he said. He opened the message in his hands and scanned it. "I received word on our inquiries and thought you would wish to hear. Those farms were a bountiful bequest. They've been yielding good harvests for the past two years, and we've been able to add to our stores thanks to that."

Nebamun retrieved his arrows and frowned at the tips. "Increasing yield each year?" he said. "Let me see..." He took the scroll, scanned it, and then nodded. "What of the other heirs? Did you find any?"

"A grandson," Perineb said.

"Why was he cut out?"

"I am not sure," Perineb said. "The benefactors were quite elderly by the time the bequest was made..."

Nebamun settled the arrows in their quiver. "Have someone look into it. If there was no reason for that grandson to lose his inheritance, we will cede him half the land. The best half." He nodded at Perineb's expression. "I thought you'd approve. I don't want to benefit from injustice."

Perineb rolled the scroll and set it aside. "I can send Sarenput with some of the older temple scribes."

Nebamun raised his eyebrows. "Sarenput? He's young, isn't he?"

"He's intelligent, fair-minded and has a sense of humor," Perineb said. "Though it does tend to run away with him if he's with young Bekhenkhons. If he can learn to control his temper he will be most impressive. At any rate, he will learn the truth and bring it back."

"Then we will send him." Nebamun broke off, frowning, and listened. Voices, the sound of a trumpet, then shouts.

A We'eb priest was coming at a run. He bowed to Nebamun and Father Perineb. "*Sceptre of Ptah* is approaching the docks," he said.

"So early?" Perineb exclaimed. "It's only been a fortnight... Less..."

Nebamun straightened and traded grim looks with Perineb. "They certainly made good time. I will admit to wishing that it had taken longer."

** ** **

They arrived as *Sceptre of Ptah* was being made fast in the growing light of dawn. Ramesses was there before them, eagerly scanning the decks. He bowed to Nebamun and turned back to the ship. "I don't see him," he said. "No, wait! There he is!" He stepped forward with a relieved smile as Pharaoh appeared at the head of the gangplank. Count Pasenhor was before him.

A brief nod from Pharaoh. "Thank you, Count," he said. His voice was very dry. "Go to your family. You have my leave to rest for the next day."

Pasenhor bowed again and moved down the gangplank. He bowed hurriedly to Prince Ramesses and left, moving briskly.

Nebamun scowled after him and then turned back to watch with anxious eyes as King Seti descended the gangplank with the energy of a man half his fifty-two years.

Seti smiled at Nebamun and nodded to Perineb as he hurried forward to embrace Ramesses with a wide smile. "It's good to see you, lad," he said, holding him away for a moment to scan his face before embracing him again. "Is all well? Intef sent letters for you and your brother." And then, still holding Ramesses, he looked around and said, "Where's Nakhtamun?"

Ramesses' eyes widened with shock. "Nakhtamun?" he stammered.

Seti had been scanning the crowd. "And there are your sisters," he said with a nod to his daughters Tia and Iset. He turned back to Ramesses and released him. "Yes. Your brother, who else? Where is he? Hunting, maybe? We made

[37]

better time than we expected. I was in Thebes and about to embark when Pasenhor arrived."

His words echoed in the sudden silence.

Nebamun hurried forward, his hands outstretched. Seti gripped them, smiling, and looked back at Ramesses with raised eyebrows.

Ramesses' voice shook. "I grieve to tell you, Sire—" he said. "Father..."

"To tell me what?" Seti's voice was suddenly quiet.

"Nakhtamun is dead." The words were stark, final and as cold as pebbles dropped in the river.

Pharaoh's lips formed the word silently. Dead. "When?"

"A month ago."

Seti's hands fell away from his son's shoulders. "So that is why..." he whispered. He straightened. "How did this happen? An accident?"

"He died in Palestine," Ramesses said.

"Palestine? Where is he now?" Seti demanded. "I have to see him!"

Ramesses moistened his lips. "He has been put to rest in a tomb in Thebes... In the small tomb." He realized that he was stammering and stopped.

Seti's eyes seemed wide and somehow blind. "The small tomb... The one I commissioned..." He closed his eyes, opened them, and turned to Ramesses. When was this done?"

"There was need of haste."

"*When* was it done?"

"Two weeks ago. Father, I had to–"

"Two *weeks*! Why wasn't I told at that time?"

"I sent word! Didn't you get it?"

Seti turned away from him and stared out over the river. His face was ashen when he turned back. "I received no message," he said. "I decided to return to Memphis a month ago. And I come to learn *this* in *this* fashion! Surely *someone* could have come to me to warn me that one of my children was killed!"

"No word?" Ramesses repeated.

Nebamun stepped forward. Seti stopped him with a motion of his hand and turned back to his son. "Idiot! No, I did not get word! Why else would I ask?" He took a turn around the dock. "Tell me what happened!"

Ramesses collected his thoughts. "Nakhtamun was leading a campaign in Palestine."

[38]

"And I was not told of this?"

"He chose to go on an inspection of the coastal forts that were—"

"And I was not told?" The words were almost shouted.

Ramesses' eyes flashed. He drew himself to his full height and looked his father in the face. "He judged that as co-regent he had the right to decide where he was going, and when. I tried to argue with him."

Seti's eyes narrowed. "Don't waste my time with excuses!" he snapped. "You let him go to his death!"

Ramesses' eyes grew stricken.

Seti scowled at him. "So. Your brother is dead. Tell me how."

"His force was ambushed, and he died in the fighting," Ramesses said, thinking of Senwadjet's account and his brother's body. "The attackers were defeated. But Nakhtamun was killed."

"And when did this happen?"

Ramesses closed his eyes. "He was killed nearly two months ago. The word came to me three weeks after that. I judged it best to take care of the entombment, and I sent word to you that very day."

His Majesty's brows drove together. "I received no word at any time."

Ramesses faltered. "But I gave one to—"

"No message was given to me until I met Pasenhor in Thebes," Seti said with cutting precision. "I was getting ready to embark when he arrived with the word that I was urgently needed in Memphis. Ptah's beard! Can you think I would have gone more slowly if I had known that I was coming back to deal with a death among my best-loved? It was ill done, and I cannot understand how any child of mine could be stupid and heartless enough deal with me in *this* fashion! I thank the gods that your mother is not alive to see this!"

Nebamun stepped forward. "Sire..."

"Silence!" Seti snapped. He rounded on Ramesses. "Get out of my sight!"

Ramesses bowed, turned and left.

X

Turquoise tiles mirrored the midday sky through a screen of roses and heliotrope. The sun had passed beyond its zenith, but the pool brimmed with water that bore its lingering warmth as it lapped over two hands, clenched at the rim.

They rose, dripping, cupped and covered the man's face. Prince Ramesses drew them away and stared down at them as though they belonged to another. The thought was briefly amusing, but the faint smile that sparked from the absurdity wavered and faded as he buried his head in his folded arms and wept against his drawn-up knees.

How could things have gone so amiss? It had been as though he were facing a stranger, not his own father. Nothing made sense, though his thoughts had circled round the shattering scene until he thought it was burned into his brain.

No word? How could that be when he had sent the letter? ...or had he?

He reared upright, knees against the ground, and drew a shaking breath, his hand to his eyes. Yes, he had! If he had erred at all, it had been out of love for his father.

He propped his elbow on the pool's apron, dipped his hands, and cupped the warm water in his palms. The water cooled in the breeze, soothing his burning eyes. He scooped up palmfuls, bathed his face again and again, until the stinging heat was gone.

He had wept enough. It was time to think. He raised his head, his eyes narrowed into the distance. He slammed his fist on the ground beside him with an oath from the barracks. "That cowardly *bastard*!" he said through his teeth. "*He didn't deliver my letter!*"

He pushed to his feet and stalked through the wide doorway and into the anteroom of his house. Four guardsmen were just inside, playing one of their everlasting games of knucklebones. One of them looked up, elbowed his fellow and scrambled to his feet, followed by the rest of the group.

Ramesses acknowledged their bows and wrestled his voice into gentleness. "I would be obliged if one of you would kindly locate Count Pasenhor and tell him the Crown Prince of Egypt requests the favor of his immediate presence."

The men traded looks before one stepped forward. "I will go, Highness," he said. "I believe I know where His Lordship may be."

"Thank you, good sir," Ramesses said with the bend of an ominous smile. "If you would make haste... And tell me your name."

The man looked startled. "I am Sokhari, Highness," he said.

"I will be grateful, Sokhari." He waited until the slap of the guardsman's sandals had faded before he strode into his chambers and slammed the door with all the strength of his chest and shoulder.

** ** **

It took some time for Sokhari to run Pasenhor to earth. He was at the Temple of Ptah, where he had gone to discuss some issues with the government of Memphis in his absence. Sokhari presented his credentials and commission to the senior priest who received him.

Perineb lifted his eyebrows. "So, His Royal Highness wants the Vizier immediately?" he mused. "Then he shall be sent. I will escort you to His Holiness and Count Pasenhor at once."

** ** **

At that moment Nebamun sat back in his chair and frowned at Pasenhor. "Now that matter is dealt with, I have a question for you: how did His Majesty receive Prince Ramesses' letter?"

"The letter?"

"Yes. The one Ramesses spent an entire evening writing. He gave it to you when *Sceptre of Ptah* was about to sail."

Pasenhor stared. "Why do you ask?"

"His Majesty's reaction puzzles me. It was as though it was the first he had learned of the tragedy." He paused, his expression ominous. "You never delivered it, did you, Pasenhor?"

"Why do you ask, Holiness?"

"As I said, His Majesty did not act as a man who has received bad news and had time to understand and accept it might. If I did not rely on your word and goodwill, I would think that he never heard of Nakhtamun's death until today."

Lord Nebamun paused. When Pasenhor did not speak he continued. "The letter would have given him time to absorb the blow, as it was meant to. You say you were with him all the way from Thebes. You are a father, yourself. Surely you had the kindness to tell him of the tragedy awaiting him in

Memphis and give Intef the letter as you promised and give him the chance to speak with His Majesty!"

Pasenhor looked away.

"You *didn't*! Why not?"

The Vizier moistened his lips. "Intef was gone and His Majesty had just boarded a ship that would take him to Memphis. I took steps to transfer him to *Sceptre of* Ptah."

"Yes?"

"I could not give it to Intef."

"You...could not give it to Intef," Nebamun repeated. He rose to his feet and paced toward the door, his hands gripped behind him. "My lord Vizier, to whom was Prince Ramesses' letter directed?"

"I beg your pardon?"

Nebamun repeated the question.

"His Highness commanded that I give the letter to Intef. The man was not there, and so I could not complete my task."

"What!"

Pasenhor looked at him with a touch of defiance. "What are you implying, My Lord?"

"*Implying!*" Nebamun repeated. "Unbelievable!" He paced to the window. Children were playing in the courtyard outside. One of them looked up and beamed at him. He smiled back and then turned to face Pasenhor.

"You didn't have the courage to deliver the letter! What did you think he would do? Order your execution? All you had to do was say to him, 'Sire, I bring sad news. Prince Ramesses has written this letter for you." You could have handed over the note, bowed, and left immediately, giving him privacy to receive the blow and collect his thoughts!"

"I am sorry."

"*Sorry!*" Nebamun took a turn around the room. "I can't understand how—" he began. He stopped and stared. "Ye gods, man! Has no one ever shown you such grace that you should shrink from giving it to one who so desperately needed it!"

"How could I face His Majesty's anger?"

"Anger! His Majesty would have gone to his cabin. Instead, thanks to your bungling, Prince Ramesses received a dose of rage! Ptah save us!" He broke off to stare blankly before him. "You only needed to give him the letter! What sort of spineless coward *are* you? You are Vizier of this land, man!" His stare narrowed. "*Vizier*, by the gods! You are a disgrace to your office!"

Pasenhor drew himself up. "I could make amends."

"How would you go about it?" Nebamun demanded through his teeth. "The only thing that might fit the injury would be to stretch your neck out across a log and let His Majesty and Prince Ramesses go at it with a war ax!" He paused and then added angrily, "We can invite Intef to participate!"

Pasenhor's eyes were as round as cart wheels. "But I couldn't!"

"Damn you, it's too late!"

A fist thudded on the door; Nebamun turned and opened it as Pasenhor looked up. A murmur of words....

Nebamun began to smile. He stood aside to allow a royal guardsman to enter the room. "I believe this man is looking for you, Count," he said as the guardsman's eyes fixed on Pasenhor and narrowed.

The man bowed to them and then straightened. "My Lord, I am sent to summon you to His Royal Highness the Crown Prince of Egypt."

The full title made Pasenhor jump as though someone had jabbed him with the point of a dagger. "*What?*" he demanded.

Nebamun had been standing with his arms folded. He lifted his eyebrows.

"The Crown Prince of Egypt commands that you wait on him in the audience hall," Sokhari said with slow precision.

Pasenhor's round-eyed stare made Nebamun look away and cough. "It would appear that it is later than you thought, Count. If Prince Ramesses has summoned you, then it is best to obey at once." He nodded to Sokhari, who bowed very low to him. "And do you, Guardsman, give His Royal Highness my most respectful greetings."

The door shut behind them. 'Hee-haw," Nebamun said under his breath.

XI

Count Pasenhor paused outside the audience chamber, aware of the guardsman's expressionless gaze. A peon should not discomfit a Vizier! He looked the man straight in the eye and curled his lip. The calm, measuring stare that met the sneer caused him to drop his eyes with a grimace. Commoners!

He eyed the closed door. A Crown Prince, however young, was a different matter. "Announce me," he said.

Sokhari inclined his head and stepped into the hall.

Pasenhor heard the man's footsteps, then a murmur of words. He waited for a long moment before Prince Ramesses' voice came "Send him in, good Sokhari. And thank you. You are relieved for the rest of the day."

Pasenhor stepped into the room.

Prince Ramesses was seated on the dais, in the smaller throne to the left of Pharaoh's gilded chair. He wore the cobra diadem and pendant sidelock of the Crown Prince. His eyes were black in the torchlight.

"Good afternoon, Highness," Pasenhor began.

"You were to tell Intef that sad news awaited my father and then hand over my letter. It appears now that you did not. Why not?"

"I thought it would be kinder."

"Kinder."

"T-to cushion the blow until a kinsman could deliver it."

Ramesses frowned. "Perhaps my advancing age has blunted my recollection. But I seem to recall a discussion among the lords governing this land in His Majesty's absence in which you, as Vizier, counseled for advising His Majesty at once so that he might know the truth and be prepared to deal with it on the long journey home. The memory is clear, but perhaps I am growing senile. I do remember, or I *think* I do, that you volunteered to go and tell His Majesty, gently, of the death of his son. Am I wrong? Did we discuss anything else, and I dreamed the conversation?"

"No, Highness."

"You cannot imagine what a relief that is," Prince Ramesses said. "But I may have mistaken our discussions. My disordered mind keeps presenting me with the memory of an interminable time spent composing a letter to be ultimately given to His Majesty. I seem to recall putting it into your hands just before you departed and asking you to hand it over to Intef, who would give it to my father in due time. I asked that you be prepared to answer the questions he naturally would have. I *seem* to recall saying that I relied, as a son, on your kindness toward my father in my absence. Did you give him that note, at least?"

"My Prince, I judged it best—"

"Was the letter put into my father's hands at all?"

Pasenhor stared. For a moment, the Crown Prince resembled his grandfather and namesake in all regards. He swallowed. "Intef was not there."

"The letter was addressed to His Majesty."

"Yes, Highness, but you said `I was to give—"

"The letter was addressed to His Majesty. Did you give it to him or did you not?" The words were not quite shouted.

Pasenhor lowered his head. "I did not," he said.

"My father never received the letter."

"No, Highness."

Ramesses straightened. "Get out of my sight at once. And do not return until I summon you."

"But His Majesty—"

"You will make your excuses. Now get out. And Pasenhor," his eyes were narrowed into chips of obsidian. "I will decide what to do about your dereliction. Go!"

** ** **

Lord Nebamun had spent the time after Pasenhor's departure frowning into space. His Majesty had arrived weeks earlier than expected... He stepped into the hallway and stopped a passing we'eb priest. Commander Ptahemhat was needed at once.

And then he sat down to write a quick note.

The Commander of the Corps of Temple Guards came briskly into the garden, bowed to Nebamun, and disposed himself to wait.

Nebamun looked up with a warm smile. "I have an assignment for those clever, discreet fellows you have in your corps, Ptahu. I need them to find a letter addressed to His Majesty from the Crown Prince. It was taken aboard *Sceptre of Ptah* the day she sailed for Semna. Count Pasenhor had it on the journey to Thebes. The letter was somehow misplaced; I doubt that horse's ass had the guts to burn it. He left the ship in a hurry, I know. His belongings may be there yet. Find it."

"Find it?"

[45]

"Yes. Here is a message for the captain, as well. Give it to him when you arrive. You both can search. Time is of the essence since the situation has just developed. You have a brief moment to act. Do so."

Ptahemhat nodded. "And when I have found it, Father?"

"Have it brought to me, of course. It may, possibly, save a tragedy from becoming a disaster."

XII

The stones rise about him, black as shadows at noonday, insubstantial as smoke. He has been near this place, he knows. He passed it on the way to Kadesh and victory against the Hittites. A fortress, even a ruined one, is something to be wary of.

A rectangle of sun-washed space is before him. Beyond it, the hills smooth to grassy flatlands that he crossed years before at the head of his armies.

He feels presences around him; men, armed and waiting.

Voices: He comes!!

Movement, shifting gazes.

Sudden concentrated stares, fingers tightening on weapons. Arrows hiss from quivers.

He can see flickering in the brightness beyond him. Horses approaching, plumed headdresses nodding in the wind— chariots—

His breath freezes in his throat.

The lead chariot is close now, the horses squealing and rearing. A whip cracks in the air. He can see the driver now, dark eyes narrowed and intent.

He tries to put himself between the others and the approaching man, to shout a warning, but he is silent, bound, motionless.

The light vehicle circles, then comes straight toward him, passing through him as though he is a twist of smoke. He can see his son's face, taut and exultant.

He tries to shout again.

Arrows sing through the air. He can see the triumphant expressions around him intensify as the arrows strike his son over and over. `

A river of shadows engulfs him, moves beyond him and he hears shouts and sees the flash of weapons raising and descending as the sound of laughter builds until a scream shatters them—

Father!

Now he can speak. "Kill me! Not him!"

A face before his, an upraised, bloody knife... The sound of laughter. "It is too late!"

He sees them crowding around...

Seti awoke with an inverted scream of indrawn breath. He could still see Nakhtamun on the ground, could feel the blows in his own flesh, and he, powerless to do anything other than watch as his son was killed and mutilated. Every night since his return, the dream had sent him rearing into wakefulness to spend the rest of the night wide-eyed and shaking.

Worst of all this night, in the moment between dreaming and waking, he had sensed his wife beside him, reaching out to comfort him. But she was dead a year now. If only he could speak to her...

He turned from the memories to face the nightmare.

The thing had happened weeks ago. It was done and over with, but he somehow could not keep his mind and heart from circling around the death, gazing upon the horror, powerless to change anything.

Moving through the past days had been like fighting his way through a sandstorm. He had spoken words, read documents, received envoys, all the things a King must do, and within his collected self it was as though his heart was drawn in upon itself, crying silently with no one to listen.

And his children, those still alive... He had greeted them after Ramesses had left, smiled upon them even as his face felt stiff and his eyes too wide. His eldest, his daughter Iset, understood. She was so much like her mother, but her home in Sais lay far to the north, in the delta. She had taken up residence in the palace to care for him.

He was glad of her presence, but he was still alone, unable to move through the numbness that bound him more effectively than ropes made of the cold gray metal from the north.

And Ramesses...

He turned on his side and stared into the darkness. How to deal with Ramesses when he could not bear to look at him? He knew he was being unreasonable. The boy...the man...was young. He had no doubt been overwhelmed and done what he could, but the fact that he had let his father receive publicly the worst news a father could ever hear, to expose him to that sickening pain and betrayal, for that is the only way he could view the complete disregard for his emotions, before the gaze of all! How could he have done such a thing? How?

And he had loved Ramesses. He loved him still, but he could not—

For the first time since that terrible moment when he learned that his son was killed, Seti closed his eyes and wept.

✶✶   ✶✶   ✶✶

Nebamun took the crumpled packet of papyrus and frowned at it. "Where was it?" he asked.

The Captain of *Sceptre of Ptah* raised his eyes to Nebamun's. "My men found it wedged against the timbers, near the mast, Holiness," he said. "It was well-hidden. We had to shift the mast to get it out. It took all my crew and Captain Ptahemhat's men." He hesitated and then said, "I thought it best to bring it straight to you, in view of the name on it and... and everything. Knowing how you and His Majesty... I brought it to you."

"Thank you, Captain," Nebamun said. "And thank your men for me. I will make sure that His Majesty receives it unopened."

"Yes, Holiness." The man paused, frowning, and then said, "I don't understand why Lord Pasenhor did not give it over. Or, if not, why he did not burn it."

"He was probably afraid that someone would smell it and ask questions," said Nebamun. "It will be set right at once."

He turned the message over in his hands after the man left, seeing the agitation in the handwriting. The galley he had sent to Semna had arrived with the dawn and the captain had come straight to him. He had reported that they must have passed Pharaoh's ship on the river, just south of Thebes and did not get the word until they docked a day's journey beyond the city.

Mistake piled upon mistake, Nebamun thought. *How to retrieve them?*

He raised his head as a tap sounded at the door. "Yes?"

Perineb entered. A scent of incense clung to him. "A fine morning," he said.

Nebamun looked up from the message. "It could be. Perhaps even a splendid day."

Perineb lifted his brows and sat. He met Nebamun's eyes. "It has come back, I see."

Nebamun balanced the package between his fingertips. "It is odd, Perineb, to have in my hands something that can heal a heart quickly."

Perineb's smile took a mischievous tilt. "We have many means for that. Right at our fingertips."

[49]

Nebamun lifted an eyebrow. "It is a very good thing, Perineb, that I am not widely known as a man of great wisdom and goodness. I would have to gather a store of such platitudes to be trotted out as needed."

Perineb grinned. "It does wear somewhat. But that does not negate the truth." He folded his hands before him. "Fortunately, children don't have such expectations."

Nebamun chuckled. "They are certainly refreshing. Disconcerting, as well, if you aren't prepared for it. You're teaching Ramesses' son, Hori. How is he doing now?"

"He's an engaging little scamp," Perineb said with a warm smile. "But a little subdued at the moment."

"By this time tomorrow, Perineb, Hori will be chattering and up to his usual mischief. If, that is, his father hasn't called for a general celebration."

Nebamun rose, squared his shoulders and nodded to Perineb. "I will be away for the rest of the day. His Majesty is holding an audience, and I must speak with him at once."

**   **   **

Another day at court. The death was old news and people had passed through their grief, as little as it had been, and were clamoring for the bright times to come again, as they appeared to be.

Perhaps they are, but they do not touch me, Seti thought, wearily considering the next item of concern. Ships from Nubia had arrived with treasure to be presented to the Temple.

Seti speared Prince Ramesses with a look. "The offerings from Kush must be presented to Ptah. You will take them without delay."

Ramesses looked up, startled. "I?" His voice was shaking with pleased surprise.

"Who else?" Seti sighed. "Your brother? Go and make the presentation, and then be about your business. I won't need you any further this day."

He stopped at the sound of a fist banging against the door to the chamber.

Ramesses started forward. Seti motioned him back and nodded to the Master at Arms.

Quiet voices; the man bowed and strode back up the aisle to drop to one knee. "The High Priest of Ptah requests an audience with The Lord of the Two Lands," he said.

Seti's weary face eased a little. "His Holiness is welcome whenever he comes, as he well knows. Bid him enter."

[50]

Lord Nebamun came up the aisle, the sound of his footsteps underscored by the tapping of his scepter on the paving. He was dressed in none of the usual finery of his rank. He looked, in fact, like a retired army officer. He came to the foot of the dais and began to kneel.

Seti stopped him. "No kneeling, Holiness."

Nebamun smiled and straightened. "I thank Your Majesty," he said. "It is good of you to receive me." His eyes lingered on Seti's face before turning to Ramesses, who had stepped forward to offer his arm.

Nebamun took it with a humorous smile and gripped his hand for a moment before turning to Seti. "If I may speak with Your Majesty?"

"Speak." Seti said.

"...in private."

Seti frowned and then nodded. He raised his voice to the room. "Leave us. I will summon you back when it is time."

Nebamun watched the room empty. Ramesses was lingering in the doorway, his expression doubtful. "Go ahead, lad," Nebamun said. "You have a commission from your father, as I have heard: go and perform it."

Ramesses lowered his head and left.

Nebamun eyed the guards who remained by the doors. "I asked to speak with you in private, Sire," he said. "I will be happy to surrender anything that may be considered a weapon if that will satisfy these strapping fellows. Or they are welcome to tie my hands behind me if they think it will ensure your safety."

Seti stared at him for a pained moment. "Tie your *hands*!" He stopped and motioned to the men. He turned to Nebamun as the doors closed and motioned to the smaller throne beside him. "Please. Sit down. You wanted to speak with me. You said it was urgent?"

Nebamun sat back and arranged his arms along the carved arms of the chair. "It is a matter of the greatest urgency," he said. "And you need to listen very carefully to me."

Seti sighed. "I am listening. What do you want to say that I must hear?"

Nebamun's smile faded at the acid tones. "It is this. Tuia bore you two sons. It is time for you to shake off the despair that you have been wallowing in and be a father again to the remaining one."

XIII

Prince Ramesses moved through the pylon gateway of the Temple of Ptah as His Majesty's envoy presenting gifts from Kush. The ceremony was brief: the announcement of Pharaoh's gift, acceptance by the Second Prophet, the goods and animals taken toward the sanctuary. Father Perineb bowed to Ramesses, who inclined his head, turned and went deeper into the temple.

The thought of returning to his life was too much to bear at that moment. Pasenhor's betrayal had been completely unexpected. The anger in his father's voice and face had been a blow to the heart. He had had no chance to plead his own case. And now his life seemed to be in ruins at his feet. He needed to catch his breath and regain his strength in the face of all that had changed.

The warm, old stones rose around him like a promise of protection. He saw a carving on the door post flanking the entrance to an inner courtyard, a bird with human arms upraised in worship: two hieroglyphs signifying the non-priestly. He was not a priest. He stepped inside.

A stream of worshipers was bringing their own offerings, bits of precious metal, animals for sacrifice, flowers. Cattle were lowing nearby. He could see the courtyard set aside for the slaughter of beasts for offerings. A cacophony of squawking geese, roaring bulls, the bleating of goats, cooing doves.

He needed peace. He turned and went out. A shady courtyard lay close by, the door marked by another carved lapwing. He moved through the gateway and looked around.

The pillars clustered about him, tapering like great papyrus stalks, brilliant with bright reliefs, channeling his gaze upward toward the great Pylon.

He lowered his eyes again. The courtyard was empty, though he could hear the whisper of sandals on the stone floors. He settled on his knees, his hands loosely clasped on his thighs, closed his eyes and lifted his face into the breeze that had pushed its way into the courtyard. The coiled tension within him eased a little as he drew breath and released it.

"Highness?"

The voice was quiet and respectful but somehow questioning. He opened his eyes and turned toward it.

Perineb stood before him. "The treasure from Kush has been bestowed, and we are cooking the offerings. Would you care to take some refreshment by the lake?"

Ramesses lowered his eyes and then nodded. "Yes, Your Grace," he said. "It would be welcome."

** ** **

The stream of wine chimed softly against the side of the lotus cup. Perineb set the jug aside and offered the cup to Ramesses. "There," he said. "Part of the governor's gifts, his choicest vintage, he tells us. See what you think."

Ramesses cupped the chalice between his hands, his fingers tracing the crisp, flowing lines of the carved petals. The wine held the scent of warm nights. He lowered his head and sipped.

"Well?"

Ramesses let the wine linger a moment, and then swallowed. It seemed to leave a glow. "It is wonderful," he said.

"Wine that gladdens the heart," Perineb said. "An old description, but true. Gladdens the heart and soothes the weary soul."

"Yes..." The word was almost inaudible.

"I am sorry, Sesse," Perineb said. "It has been a terrible time for you."

Ramesses sipped again. "I don't know what to do. If I try to speak he will look at me with cold eyes and hate me for something did not do. And if I force him to listen, and I could do it, it will hurt him. And so I see my father looking for Nakhtamun and seeing me and flinching."

"He is grieving for a son he lost suddenly and painfully. It has nothing to do with his love for you. It will pass."

Ramesses set his cup on the rim of the pond and trailed his fingers in the water. "I am not so sure," he said.

"You will be," Perineb said. "You have your own skills and blessings, and your father is aware of them. He is grieving, and it is very soon after he learned of Nakhtamun's death."

Ramesses' eyes widened and filled with tears.

Perineb poured a little more wine in Ramesses' cup. "Your father is not what is troubling you now," he said. "What is wrong?"

Ramesses drew a breath, tried to speak, swallowed the words and buried his face in his hands.

[53]

"What is it, Ramessu?" Perineb asked again. "As terrible as you think it, it will not make me hate you."

Ramesses looked up at Perineb and heard his father's voice in his mind. *You let him go to his death!*

"I am afraid."

"Yes?" the word was quiet, calm.

"I may have brought my brother's death." Ramesses said. "The week before he left. I asked him why. He was being autocratic." Ramesses stopped, gnawing his lip. "He had been increasingly so, and short-tempered, but—" he drew a shaking breath. "I asked him why he was going, and he said that he was King, and he would damned well do what he wanted to! I asked again: why was he taking the army north, and he answered again."

"He could indeed be autocratic," Perineb murmured with the hint of a smile. "And it could be annoying..."

"And I said that he could go with my blessing. That he was certain to do something stupid and get killed. I said they'd drag what was l-left of him back here and I'd have to clean up the mess!"

Perineb shifted his gaze to Ramesses' face. His mouth straightened and his smile faded. "And you have been remembering the words you said during that burst of vexation and thinking that somehow you brought it about?"

Ramesses lowered his head. "I know it is foolish, but I keep thinking that I might have. Father said I had sent him to his death. And then I think that no, I would have died rather than wish that on him! But I can't forget the words."

"We remember the most foolish things," Perineb said, "And we forget what is important." He looked down at his loosely clasped hands, choosing his words with great care.

"Listen to me, son. Nakhtamun met his own fate through his own actions, against the advice of all his advisors. He met it through the actions of the enemy he sought to fight. Forgive me, but it was a piece of unmatched stupidity that should have been beneath an experienced soldier like him. Your heedless words, said to stop him, did nothing to make him go or stay and did not somehow place a curse of destiny on him. If such a thing were possible, you would have died rather than let it happen."

"I watched him go."

"And, no doubt, thought 'Good riddance to you, you intemperate pest!' I am sorry your last days together were tainted with temper, but do you honestly think Nakhtamun didn't love you? That he left with the strong desire never to see you again?"

The bluntness of the words, despite Perineb's kind tones, made Ramesses look up sharply. The jeweled sidelock swung and chimed; Ramesses' brows drew together in a frown.

"But he didn't, you know," Perineb said. "There is much that you have forgotten, isn't there?"

Ramesses lowered his eyes. "I seem to remember all that happened," he said. "It repeats and repeats."

"But it repeats incorrectly," Perineb said. "I was there for his departure, and I saw and heard your final words. He was laughing at you, and you began to laugh, too. It was as though you were youngsters together again, with the shadow of kingship far from either of you. You kilted your robe and ran after him as he reached the gangplank. You were calling his name, and he stopped and smiled at you, and you spoke together privately. He ruffled your hair; you gripped his hands. He embraced you and continued to hold your hands and speak to you with a happy smile. And then he went on his way at last."

He watched Ramesses' expression. His voice was gentle as he said, "Do you remember now?"

"Yes," Ramesses said, half under his breath. "I said he was... the best brother I could ask for, if sometimes a pest. I told him to come again well and safe, and we could rejoice together."

"You had forgotten, hadn't you?"

"I .had." Ramesses' voice broke. "I wished him well. And he knew it. He *knew* it!"

"From what he seemed to be saying, he did the same to you."

"*I will miss you, too, best of brothers, best of friends.* He said that to me, and then he released me and went to the ship. And he waved to me as it moved away."

"You have that memory returned to you," Perineb said. "The tragedy of his death can't touch the love you had for each other."

"I thank Your Grace," he said. "With all my heart. I can't say how much..." he stopped.

"Highness?" The words were quiet, but the voice held a smile.

[55]

Ramesses opened his eyes. "I see myself stepping into Nakhtamun's position," he said. "And I think how wrong it is. I can't stop thinking that this is all a nightmare, and I will wake up and simply be myself."

Perineb smiled at him. "Ptah does nothing by accident, and He can turn tragedy into triumph." He added, "Your father will want to speak with you very soon."

XIV

Seti's eyes blazed. "Two sons!" he gasped. "Your Holiness presumes too—"

Lord Nebamun interrupted him without ceremony. "We are alone, Seti. His Majesty and His Holiness left this room with the rest of that crowd. The only people here at this moment are a retired Officer of Archers and the son of his friend Ramesses, whom he held years ago as a baby, and whom he came to know and love as a grown man. And who has now suffered a terrible loss. Your father can't be here. I am standing in his place and speaking as he would want to."

Seti stared for a moment and then closed his eyes.

"I can only imagine your grief," Nebamun said. "To have your world torn apart as cruelly and suddenly as this..."

Seti raised his face. "Of all people, you would certainly understand. But..."

Nebamun folded his arms and was silent.

Seti paused to master his voice. "...he was a soldier," he said at last. "I know that soldiers die... I am a soldier. I know it. But an ambush, and he riding along and singing, smiling as the arrows hit him one after another after another... and they coming forward as my son was dying, and they tried—" His voice broke.

"They did not succeed," Nebamun said. "Nakhtamun was rescued well before any of them could reach him. And they were all dead shortly after, along with the men who had spoken the lies that lured him there."

He met Seti's anguished gaze. "I questioned his staff exhaustively the day they arrived. I also examined Nakhtamun's body, myself, before it was made ready for the embalmers. It needed to be done. Ramesses and Perineb have never seen the aftermath of a battle, and I thought I should prepare them. I also knew that you would have specific questions. I am here to give you that report."

Seti closed his eyes. "Tell me."

"Nakhtamun reached the fortress at a gallop, well in advance of his vanguard, and the rest of his army, against their repeated advice. The ambush was awaiting him. He was struck directly to the heart with four arrows."

He nodded as Seti raised his head. "Yes. I examined the wounds. Nakhtamun was dying as he fell, with moments left to him when his staff arrived at top speed and cut their way to his side. The ambushers never touched him. He fell from his chariot into his second's arms. General Senwadjet held him as he died while the fighting went on around them."

"They never..." Seti's voice wavered.

"Senwadjet told me that Nakhtamun was smiling in his last moments. I saw the smile, myself. Perineb and Ramesses saw it when they came to prepare him. Ramesses, especially, was eased. Set your mind at rest, Seti. Nakhtamun died very quickly, he was not abused, mocked or tortured in his last moments."

Seti drew a shaking breath. "Then they didn't. The nightmares were false..."

"Nightmares usually are," Nebamun said. "It is time to wake up."

"But—" Seti's voice shook. "Such a *stupid* mistake! Letting the spies go, outrunning his vanguard, his staff arguing with him—"

"We have all made stupid mistakes," Nebamun said. "Sometimes we survive them."

"It should have been me, Nebamun! For a father to outlive his son! If only I had died in his place!"

"But you would never have made that stupid mistake. And he knew better, himself."

"He was *supposed* to remain in Memphis and learn from you and the others I had set to assist him! I ordered him-!"

"He chose not to obey. I tried to talk him out of it. He used his rank to override me after a hard argument. He told me he needed to think things over, and he thought he would be more clear-headed in the field."

Seti's anguished expression shifted to a scowl. "From what I've learned he spent very little time in thought!" He caught himself. "It should have been me." he said again.

"But it was not," Nebamun said. "It was his time, and your task is not finished." He added gently, "And you have a son to succeed you."

"Ramesses!"

"Yes. Ramesses. He's young, but he has much promise, even at eighteen years of age. By the time he is thirty, as his older brother was, he should be a man to make you proud."

Seti shook his head.

"Have you looked at him, Seti? He is young, yes. Not even twenty years old, and he is handsome. Are those faults? You share one of them in that case. He has the common touch. Crowds cheer him when he goes about. He grew up as the son of a Vizier, he moved through palaces and yet never lost his identity. He is aware of his weaknesses, and he has a good idea of his strengths. You know, as a General, how rare that is."

He drew up the low stool beside the throne.

Seti pushed himself to his feet before Nebamun could sit. "No," he said motioning to the throne. "Please, sit here."

Nebamun smiled and obeyed. "Your father was proud of you," he said. "I remember how he spoke of you as he was dying; of the good fortune in store for this land."

Seti sighed.

"But let us speak of the younger Ramesses," Nebamun said. "Faced with this unprecedented emergency, he dealt with it. He took this blow, sought counsel and then made decisions. He led this land." He smiled at Seti's stare. "He did. With the Vizier of the North, the Governor of Memphis, and myself. We advised him, but he made the decisions, and he issued all the orders. He addressed the problem of his brother's body and enlisted Perineb's help to begin the proper preparations. He ensured his brother's honorable entombment, disposed of his troops, and summoned you. And remember, to his credit, that he broke this terrible news to you, himself, even though you were caught in the first agony of grief and in a white heat. He sought to spare you as much as he could. He is a very good man, and I believe he will be a great one in time."

Seti considered this and turned his attention aside. "But I— Far away in Nubia, busy with nothings, and I received no word until my son... until my son was in his *tomb!* I came back to learn publicly that my son is dead. He is locked away in that tomb, laid to rest by strangers!"

"Nakhtamun was laid in his tomb with all ceremony by his brother who loved him. His sisters and their families were there, as were the great nobles of this land. It was done properly. I was there, and I witnessed it."

"No word at all!" Seti said through his teeth. "And all that long journey north to Memphis no one said anything to me at all. I was fearful at first, but nothing was said, even though that jackass Pasenhor was peering at me at all times. I finally demanded what was wrong, that he was staring at me so! He gaped at me, stammered 'Nothing!' and went below. And then, thinking all was well, I came home to *this!* It is more than I can understand."

"Ramesses sent this," Nebamun said.

Seti looked at the folded parcel of tattered papyrus lying across Nebamun's palm. "What is it?"

"Open it and read. It took a long time to compose."

Seti frowned, but he broke the remains of the clay seal, pushed the twine from the letter, and unfolded it, scanning the sheet. He read:

> *My Dearest Father,*
>
> *I grieve to tell you that Nakhtamun, your son and my beloved brother, was ambushed and killed while investigating a ruined fortress held by the Canaanites. He rode ahead of his force, and the foe struck stealthily. He died immediately and without pain in his second-in-command's arms. They brought his body to his camp and then to Memphis.*
>
> *Because of the time of year and the progress of nature, I have chosen to send my brother's body to the royal embalmers. If you have not returned by then, I will be overseeing his entombment along with my sisters and the princes of this land.*
>
> *It grieves me to be so far from you in this terrible time, unable to speak with you personally and give you what comfort I can. But I have given Pasenhor the task of bringing this letter and the word to Intef, who will stand by you as the good friend he has been to you and to our family all these years.*
>
> *Please believe that I do what I am doing with the conviction that it is what you yourself would direct me to do-*

Seti's voice broke. He scowled and lowered the note. "I never received this!"

"That is because the messenger chose not to deliver it. In all fairness to him, he probably judged that it would be best for you to receive the word from your son."

Seti's eyes narrowed. "But Ramesses never told me he had sent a letter."

"He tried. I heard him. Did you listen to him?"

"But now—"

"He apparently decided it was not worth pursuing the matter with you once you had returned. Ramesses is perfectly capable of dealing with the issue, himself." His expression softened. "He has been breaking his heart because it was Nakhtamun who was killed instead of him."

Seti stared. "He's a fool!" he exclaimed. "How could he think that I would welcome *his* death or that of any of my children?"

"He is young, for all that he's a father himself. Whether that is how you feel at this moment, it is what he thinks." His gaze was very direct. "What could he think after you ordered him from your sight before all of Memphis when he tried tell you what had happened?"

Seti lowered his eyes. "Oh, ye gods," he sighed.

"Few know better than I the devastating nature of tragedy," Nebamun said. "But to see a man of your intelligence and self-control lose his temper so disastrously and," his eyes narrowed, "so thoroughly 'kill the messenger' who brings bad tidings astonished me. I would not have thought it of you."

Seti's brows drew together.

"Listen to me. We are apart from others, and we can speak freely. Anyone with a heart can understand your anguish at that moment, but that moment is past. Do you want to lose your other son? I warn you; you are in danger of it!"

"No!"

"Yes! Not that he would renounce you or hate you. He is not made that way. But now that you know what happened you must mend matters, or he will go away as thoroughly as Nakhtamun did."

Seti drew himself up. "I don't believe you!" he said.

"Don't you?"

Seti looked down at his hands. "You are right, Nebamun," he said at last. "I have behaved badly."

"Not badly. But it is time to set matters straight with Ramesses."

"*Will* he forgive me?"

"You know the answer already," Nebamun said. His voice gentled. "It is not too late, I promise you. But don't delay."

Seti nodded, his mouth tight. He sank down again on the footstool. "I am lost," he said. "I have never been so...The nightmares, the memories that come unbidden…" He fell silent for a moment before looking up at Nebamun. "I don't know what to do."

"I know, Seti. Believe me. And I have been considering." Nebamun chose his words carefully. "This grief came to you without warning. You have had no chance to come to terms with it. To be alone and remember and mourn. You must do so for your own sake."

Seti lowered his head. "But I am King."

"You are also a man and a father. Go where you can be private, with no one to peer at you and point and say, 'There goes His Majesty'. Travel to your son's tomb and put offerings there, as you should, but then take steps to be private, to catch your breath. You have estates to the north. You could go to one of them with a handful of servants, as needed. Or travel to one of the great temples, where they would respect your need for solitude. We will muddle along without you for a time. We have done so before when you went to war. You have a Crown Prince who has the gift of knowing who is capable and can be allowed to run things." His voice gentled. "Ramesses will be under my care, and you know that I love him. You needn't worry about him."

Seti looked up at him.

Nebamun's eyes narrowed with the edge of a grim smile. "And when you come back, you can set about avenging a death."

Seti's expression wavered. He set his clasped hands on Nebamun's knees and gazed down at them. "I would give my life," he said, "gladly, not to have this death to avenge."

XV

Ramesses sat by the reflecting pond and laughed at Hori and Rai as they pushed palm-leaf boats into the water and tried to race them by blowing on the papyrus-scrap sails. The boats were inexpertly rigged, and the children spent a good deal of time trying to get them to sail straight ahead.

Rai, the younger by about five months, waded into the water to push his boat.

Hori watched him, shook his head, and tied a length of twine around his boat's mast. "Look!" he called, "It goes faster!" He gave the twine a sturdy yank that made the boat founder.

Rai sat down in the mud and laughed while Hori fished the boat from the pond, up-ended it, and set it back on the water. Both boys looked up at Ramesses, smiling widely.

As he watched, their expressions changed to unease. They stepped out of the water and waited.

Ramesses turned to look over his shoulder.

His father was coming quietly toward him, his hand on the major-domo's shoulder.

The man stopped and cleared his throat. "I am directed to tell you that your father asks the favor of speech with you," he said.

Ramesses pushed to his feet, awkward with haste. "Take them to their ayah," he told Teti. When they had gone he looked at Seti. "Your Majesty," he began.

"'His Majesty' is not here, Sesse," Seti said. "Only your father, and he begs to speak with you, if you will hear him."

"If I will?" Ramesses repeated. "Of course I would! How could you doubt it?"

"Easily," Seti said. "Sesse, I have done unjust things in my life. This may have been the worst of them. Have you the charity to listen to me now while I try to set things right between us?"

"But there is nothing to set right!" Ramesses said. "Ptah's beard, Father! In this time of grief for you—"

"I was not the only one to suffer a loss," Seti said. "May I sit down?"

Ramesses looked more closely at him. "Please," he said. "Sit down."

Seti hesitated at the edge of the pond and reached out to take the boat that Hori had been sailing. He lifted it in his hands and smiled down at it, seeing in his mind a small image of a child, *his* child, holding just such a boat and asking if he might go to the pond to sail it.

Oh, Nakhti, he thought. He set it on the pond and sent it skittering across the water with a gentle push.

He straightened. "I seem to have been wandering through a wasteland," he said. "After a week of strange looks from Pasenhor–and *how* did my father come to confirm him as Vizier?–I should have expected to hear what I heard when I arrived in Memphis. But I had hoped—"

"I am sorry," Ramesses said.

"Spare me unnecessary apologies," Seti said. He selected a spot by the water and sat down cross-legged, remembering for a moment the years when he had sat like that, papyrus spread across his lap, composing his reports.

"I knew you had to stay where you were, to take care of what was immediately necessary," he said. He looked up from the sun dancing on the water. "This is a hard time for corpses. I understood all that. But I kept thinking, unreasonably, that you should have come to me at once and told me."

Ramesses lowered his head. "I wanted to."

Seti looked full at him. "You did," he said. "You sent word to me by someone you trusted. You tried to spare me public pain. I know now that you wanted to come to me, yourself, but you were needed here in Memphis and then in Thebes. It was the right thing to do." He paused, choosing his words. "You are a son to make a father proud, and I want you to know it at once, and to know, as well, that I bitterly regret the things I said in my first shock on learning of Nakhtamun's death. You did nothing to hurt me. I did much to hurt you, and it was all ill-done."

He raised his eyes to his son's. "I am ashamed," he said. "Can you forgive me for my cruelty when you, yourself, were reeling from this blow and striving to do what had to be done? You did very well. I beg you to believe that I spoke on impulse, not from the heart."

"I never thought otherwise, Father," Ramesses said.

Seti smiled, though he winced. "You have a generous heart, Sesse."

He took out the message. "The word may have come to me late, but it was through no fault of yours, my son. As you see, it came at last, and I have no cause to complain of you. Had it never come I still would have no cause to complain." He set the letter between them and said quietly, "What more could you have done during this dreadful time, Sesse, than what you did?"

Ramesses stared at the packet and then lowered his eyes. "You did receive it," he said. "At last. If only it had come to you in time."

"You will learn, Sesse that the words 'if only' number among the most useless, and the most painful. You have no cause for regrets. You have been a shining example to me of excellence and courage. You have made me proud."

Ramesses eyed the letter, but did not touch it. "Thank you," he said. He frowned. "But how did you get the message?"

"Thank His Holiness," Seti said. "He would not tell me who the messenger was to have been, though I have my suspicions." He paused for a moment, waiting for his son to say the name he had written in the message. His smile assumed an ironic bend when Ramesses remained silent. "But he made sure that I had the message. It gave me some ease."

Ramesses stretched out his hand to his father.

Seti gripped it. "I must leave you once more," he said. "I will be traveling to Thebes. I want to place some offerings in Nakhtamun's tomb. His bow... Little things, but things I must do..." He smiled and rose. "You are Egypt's Crown Prince, Ramessu. Egypt could have no better man at its head than you. And you could have no better advisors than those around you. I am content."

"Will you be long? Should I come with you?"

"I must go alone," Seti said. "It may take some time..." He paused. "I will send word as I can, and return in good time. And Sesse—"

Ramesses looked up at him.

Seti's expression grew grim. "I have dealt with Pasenhor. Thoroughly. You need not give him another thought. Ever."

XVI
Northwest of Thebes

The boy tossed the pebble with his left hand, sending the flock of feeding ducks exploding upward. He hurled the bent throwing stick into their midst. *Thwack!* A duck came hurtling to earth.

"Got it!" the boy crowed, pushing his papyrus skiff into the water and paddling over. The inundation was at its full height, the marshy borders of the Nile teeming with waterfowl in pursuit of the schools of fish that darted in the shallow waters of the river's edge. This afternoon they had caught far more than their usual haul. The duck would be filleted, dried and stored against leaner times. His mother would be delighted.

"You cheated!" his friend shouted.

"Cheated!" he yelled back with an extravagant gesture he had observed among the stevedores at the docks. "You idiot! I threw it clean!"

"You used a pebble!"

"You'd have used it if you thought of it!" He reached out and lifted the floating duck onto the deck. The water beaded and ran off the iridescent feathers. The boy wrung its neck with a shout of delight. "That makes three to your two!" he said.

"Says you!" The thicket of reeds clattered in the wind; their sound was overlaid by the plash and hiss of water. Movement through the dappled shade, a rhythmic splashing...

The two boys traded surprised glances and edged their skiffs through the reeds, the bows nosing into the river.

They parted the reeds and stared across the river toward the western shore.

A huge ship was slicing through the water, heading south on the wind. Twin plumes of foam streamed to either side of her jutting prow.

The boys stared. "Look!" Khwed hissed. "On the sail!"

They frowned at the oval enclosing three symbols. Ani sounded them out. "'Men'" he said. He eyed the middle symbol, the figure of a seated woman with a feather on her head. "Maat and Re above her! Men Maat Re!" He gasped. "It's His Majesty's ship!"

**   **   **

Men-Maat-Re Seti Merneptah, King of Upper and Lower Egypt, leaned his forearms on the top rail of *Ruler of Kings* and watched as she surged along the Nile on the back of the prevailing winds. They were moving between twin ribbons of green, the cultivated land—'the black land'—bordering the great river. A veil of acacias and palm trees hid the red land of the desert that lay beyond the fertile land.

Two boys on papyrus skiffs were paddling swiftly upstream. One of them had a poacher's haul of ducks. They looked up as *Ruler of Kings* passed. He caught their wide, startled gaze and smiled. White grins split their faces and he could see them waving before a bend of the river took him far from them.

By noon, the scenery had changed from palm trees, fertile land and desert to the sprawl of Thebes, flashing and glittering in the distance like a stretch of wind-rippled water at noon. They were drawing closer. He could make out gilding on white-painted buildings, gold-sheathed obelisks rising before the temples and beyond them the stark shoulders of the hills, bordering the desert.

A trumpet sounded from the shore. *Ruler of Kings* had been sighted and the people of Thebes were assembling.

He sighed and pushed away from the rail.

XVII

Deir el Medineh Near Thebes

The old man settled his hands on the head of his staff and gazed up the sweep of the hill. He had loved traveling that path, over the years, gazing down at the river, watching the passing ships... How long had it been? A turn of the Nile? He remembered his wife with him, they laughing as they scaled the steep hillside. She had died, how many inundations ago? Four? Five?

Too many. And he had allowed himself to grow old.

He frowned at the hillside and then, thrusting his staff into the shifting earth, began to scale the heights. Not so far now. He was almost there.

Ah, it was good to remember his youth. The years he ran up this slope and gained the summit without even being winded. Gone long ago. He reached the top of the hill, steadied himself on the path, and looked down at the river. A breeze was rising from the sparkling waters, lifting his wisps of hair, cooling his cheeks. He turned his face into it and smiled again.

The notes of a trumpet, north and east of him, from one of the great temples, made him open his eyes and look upriver. The trumpet sounded again. He had heard that His Majesty was coming to Thebes. It must be him. May all the gods bless him! To lose his son so disastrously! Any father's heart would break at that news. If the gods were kind, seeing how his son was now bestowed might set his heart at rest.

A sound behind him made him shake his head and turn straight into the blaze of pale eyes in sunburned faces, hear words he could not understand.

His voice quavered, steadied. "Who are you?" he demanded.

A hand cracked across his face once.

The staff dropped from his hand. He cried out as he fell and again as the rocks of the path gouged into his shoulder.

Curses, footsteps. They were gone.

He opened his eyes to the sky and wondered for a moment why he was looking at blue... Memory came back.

He tried to move, to roll to his knees. He wept as a wave of pain made the world spin about him.

**   **   **

A grand procession of pylons and courtyards to the east was the vast bulk of Opet with its cluster of white-painted houses about its knees. Seti turned to gaze toward the west, watching the great mortuary temples slipping by against the backdrop of the hills.

The two seated colossal statues of Amenhotep the Magnificent were passing to starboard now, the waters of the inundation lapping at their plinths. He could see the temple of the great King behind it, white-painted pylons towering above the crowds below, their reliefs depicting the King at the height of his reign, symbolically smashing his foes.

Seti gazed at the carvings and then smiled ironically. He had paused there many times in his years as Commander of the Armies to bring offerings to the great temples and commission prayers for success. He had always been an historian: Egypt, not its foes, was smashed at the end of Amenhotep's reign, its disintegration hastened by his son, who called himself Akhenaten. Now Egypt was in resurgence, its armies on the march again, trade booming again...

He turned away with a sigh. This task would be behind him soon and he could breathe easily again.

He looked down at his hands, gripped together on the top rail. A flash of blue made him smile; the ring Nakhtamun had given him, inscribed with Nakhtamun's name. The lad had been all of eight years old, bringing a gift on the eve of Seti's departure for a campaign to the south. Something to keep him safe, he had said. And he had found the box containing Nakhtamun's bow among the effects that had been sent back with his body. It had been overlooked in the hurry to have him embalmed and interred. The bow had escaped the fate of other such weapons, broken so that they could not injure their owners.

Seti had shaken his head at that superstition. He had spent the better part of a day smoothing and polishing the wood and horn of the great composite bow, buffing the gold-washed bronze tips, selecting the best bowstrings, and then carefully wrapping the bow in layer upon layer of oiled leather, finally placing it in the box. He had left the box as it was, the wood scarred and battered from half a lifetime of campaigning. He could see it with the eye of memory, never far from his son.

He sighed. So many things had been left incomplete. Words he had meant to say, all the things he had meant to do. The foray into the desert to hunt gazelle. Nakhtamun had

[69]

spoken of it many times, even before he had become King. There had been so little time and so many responsibilities. He now thought, wistfully, that he would gladly trade a decade of his life just for the chance to step into the past and do the things he had always thought he might when there were no distractions.

The lowering sun was in his eyes now. He crossed the deck and gazed out across the eastern bank, watching the landscape...

** ** **

Djedi stepped from the dim coolness of His Majesty's tomb into the bright afternoon light. The hot air was pleasant against his bare arms, chasing away the lingering chill of the rock-hewn chambers. He shouldered his satchel and frowned at the damp brushes in his hands. Serving an apprenticeship under the Master Painter was not easy, he spent more time grinding pigments from the different minerals and mixing paints than he did actually painting. Drudgery, but necessary for an apprentice. If all had passed as it should have, the Master would have been his own father. But his father and mother were gone, buried among the tombs of the village.

But this day had been a good one, with Master Sennedjem complimenting him. A smile, a nod... Words to the Senior Foreman himself, who clapped him on the shoulder and smiled at him, and said he wasn't at all surprised.

Could the day get any better?

He passed through the closeness of the valley path and paused before the beginning of the track running along the crest of the hills that led to the southern end of his village. He hesitated, then chose the hilltop road... A view of the Nile would be fine, a way to withdraw from the pressure of learning and performing, a way to savor the talent he always knew he had, but which others were now recognizing.

He was near the entry now. Voices caught his attention, accents from other lands. And a cry of fear.

He dropped his satchel and ran along the track toward the sounds.

Three men moving away, a man on the ground. The fallen man lifted his head... Djedi was caught by the terror of his expression.

The others were gone. He ran to the old man's side and dropped to his knees.

[70]

Bewildered eyes raised to his. The old man's face was spattered with blood.

"Little Father? You're hurt! What happened?"

"I didn't mean to anger them."

"Anger them?" Djedi repeated. "What happened?"

But the man, blank-eyed with shock, was wavering, his speech growing fainter.

Djedi looked around. "Here, Little Father. I'll carry you home." The old man closed his eyes. Djedi set an arm about his shoulders, another beneath his knees, and rose.

Others were there now, coming from the tomb, asking questions.

"Master Kenamun must be told," said his painting master, steadying him as they moved along the track.

Nods all around.

The old man opened his eyes. He seemed more alert now, gazing at Djedi with a touch of wonder. "A warrior!" the man said. "A warrior come to save me!"

Djedi shifted the weight. "Are you better now?" he asked.

"You rescued me..."

"I wish I had come sooner. What-what did they want?"

The old man closed his eyes. "I asked. They did not answer. It was good you came when you did."

XVIII
Thebes

The Royal Palace lay before Seti, bordered by high walls, surrounded by palm trees, scented with flowers. Seti leaned his forearms on the top rail as the ship glided in to the dock and was made secure. He straightened as the gangplank was lowered and made fast, waited as they spread lengths of fine cloth over the walkway, then pushed himself to his feet and strode to the dock, smiling slightly at the bows and greetings of the others. A chair was awaiting him, as was Count Intef.

He listened to their greetings, replied suitably, and accepted Count Intef's escort to the palace of Djed-Nefer, where a gala feast awaited him. He closed his eyes for a moment and then, seeing Intef's worried expression, nodded.

He moved through the feast without heeding; responding to the speeches and music and entertainment with practiced ease that did not touch his mind. He did justice to the food, applauded the dancers, and then turned to Intef and said, "I will travel to my son's tomb tomorrow."

Count Intef blinked. He had been giving what he thought was an account of possible incursions from the west, which might possibly require the royal army's intervention, and he had received all the appropriate responses. His Majesty had not been listening. His expression shifted to worry, but his voice was level when he replied. "I will assign guards to escort you."

Seti accepted another cup of wine poured by the Vizier himself. "I will need only two men," he said. "If that many."

"Sire?"

Seti sighed. "This is not a visit of state, Intef. I want to see my son's tomb..." His smile quivered and faded. "There are things I must see, must say... it is my only chance, and I must take it."

"I will still assign an escort," Intef said. "And I will come along, myself. It will have to be more than two men, I regret to say. There have been signs of activity from the south and east... I don't want to take chances."

"Yes, well," Seti said. "I wish my son had had that caution."

Intef lifted his cup of wine. "Why didn't they tell you?" he asked quietly, under the noise of the feast.

Seti looked into his own cup. "They did," he said.

"What!" Intef blinked and then scowled. "Pasenhor knew! That is why he–"

"–behaved so oddly as he came aboard," Seti finished. His smile narrowed. "He was to give the message to you, it seems. But he could not."

"I was standing right there as he boarded!"

"You were on the point of leaving. I have learned that Pasenhor is not capable of thinking quickly."

"Or thinking at all." Intef shook his head slowly, as if clearing it. "Unbelieveable: I could throttle the man!"

"I have taken care of matters, and we needn't discuss him any further, Intef."

"We won't," Intef said. He lowered his voice. "Old friend... I wish—I wish I could have done something..."

"You already have." Seti set his cup down and reached for more meat as the sounds of flutes and drums rose around him.

XIX

Kenamun, the senior foreman of the village of Tomb-Workers, stood at the juncture of the two valley paths and waited. His Majesty was coming to the Valley of the Kings to see with his own eyes the tomb of his son. Kenamun had been present at the entombment over a moon ago. Pharaoh, far to the south, as he had been told, was not there. The Crown Prince, who had performed the offices along with the priests, had been composed and capable, but Kenamun had caught a sense of rigidly controlled uncertainty. He had smiled at the prince and received a startled, somehow shy nod in return.

A shout: His Majesty was arriving. Kenamun turned to gaze along the processional way.

Pharaoh was in full regalia, wearing the garments and jewels of his station, a sphinx headdress laying on his shoulders, the Cobra rearing above his brow, the Gold of Honor around his neck and wrists. His eyes were outlined with kohl, the corners drawn to meet the brows. He held a long, narrow box of scarred wood on his lap.

The procession approached along the hot track, bumping over rocks and scree, the attendants, conscious of the gravity of the visit, moving in silence, the corps of guards looking around with narrowed eyes. And then they stopped at the base of the valley, in a spot where the surrounding cliffs channeled the eyes upward to the ridge bordering the desert.

Pharaoh stepped down from the chair and frowned up the cliff face.

Kenamun caught Count Intef's nod and came forward to kneel before the King and bow his head to the ground.

"Get to your feet, my good man," His Majesty said. The voice was controlled, but Kenamun caught the hint of a quiver.

Intef stepped forward. "Master Kenamun is the senior foreman of the city of workmen at Deir el Medineh. He has come in answer to your summons."

Kenamun pushed to his feet and waited as they gazed up the escarpment.

Pharaoh turned to him, frowning. "Where is it?".

"Up the hillside, Sire. There is an irregularity in the ground. It is very slight, but visible. Can Your Majesty see it?"

Pharaoh frowned and then shook his head. "If you can see it, Master Foreman, I am content," he said. "But how do we go up there?" He paused. "Is there an entrance from higher ground?"

Kenamun darted a surprised look at Intef. "I wasn't told that Your Majesty wanted to enter the tomb," he said. "It could be done with some— Sire!'

Pharaoh, the box clutched in his arms. was striding toward the vertical cliff face at a pace that left Kenamun and Intef puffing behind him.

Intef caught up with him, Kenamun right behind him. "What are you doing?" the Vizier demanded in a whisper.

"I am trying to see my son's tomb," Pharaoh said through his teeth. "He was buried over a month ago. That's what I was told. Where is it? Are we in the wrong place? I can't see it." His voice wavered. "I can't see it, Intef..."

Intef's hand stretched out toward him, hesitated, settled on his shoulder. His voice was quiet. "Seti..."

Kenamun had come up behind them. "If it please Your Majesty—"

Seti rounded on him. "What do you want?"

"The tomb is up in the hillside, Sire," Kenamun began.

"But I don't see it," Pharaoh said wearily. "I brought these for him. He needs them and nobody thought to put them in the tomb with him. It was so sudden... I did not know he was gone. I never had the chance to say goodbye, and I thought these... but..." His voice quivered. Kenamun caught the glint of tears in his eyes before he looked down and away.

Kenamun thought, *He is still grieving... and he is exhausted.* "Sire," he said. He hesitated as Pharaoh turned to look at him, his hand at his eyes. "There is no mistake. The tomb is there and safe. The entry is disguised by plaster tinted to match the rocks, as is our practice. If you are not trained to look for it, then it will be invisible to you. It is what we intended, and you can see how effective it is."

His Majesty's expression eased. He lowered his hand and gazed at Kenamun with a sort of agonized hope that made the foreman's heart contract.

Kenamun continued, "We erected scaffolding during the years that the tomb was being constructed. I did much of the carving, myself. The workers climbed the scaffolding to get in there. The stone chips were carried to the entryway and emptied down the cliff face at the end of each day. You can see the lighter stone there, Sire-if you look. I promise, Sire. Your son's body is there, safe and secure."

"But to get there—"

Kenamun drew a careful breath. This was Pharaoh, but he was also a sorrowing father. "My men and I will rebuild the scaffolding so that you may climb to the tomb," he said. "If Your Majesty will come back in two days' time, you will be able to go there." He hesitated and then added, "And we will open the entryway for you, so that Your Majesty may enter and see how your son has been bestowed and provided for."

Pharaoh turned and looked at him for an anguished moment. Kenamun, lowering his eyes in the face of that gaze, thought, *The lines of his skull are very clear. If I were to see him again, without the robes or the jewelry or the kohl, I would still know him.*

His Majesty finally nodded. "I thank you, good Foreman," he said. The back of his hand was before his eyes again, but his voice was steadier. "I will return as you have said." He turned and stepped into his chair. The servants hoisted it, turned, and went back toward the city in silence.

**   **   **

Kenamun paused at the crest of the hillside overlooking Deir el Medineh and let his eyes linger on the blue-green ribbon of the Nile. The first Thutmose had established the village to house workmen and artists who built and decorated the royal tombs outside Thebes. It was situated between the Valley of the Kings and the Valley of the Queens. All royal tombs had been constructed by the residents of the town for over two hundred years, except for a brief time when Akhenaten used his own men to build the tombs in and around Akhet-Aten.

The village's cemeteries covered the hillsides to his left. After all this time, the tombs of the Deir el Medineh workmen took up more space than the town itself. While the town was comfortably situated in a valley, the tombs, terraced and topped with small pyramids, climbed the hillside, a reminder of centuries of service.

Kenamun paused as he always did, looking down over the tombs to the village itself, laid out neatly in its fold of valley. He smiled and went to the cemetery. His parents were buried there. He paused to place a small offering before their grave. His oldest child was there with them. The memory still hurt after ten years. He remembered the pain in Pharaoh's voice. *It fades,* he thought. *But it never fades entirely.*

He returned to the path and began the descent to the town. Moments later he was abreast of the walls. He could see people moving about in the coolness of the afternoon; heads were raised, someone called his name. He smiled and quickened his pace. Moments later he was by the village well, greeting his fellows, smiling at the children.

"Welcome back," said his nephew, Neferhotep, the Junior Foreman of the village. "An eventful day, certainly."

The tone was dry. Kenamun smiled wryly. "Eventful," he said. "But all is well. Come to my house for a cup of beer. I have a great deal to report."

**   **   **

Kenamun lifted his cup and sipped, suppressing a smile at the curious gazes of the others. He had been greeted, escorted to a seat of honor in the town square, and presented with the first cup of beer. "His Majesty will return in two days' time," he said. "It will give us time to rebuild the scaffolding and reopen the tomb."

"Can we even do that?" asked the Senior Stonemason.

"*He* can," Kenamun said. "He wants it done, and we are going to do it."

"But shouldn't we have a priest presiding?" asked Kenamun's son-in-law, offering more beer and some bread.

Kenamun selected a small loaf and broke the tip off. "It is a good idea," he said slowly. "See to it; Father Peri would be the best. For the rest, it will take a day at most to throw the scaffolding back up if we hurry, but we'd best be careful. And not much time to open the tomb." He frowned thoughtfully and added, "I must go to Abydos, but I can delay until His Majesty has done what he came to do."

"But I don't understand why His Majesty is doing this! The burial was done, the tomb was closed, and the Osiris Nakhtamun is safe."

Kenamun looked at the Stonemason. "His Majesty is a man, Isesi, whose son was killed, embalmed and shut away in a tomb while he was far away and without any notion of what was happening. Who am I to deny a father the right to weep for his lost child?"

Sidelong looks, slow nods.

"Well, then," said Kenamun. "We'd best get to work at first light."

"But what of His Majesty's own tomb?"

[77]

"He won't grudge the time away from it," Kenamun said. "This is far more important to him."

XX

Kenamun stood on the platform before the tomb opening. The tinted plaster had been broken away by the blows of a maul that had bitten into it again and again, cutting it away in great, uncured chunks. The work had gone slowly, late into the night, though the plaster had been slightly wet and friable still.

"I don't want a mess," Kenamun had said. "His Majesty is here because he wants to lay his son to rest personally."

"But His Majesty—"

"—is a father. Do the job right." He smiled at them. "Or answer to me."

He had heard some suppressed grumbling, but the plastered edges were smooth and clean, the entry swept clear of debris. Father Peri had said the proper prayers and had lingered by the tomb more, Kenamun thought, to reassure His Majesty that all had been done properly than to promote himself.

Pharaoh was standing before the doorway, looking up at the hewn, living rock, his hand upon the crisply cut edges. He had carried the long, battered box up the narrow steps; it rested against his shoulder, almost like the shaft of a spear.

"As you see, Majesty," Kenamun said. "It is ready for you."

"Thank you," Pharaoh said. "I will come down when I have finished."

Kenamun bowed as His Majesty took the torch, lifted the dark box and went into the tomb. He descended the steps to the valley floor and sat down with Pharaoh's escort to wait.

**   **   **

Seti stepped into the anteroom and looked around with dazzled eyes. It appeared to be filled from floor to ceiling with a jumble of goods. Vases, bowls, pots, baskets tied with rope. Figures of gods and goddesses; in the corner of the first room, he could see his son's dismantled chariot, the gold-mounted harness-tree and yokes flashing bright in the fitful torchlight. Had Nakhtamun been riding in that when the arrows struck him?

He could see boxes. Filled with his clothing, maybe? His robes, his sandals, no doubt. Boxes of jewelry, the gold of honor Nakhtamun had won for valor in battle in the years before his father died, Seti became King, and Nakhtamun began to pace in his cage.

Had he done ill to-his mind shuddered to a halt for a moment, his breath catching in his throat. And then he relaxed. Done ill to what? Inherit a Kingdom? What choice had he? Could he honestly say he had done ill deliberately? And had Nakhtamun possibly thought that? No. His Nakhti had not thought such a thing. What other choice had they when he, Seti, was King and Nakhtamun was his eldest son? Nakhti knew now; he was among the Blest.

He frowned and looked down the length of the tomb. The burial chamber was at the back. He nodded, lifted his torch and moved toward it.

Guardian statues, painted the black of the fertile earth of Egypt, leapt into being, picked out by the torchlight. They flanked the doorways, their gold garments and crowns glinting, their wide, inlaid eyes eerily bright. One of them held a mace, the other gripped a spear. He moved between them with a nod, one eye on the mace, remembering another time, years ago in another tomb.

A large, white mass in the corner revealed itself as the huge limestone sarcophagus, severe and chaste in its shape. He had wanted to set the box in there, but the lid was too heavy to lift, and he had no time to call in the workers. And his mind shied away from breaking the seal. He set the box beside the sarcophagus, as though it were within easy reach of a sleeping man and stepped back.

Eyes upon him— He turned quickly, hasty words rising to his lips. Nakhtamun was seated in upright, elegant ease, his palms on his thighs, gazing at him with a pensive, slightly melancholy expression.

Seti's breath froze in his throat. For a moment it had seemed to his weary heart that he had been mistaken; his son was *not* dead, *not* gone. He was sitting there, ready to speak with him—And then he realized that he was looking at the statue he had commissioned years before, when kingship for Nakhtamun was merely thunder upon the horizon. Now it was in his tomb. How had it come to this remote place?

The reality smote him like a blow to the breastbone. He dropped to his knees before his son's memorial statue and wept. It was time to accept the truth. His firstborn was dead, gone beyond his voice, beyond his touch, into that land...

So just and fair
Where fear is not...

He felt as though another had spoken through a smile. Just and fair, free of fear... There were so many things to fear, he thought. Loneliness, violence, the disintegration of one's character, betrayal, loss. But that fair land was far from him, and he had not been prepared for this separation. He lingered, there on his knees, his hands loosely linked on his thighs, his eyes gazing inward, remembering.

It was as though in that space of time he lived through the moments of his son's life, from the time that he lifted the newborn in his arms, smiling at his father's beaming face, to this moment, before a statue carved of stone. It was complete, and if he was unprepared for it, what help was there? It was time to let his son go.

He pushed to his feet, knuckles against the floor, and lifted the box with the bow.

"I have come, Nakhti," he said into the thick silence. "I am here beside you." He paused, almost expecting his son's smile-tinged voice to answer. But the silence remained untouched. "I have come all the long way from Memphis. I... had to come. They forgot to bring your bow, Nakhti, so I have it here, protected against the dryness here, and the dust. I brought extra bowstrings, as well. They said it should be broken, lest it hurt you in the fields of Yaru. They were fools who said it. I didn't do that. It's here, to hand, for your use if ever you have need of it."

He looked down at his hand and slid the small ring from his finger. "I have your ring here. Do you remember? You brought it to me just before I left to fight in the south. You said it would keep you with me and keep me safe. I saved it all these years. I never thought I would return to you in your tomb. You will have it in the Fields of the West. You can fit it on your little finger s-still..."

His voice wavered, broke, and he doubled against his knees, the ring in his hands. "My little boy... Oh, my little boy... I should have died, not you! If I could turn the sun back all those days and step in front of those arrows— If it meant that you would still be alive and well under the warm sun— I would do it gladly if I had known that our parting that day in Memphis would be the last in this life ..."

He opened his hand and stared at the ring, his other hand to his eyes. After a long moment he opened the bow's box and put the ring there, then closed it.

He set the box beside the sarcophagus and looked down at it, remembering times and days. The flash of sun on a papyrus skiff among the reeds outside Memphis. He had been Vizier then, his son nearly twenty. They had laughed, so much at ease together that they might have been friends rather than father and son. And the time had passed with such heartbreaking speed. He had not known how swiftly his son's life would run out.

He drew a shaking breath. "Soldiers die, and you did. Now you are in the Fields of the West, under the eternal sun."

He fell silent for a long time. "I have brought your bow," he said at last. "It is here, for your use. I must go on now. As must you. We will meet again."

He pushed to his feet, gazed at the statue, and slowly, carefully, brought his hand up to the carved face, touching it lightly with his fingertips, feeling the shape of the face depicted in the stone. "Goodbye, Nakhti," he said.

** ** **

"You may seal it now," he said as he stepped into the fading light.

He descended the rickety steps, mounted his chariot, nodded to Kenamun and the tomb crew, and left.

XXI

The sun sparked a line of fire along the Libyan hills when Seti arrived in the palace courtyard in a whirl of dust. His horses were lathered and blown; the time he had spent tearing across the flatlands, circling almost to the river and racing the gazelles in the desert lands had devoured the afternoon and left him weary and more content than he had been since he had first learned of his son's death.

He tightened his grip on the reins; the pressure on their bits brought the horses to a collected trot that eased into an amble.

Seti stepped down from the chariot and went to their heads. The near horse tossed his head and champed on the foam-spattered bit. He smiled and gave the horse's forehead an admonitory rub. "You've had a hard afternoon," he said. "Have faith. You will be fed!" He caught the eye of the nearest guard. "Take this team to the stable master," he said, dragging the rich headdress and gilded browband from his head and tossing it over one arm, along with his pleated tunic. "I am in haste."

The man went to one knee, rose and took the reins. The horses seemed to like him. Seti nodded to the man, turned on his heel, and strode into the palace's dim coolness. His footsteps seemed to echo down the hallways, as though everyone held their breath as he passed.

He was at his chambers. The guards flanking the doors knelt and then swung them open. He nodded to them, went into his chambers and gazed around as he pulled off his damp driving gloves.

The luxurious appointments appeared to his suddenly weary gaze as a jumble of color and glitter. Piles of pillows, gilded chairs, a harp in the corner (when had he *ever* played a harp?) elegant vases in gilded bronze ring stands. He thought a cup of wine would be welcome. And then he remembered that His Majesty had to call for wine whenever he wanted a sip. It would never do to have one's wine sitting untended. What if there was an assassination attempt?

"He could certainly try!" Seti growled, thinking that he would enjoy throttling someone.

He pulled one of the gilded stools forward, sank into it and scowled at the frescoed walls. People would think him mad if he told them that he wanted nothing more than to be in a tent, in the field, planning a campaign to smash the tribes that were disrupting the trade routes to the north. He *would* be doing that when he had finished this task. Yes, and he would be pursuing the campaign with a good heart.

He looked at the tray with gold cups and cursed as he remembered once again that he had not ordered any wine.

A tap at the door. Murmurs... His major domo, Kha, had come in silently and was addressing the commotion.

He raised his head, watched a man enter, flanked by two guards. He looked familiar... Of course. The Governor of the Third Nome, headquartered in Thebes. What the devil was his name?

He searched for it in his memory. Gone. He rose, greeted the man, and accepted his homage with a kind smile.

The man was talking. He was a great talker, Seti remembered. And he liked anise seeds and onions. He was always chewing them, too. How odd that he could remember all this and still not be able to recall the fellow's name!

He made some response, still smiling, watching the happiness bloom in the man's eyes. *What, in Ptah's name, was his name?*

"Thank you, Sire!" the man said. "Till this evening!" And he bowed himself out of the room.

Seti closed his eyes. He could picture himself telling his corps of guards that the great lords of the third Nome could damned well eat their meals in garrulous comfort and leave him in peace.

What a pity he would never respond that way.

He nodded to the major-domo. "Send my servants in, Kha," he said. "I will prepare for the feast."

The door closed softly. He watched and then sat down with a scowl.

Ye gods! he thought. *Another damned feast. My life is one long feast, here in Thebes. There is no way to escape.* The thought caught him up short. *Or is there?*

He decided that it was time to do something about that. He could make plans at the feast.

** ** **

Djedi pushed the hair from his forehead and frowned at the blood. He could sense the junior foreman, Neferhotep, bending over him. He raised his eyes.

"They came in force," he said. "They were there, surrounding old Master Akhti. He was screaming. I have never heard him make such a sound, and they laughed.

[84]

"I ran toward them, but Kaya was there first. They pushed him and he fell..."

He looked down at the body in his arms. "He's—he's dying, isn't he? I heard his head strike the step."

The others traded looks. The physician sat back on his heels and shook his head.

"He is dead."

Djedi repeated the word. Dead...

"Set him down," the Junior Foreman said. "There is nothing more you can do."

"We can do something, he said, holding the other closer, as though his own warmth would make the other's blood move and warm and bring him back. "This should not happen!"

"Master Kenamun can speak to Lord Intef when he comes back. He mentioned the first attack... Though it seemed to me an unfortunate encounter. I don't think they were trying to hurt him."

Djedi sat back on his heels. "This makes two! Two in a sevenday!"

"We do what we can."

"Is it enough?" he demanded.

"Kenamun will say something to Count Intef. When he returns. These are isolated incidents."

Djedi frowned. "Make a spot on papyrus, he said. Make another and another. Suddenly your papyrus is covered with paint, just through drawing dots! We must do something!"

XXII

The moon was riding at the top of the night sky when Seti returned to his chambers. He disrobed, suffered his servants to bathe and oil him, and then dismissed them. The night was relatively young. He went to the balcony and looked across the Nile toward the east, warming with the first, faint light of false dawn.

False dawn... His mind circled around the term. A precursor to dawn, an indication of dawn's approach while still in the night.

He smiled to himself. *Well and good*, he thought. He had to move forward. Nebamun had been right to tell him to go away, but he could not return to the great temples or his estates to rest and recover. They would hover, treat him like a delicate youth with dyspepsia. He was a grown man. He wanted to be about and doing, relying on himself, not the tender care of servants.

He looked around his chambers. There were so many things there that he did not need, things that had only become necessities since the death of Horemheb when his line had become entangled with the exigencies of royalty. He could still live frugally and comfortably with what could be packed in one small satchel.

His smile widened. It was almost time to do so. He had made plans while moving through the feast and acting like a King. He might be a King, but he was still a General, and could still out-think just about anyone. And the one whom he could not out-think was a hundred leagues to the north, among the pyramids, watching over his son.

He had given some thought to distance and timing, and his plan was in place.

No time like the present. He took up a sheet of papyrus that was always kept to hand by his command, eyed his scribe's kit and reached for his brush. The note would go out by messenger in the morning. He had plenty of time to compose this one. The others would be finalized over the next five days.

XXXIII

Another attack? How could they be so bold? Djedi tore down the path that threaded down from the hills to the town.

And then the screams started. *What are they doing? Torturing him*

He shouted a warning, saw them turn and eye him. They were different people this time, narrow-eyed, somehow more dangerous. There were more of them, as well.

He was carrying a staff. He raised it over his head and increased his speed...

** ** **

His neighbors surrounded him. "You were brave!"

"I did what I had to. Will we send to Count Intef now?"

He saw them exchanging looks. "Kenamun has Intef's ear," Neferhotep said. "Yes, and His Majesty's too. When he returns–"

"What about now?" Djedi demanded. "We can't stay as we are!"

Neferhotep frowned. "When Master Kenamun gets back."

"We need to do something now!"

They traded glances. "And what do you suggest?"

Djedi closed his eyes and saw old Akhti's disintegrated face before him. "I will serve as guard for now. We need to get everyone together to help."

More glances.

"Very well," they said. "You will be the guard..."

Later, as the moon mounted the sky, he walked along the dark pathways, raised his head to the pale light and wondered what he had done.

If only, somehow, someone could show him what to do.

** ** **

The papyrus was awaiting Seti, as he had ordered. He had his own writing kit. He eyed the reed brushes and thought for a moment. And then he composed the second set of messages, smiling as he imagined the various responses they were likely to cause. He almost regretted the fact that he would not be around to watch.

He folded the last of the packets, tied it with fine linen string, set a pinch of clay over the knot, and pressed his private seal into it.

Done.

[87]

He rose and stretched. His belongings—three tunics, three kilts, several shentis, other miscellaneous items—were in his pack. He wore the lion pendant Gold of Honor that he won a lifetime ago, with his wife's ring on its cord. He needed nothing else, and it was time. He had an idea where he could go. He had read documents concerning Nakhtamun's burial, sent from that little village of craftsmen who had constructed his son's tomb. Based on the terrible scribbling, they certainly needed a scribe who knew what he was doing. No one would recognize him. Who would expect to find him at Deir el Medineh, certainly not unadorned and carrying a writing kit?

He strolled through the hallways of the palace, bowing to the guards, who did not recognize him, bareheaded and humble as he was. He spoke briefly with the gate guard, who eyed him and concluded that he was a middle-aged man who wanted companionship that night and was going to the docks to find it.

If he only knew, Seti thought as he moved through the gateway and out onto the street.

And so, in the third hour before dawn, Men-Maat-Re Seti Merneptah, King of Upper and Lower Egypt, stepped out of his world and left it behind as completely as a man boarding a ship that will take him to another land.

XXIV

Word of Pharaoh's disappearance did not come until long after dawn. Thebes was a tolerant and understanding city. His Majesty had suffered a severe blow, and he had borne it with pride and courage. Who could blame him if he lay abed late? Or if he chose to pass that time warming his bed with the caresses of a woman? Indeed, it was a wise thing to do.

But when the silence continued and there was no sign of activity, and Kha his servant timidly entered the Royal bedchamber, he found no woman, and the bed was cold and unmarked.

**   **   **

Intef sat back in his chair and tilted his chin back to allow his manservant to shave him. The scent of the unguents was almost intoxicating, and the action had become a morning ritual that helped to soothe him and prepare him for the day. He let himself drift, thinking over what had happened and what would happen... he prided himself on his ability to prepare for whatever came.

He thought nothing of the slap-slap of sandals on the packed earthen floors, and when reality burst into his chambers and shouted the news, his first thought was to regret not having that second cup of wine with his breakfast.

**   **   **

The Great Temple of Ptah at Memphis lay beneath the thick morning sunlight, its progression of pylons, gateways and courtyards as filled with light as a lotus bud is filled with shimmering water. The air rang with the soft chime of sistra, voices raised in laughter, in prayer. The sound of children playing. Incense rose in tendrils from the sanctuaries, heavier toward the holy of holies, the heart of the great complex. People came in through the gateways in throngs, bearing gifts and offerings; near the river, people gathered at the side portal to be served with food from the temple's store.

And the High Priest of Ptah was enjoying his leisurely breakfast on the terrace of his estate.

Nebamun raised his face to the sun's morning rays with a smile. This was his favorite time of the day, a time of renewal, the sun demonstrating the fulfilled promise of another day.

Rising without ceasing. He could hear the chorus of birds in the trees of his garden; farther away some children were laughing. He paused to listen; it was a game of tag with some complications to its rules. His grandchildren, no doubt, though the temple had a large and busy group of children sheltered within it, the children of the workers there, or children brought to the Temple to live and learn.

He raised his morning cup of watered wine to his lips and sipped. A bowl of warmed, sweetened gruel lay before him, with some broiled fish.

"Holiness?"

He looked up to see his Major-Domo approaching. "Yes, Si-Ptah?"

"Her Ladyship sends this fruit from the country and bids me tell you they are the choicest she has seen in years."

Nebamun smiled. "Her Ladyship is trying to get me to live to the century mark," he said. "Thirty more years..." He eyed the fruit, took one and raised it to his nose. "Very choice," he said. "Thank you and thank Her Ladyship. I will call on her shortly."

A tap at the door. One of the junior priests entered, performed a breathless bow, and took a packet from the folds of his tunic. "This came for you by royal messenger. The officer said it was urgent, so I bring it to you."

Nebamun took it from him, eyeing the strong, elegant writing. His brows drew together fractionally, but he nodded. "Thank you. Have you breakfasted yet? No? Then do so at once."

When the man had gone Nebamun swore under his breath, took the small fruit knife beside him and cut the twine that tied the packet. He spread the letter open.

My dearest friend,

I am writing to you in this manner to tell you that I have gone into hiding, after a fashion. As you know, I traveled to Thebes to visit Nakhtamun's tomb and place some offerings there. Among them was the bow he carried on campaign. I had to go, Nebamun. If I could not see him, myself, in the flesh, at least I had to near where he was, to see for myself. You understand this, I know.

I did as I resolved, and it was well done. But I am now at a standstill, and I need to take time to catch my breath.

While I intend to rest and recover, I am keenly aware that my disappearance and death, if something happens to me, would lead to complex problems for Egypt and for that young man who is currently taking my place at its helm. Until such time as matters settle, you, my dear Nebamun, are Vizier of the North. I have sent documents to that effect through official channels; they should reach you shortly after this message.

The cup crashed to the floor, wine splashing everywhere as Nebamun leaped to his feet with an agility that would have done credit to a man half his age, the message clutched between his hands. "Ptah's *beard!*" he shouted.

**   **   **

Count Intef set the message atop the pile of documents. "His Majesty has certainly neglected no one," he said, reaching for the last packet. He lifted it, frowned at the superscription: his name, and the note that it was to be opened last.

Very well, Seti, he thought, and broke the seal.

Kha was wringing his hands, to the amusement of the Commander of Pharaoh's Guard, who was holding his staff of office as though it were a weapon.

"Well, My Lord?" Kha demanded. "What does His Majesty say?"

Intef looked down at the writing, hesitated over the question of whether he wished to be kind and diplomatic or completely factual. Kha had been fluttering through the King's rooms, giving orders, getting underfoot and talking about disaster. The temptation was very great...

"It is a final piece of instruction, Master Kha. Addressed to you and to the rest of his household. I have been asked to read it to you."

The guard commander straightened. The various body servants lifted their heads. Kha clutched his hands together at his breast.

"He says this: 'Instruct all my good followers to return to Memphis as quickly as may be arranged. His Royal Highness

[91]

will have need of their assistance during my absence. Thank them for their service and tell them that I send them forth with my thanks and my blessing.'"

"Leave?" Kha exclaimed.

"At once."

Kha burst into tears. The Guard commander traded looks with Intef and shepherded him from the room, followed by the others.

Intef chuckled as he read the writing again.

> *By this time, no doubt, Kha is driving everyone mad with his vapours. Tell him to hold his tongue, stop getting underfoot, and be prepared to leave for Memphis. A ship is waiting as you read this. I have confidence in Ramesses' ability to make him feel valued. I am out of all patience with him.*

Intef found himself wondering what Nebamun in Memphis thought of all this.

XXV

Nebamun clapped a hand over his mouth. His servants were very solicitous, thanks to their mistress. He had a handful of heartbeats to read and understand what he just read. He pushed away from his seat, shook his robes out, and continued reading.

> *I have this date appointed Pasenhor as Governor of the Faiyyum. It is a position well-suited to his unique abilities. It will save his pride, I think, though I question my sanity for troubling with such a fool, no matter how great a friendship my father had for his. I nearly sent him to administer the mines at Sinai. But he would have had too much scope to foul up matters there, so the Faiyyum was selected. I am inclined to think that if there is a billet for which his abilities are suited, it should be immediately abolished.*
>
> *I have not settled on a place to stay during this time. Be assured that I will get word to you and to Intef. Should things happen, you will have full power to step in, with all my power, in my place and deal with matters with your usual wisdom, grace and subtlety. Egypt and my son will be safe in your hands. I do not wish anyone else to know where I am. I have Ramesses' promise not to pry. The others are not so trusted.*
>
> *You may attempt to kill me at singlestick when I return. You may, perhaps, succeed.*
>
> *I know you will do what is best, as you always have, my good friend.*
>
> *Seti*

He swore and threw the letter down as the slap of sandals on pavement was immediately followed by, a bevy of wide-eyed faces peering at him. "Holiness?"

He mastered himself and pushed at the shards of the cup with a sandaled toe. "I've spilled my wine," he said, "Of your courtesy, send someone to clean the spill and bring me some more."

Smiles, nods. All was well. The servants left.

Sink me all devoted servants! Nebamun thought savagely. He looked at the message. "That *bastard!*" he said through his teeth. He saw one of the servants approaching with a pitcher of watered wine. "Thank you," he said.

He eyed the letter again and smiled grimly as he heard an official-sounding commotion at the door.

Vizier! That *Bastard!*'

**   **   **

"I had a letter from Father," Ramesses said. He had come briskly into Nebamun's presence, beaming. He had brought Hori with him. "He told me that you have been appointed Vizier of the North in that idiot Pasenhor's place, and good riddance to him! He has been ordered to the Faiyyum.

"Father said I could rely on you, and all would be well."

He eyed Nebamun's expression. "I know you are angry, but it's the best news for me. I feel as though I can breathe again." his voice wavered; he bent to lift Hori to cover it. "May I sit down?"

"Your Royal Highness—"

"My name is Ramessu."

Nebamun sketched a bow. "You can always be at ease with me, Ramessu," he said with a smile. "You're another grandson to me."

"I wish it were true."

"So do I," Nebamun said. He held out his hand to Hori. "Well," he said. "I have received His Majesty's edict this morning naming me Vizier of the North. He said that Lower Egypt would be blessed to have at its helm one such as myself, who will serve with distinction as did my father before me. Considering that I am nearly half again my father's age at the time of his death, with no experience of being Vizier, it should be interesting to watch. At least I had a chance to watch him. *And,*" he added with the bend of a slightly malicious smile, "It will be fascinating to see the reactions of various folk. Will you grace my afternoon audience with your presence?"

"Of course!" Ramesses said. His expression grew thoughtful. "I must." He frowned at his hands. "Father sent me a letter. He said that he would be away for a time. I think he may be doing something dangerous, but he told me not to worry."

"Your father is an intelligent man," Nebamun said, lifting Hori to his lap. "He has trusted Egypt to you, and you to my guidance if you need it." He paused as Ramesses took his hand between his own and gripped it.

He returned the clasp. "He knows who he can trust, and he trusts you. But this is not what is troubling you, is it?"

"No," Ramesses said. "I would at least like some assurance that he is safe, especially after all that has happened." He raised his eyes to Nebamun's. "Father may be an intelligent man, but even intelligent people make missteps. Here in Memphis, I have people that I can rely on." He smiled as Nebamun lifted his eyebrows. "I grew up the son of a Vizier," he said. "And I enjoy watching things develop. But there are limits to my-my influence."

"That will change," Nebamun said. "For the rest, I can deal with that for you, if you like. Will you trust me to do so?"

"Father says *you* can do *anything!*" Hori said.

Nebamun smiled down into the black eyes and dropped a kiss on the boy's cheek. "Never forget that you can, yourself," he said. Hori startled him by putting his arms around his neck and almost throttling him with a hug, then settling against his shoulder and demanding food.

Ramesses laughed and sat back. After a moment he said, "I was thinking... the word is very new, but it does come from His Majesty. Would it be perhaps wiser to simply announce the change this afternoon, then hold your first, formal audience after a passage of days?"

Nebamun sat back with a frown. "I had not thought of that..."

"It would give you time to accustom yourself to the change," Ramesses said. "I know that I needed that, myself, when Nakhtamun died, and I would imagine your situation is similar." He smiled across at Hori, who was watching him. "Time is always useful."

Nebamun was frowning now, but it lightened. "Your Royal Highness has a point."

"I thought so," Ramesses said. He lifted his cup of beer. "...and, as I said, my dear sir, my name is Ramessu."

XXVI

Neferhotep, the Junior Foreman of Deir el Medineh, stirred his morning gruel and raised his spoon to his lips. It had been a long night, what with a restive baby, a pregnant wife inclined to argue, and his indiscretion with honey-soaked dates right before retiring. The thought of a day at His Majesty's tomb was not a happy one, but he had some time to regain his serenity before he had to set out for the tomb.

He sipped his gruel with slurping noises, enjoying the flavor and mulling over the day's impending tasks, when his son came to him with word of a visitor asking for him.

"A visitor?" he repeated. "At this hour?"

"Kheti brought him, since he was making the rounds and this man was asking for you," his son, Iry, said. "He apologized for coming early. I told him you weren't out of bed yet."

"*What?*"

"Well, you weren't out and about," Iry said, "and I thought that would be the best explanation."

"So, this man thinks I am lying abed now?"

"You just said it was early," Iry pointed out.

Neferhotep frowned at his son. With one son grown, he had forgotten how it was with striplings. Iry had developed a deplorably pert streak. He had forgotten that children his age developed attitudes of disrespect toward their elders.

"Tell him I will be out directly, Iry," he said. When his son turned he said, "Wait— What's he like?"

Iry raised his eyebrows. "He is bigger than the people here–"

"Well-spoken?"

Iry considered this. "He's good to talk to," he said. "I think he's a soldier..." His eyes shone. Iry had started talking about being a soldier. Neferhotep was hoping that the boy wouldn't take himself off to join the Necropolis Police.

"Well, go ahead, Iry, and tell him," he said. "And for heaven's sake, if you think he is a soldier—"

"He says he's a scribe," Iry interrupted.

"Don't interrupt your elders!" Neferhotep said.

Iry opened his eyes at him.

It made Neferhotep laugh, as Iry had intended. "—don't pester him for war stories," he finished.

Iry snapped his right fist to his left shoulder in the salute he'd seen the royal troops give, bowed, and marched from the room.

Neferhotep shook his head, but he was smiling. This youngest boy of his was proving to be quite a trial. His smile deepened, an engaging trial, at any rate. And there was the baby after him... He finished his bowl, rose and went out.

The visitor was standing in the living area of the house, facing his son. Neferhotep had a moment to look the man over before they were aware of him. He was a dark-eyed man, tall and strongly built, with graying black hair. His clothing was well-worn but neat. A gold pendant, shaped like a lion's head, hung from a leather cord about his neck, and he carried a scribe's kit. A long dagger was sheathed at his belt. The sheath was worn, though the hilt was bright.

Iry was right; he had the look of a soldier. In fact, he was speaking of being on campaign as Neferhotep entered.

"For every moment of glory, son, there are weeks of work and a good deal of discomfort. It's that way with anything worth doing, and while the moments of glory do come, no matter what your calling, they are brief."

Iry looked disappointed. The man smiled at the boy's expression. "People are always telling you to wait, aren't they?" he said. "They will stop, I promise. And it will be your turn to tell them to wait."

Iry looked over and saw his father. The hero-worship was replaced by something deeper.

"Here is my father, sir. He is the Foreman of the Village."

"The junior one," Neferhotep corrected automatically as the man bowed. "My uncle, Kenamun, is the senior. Good morning. I am Neferhotep."

"I am Sa-Ramses, Master Neferhotep," the man said. "It is good of you to receive me this early."

"I was eating my breakfast," Neferhotep said with a look at Iry.

"So I thought," Sa-Ramses said. He was a handsome man with a measured way of speaking. "I apologize for the early hour."

Neferhotep straightened. "You came in good time, Master Sa-Ramses," he said, "and it's a pleasure to receive you." He paused and then said, "Is there a way that I can serve you?"

The man smiled; it appeared that Neferhotep's liking was mutual. "Well," he said, "I was hoping that there was something I might perhaps be able to do for the town. I am, in fact, looking for employment at the moment."

"What sort? My son says you are a scribe."

"I am," he said. "I was an army scribe for a time, but I have also had experience with royal correspondence."

"Is that so?" Neferhotep repeated. "Then you can do numbers?"

"Yes, sir."

Neferhotep's smile widened. "Wahankh, our chief scribe, was called away on family business and we're in need... You *can* write, you say?"

"I am a scribe."

Neferhotep nodded. "Could you give me a sample of your writing?"

"I would be happy to," Sa-Ramses said. "Dictate a letter. I will write it."

Neferhotep stared at him and then nodded.

Sa-Ramses sat down, stretched the skirt of his kilt across his knees and took a sheet of surprisingly fine papyrus from his kit. He spread the sheet of papyrus, across his kilt, and reached for his writing kit. A quick spit on the cake of black, the brush dipped, he looked up. "I am at your service," he said.

Neferhotep groped for words. "My dear mother..."

The brush scratched across the papyrus.

"My dear mother," he repeated. Encountering a suppressed smile in Sa-Ramses' dark gaze he cleared his throat. "Oh, all right," he said. "I will do it right." He cleared his throat again. "Neferhotep writes to his mother Henetre; the son Neferhotep to his beloved mother Henetre: The son says to his mother, how are you? Are you well and content? Behold, I am well and happy in my heart."

He watched Sa-Ramses' brush flow across the page without a pause.

He continued, "I have learned that my wife's confinement will be in the high inundation, and while I have arranged for servants to be there to assist, I do feel that another lady, experienced in such things, would be good to have beside her." He paused and added, "Although it would tend to darken our rejoicing if you and she came to blows and killed each other in the course of the birthing..."

[98]

Sa-Ramses put down his brush, gazed at the papyrus and began to laugh. "My wife would not have been happy to be attended by my mother," he said.

"She is a kindred spirit to my wife, then," Neferhotep said. He frowned and continued dictating. "I have thought, instead, to send my sons, my daughter and the baby to your dwelling, to be cared for by you, since you speak wistfully of the days of children, and this will bring the memories back."

A crack of laughter, hastily suppressed, stopped him. Sa-Ramses was smiling widely as he finished the line, blew across the page and then offered it to Neferhotep.

Neferhotep took it. The writing was firm, flowing and elegant. "My wife would have killed *me*," he said. "And my mother would have helped her. Well, you write beautifully, better than Wahank. A scribe of your quality is always welcome. But..."

Sa-Ramses lifted his eyebrows.

"You have the look of a soldier about you. Oh, I don't mean hacked and grizzled! But you look as though you would be at home in a fight. Have you been in the army?"

Sa-Ramses gazed down at the papyrus with an odd bend to his mouth. "I have been a soldier," he said.

"Can you shoot a bow?"

"Of course."

"Fight hand to hand?"

"I have been a soldier," Sa-Ramses said.

"If that is so, Neferhotep said, "We need you and any able-bodied man. There have been incursions, and the town is worried."

Sa-Ramses nodded. "Tell me."

"One of the young fellows here told us we needed a group of guards. He said he'd be one, and he is trying to get others to join him."

Sa-Ramses frowned thoughtfully. "And he is doing this himself?"

"Yes."

"Is no one joining him?"

Neferhotep eyed his expression. "He is young," he said. "No one takes him seriously. He was something of a troublemaker as a youngster after his parents died. My uncle took him in hand, but the reputation remains."

"Tell me more," Sa-Ramses said. He blinked and added, "It interests me."

The frown continued as Neferhotep told him, giving all the details, a bleak story of bullying, intimidation and stealth. By the time the tale was told, the frown was very black. "This is vile," he said.

"Then you will join us?"

XXVII

Ramesses set his brush aside and scanned the sheet he had just filled. Short and specific, direct and to the point. His father would approve. He, on the other hand, preferred to set the stage for communications and proceed in a more ceremonious fashion. Graceful turns of phrase, ambivalent expressions that pointed to a conclusion, involving intelligence and puzzle-solving. It was almost like a sort of dance, he thought. Intriguing, enjoyable, playing personality upon personality with everyone convinced that he had come out the winner...

The writing done, he sat back and indulged in a luxuriant stretch accompanied by a full-throated yawn. Writing always did that to him; put him before a piece of papyrus, a palette, brush and well-moistened pigment cake and he was yawning before a hundred heartbeats had passed. He had no such problem if he sat down before a scribe and spoke the words he wanted written. The words came easily, flowed precisely, and were written beautifully. This time he had said what he wanted, and it could be understood. The next time he would engage a scribe.

** ** **

Sokhari set the small whetstone to the side and ran a fingertip along the edge of his curved sword, testing its sharpness.

"Guardsman!"

He started, swore and put his bleeding fingertip in his mouth as he turned to find his division commander, Lord Hesira, holding a sheet of papyrus in his hands, standing at the doorway and frowning at him while his phylarch signaled to him behind the man's back.

"You are summoned to His Royal Highness."

Sokhari stared.

Hesira lowered the papyrus. "You are wanted at once. He asked for you by name." The man's gaze shortened, drove to a frown. "What the devil are you doing with your finger in your mouth like a baby?"

"I cut it."

"Keep your blade sharp and it won't happen!" he snapped.

"Sir."

"His Royal Highness has an assignment for you. You apparently made yourself useful some time back..." He paused as though this thought was too miraculous to contemplate. He finally shrugged. "Well. He has asked you to go to him 'of your courtesy'-Hah! To hear a great lord say *that*—*!*" He cleared his throat. "At any rate, you are to report to His Royal Highness. He *said* 'when it is convenient'. You will learn, my lad, that it means 'straightaway'! So, you'd best go now."

Hesira drew a breath, straightened and then frowned at the patch of red on the floor. "What's *this*?"

Sokhari showed his finger.

"You're letting it bleed all over the floor? Ptah save us!"

"You told me to take my finger out of my mouth, sir."

"Well, there's no help for it. Go to His Royal Highness immediately. It doesn't do to dally!"

** ** **

"How did you come to cut yourself so?" Ramesses, Crown Prince of Egypt said, tying the strip of linen more firmly around Sokhari's finger.

"I was sharpening my blade, Highness, and just as I was testing it someone called my name."

"Is there such a thing as too sharp?" Prince Ramesses mused. He dismissed the question with a lift of his eyebrows. "There. This will do for now. Please sit down."

Sokhari looked at his bandaged finger and then at the Prince, who was tidying things with a smile. "I thank Your Highness."

"Not at all." Ramesses set the bloodied cloths aside. "I have asked that you come to me. Some time ago you performed an important service very well. I have need of one who knows his way about the men here. You showed that you do. Would you be willing to serve in my personal guard?"

Sokhari stood straighter, suddenly aware with a flash of happiness that there was no one he would rather serve. "I would be honored, Highness."

"Excellent. I put in a word with your commanding officer. You may tell Lord Ankhu, if you will, that you have accepted the position."

Sokhari indulged in a mental picture of his division commander's reaction to the news. The thought made his eyes dance.

A small hand slipped into his. He started and looked down into a pair of black eyes in a boy's face.

[102]

"Hi," the boy said.

Ramesses set his writing tools aside. "That is Captain Sokhari, Hori. See that you're respectful with him."

Sokhari returned the boy's grin and went down on one knee to bring their eyes level. "Hello, Prince."

"I like you," said Hori.

Ramesses nodded. "Now:" he said. "I want you to assemble for me ten men of firmness, courage and intelligence. I want those who can be respectful but also firm. Do you know any such men?"

"I can find them, My Prince."

"Excellent," Ramesses said again. He eyed the bandage. "Now go to Master Sennefer and have that properly looked at."

** ** **

The port of Peru-Nefer served as the hub of northern Egypt's trade and transportation. Navies sailed from its docks, ambassadors arrived to speak with His Majesty or the Northern Vizier. The docks themselves were often adorned with flowers and furs to be set under the feet of important visitors. It was a place of rejoicing, of splendor and ceremony.

A bustling, bawdy hell-hole thrived eight streets from those docks, in a section full of loud chatter, the smell of sweat and cheap beer and the sound of quarreling. A great Vizier of the past had commented once that more urgent business was transacted in that area than in all of Egypt.

** ** **

"You understand what you are to do? I want any word-any at all!-of unrest, of anger, of jealousy. Plots, threats-anything you find; send it to me. Written, if possible. Spoken if not. I don't want old news of jealousy or dislike. Substantial things. And I want names, times, locations, and listeners."

The man's dark eyes narrowed. "Bring what you find at once. Never mind if it seems small. I want to see all of it." The smile grew wider. "We have, of course, settled the method of payment..."

Nods all around.

"When does your principal need it?"

The man sat back. The floor was not a comfortable place for him; he adjusted his knees, went back on one elbow, and frowned thoughtfully. "As the information comes," he said finally. "Right away. It does not matter when or where you

[103]

are; get the information to me. I will pay." His eyes narrowed. "But I will also read it, and if it is not genuine..."

Sidewise glances. Nods. This man was not one to toy with, for all that he looked like a prince...

XXVIII

Djedi stood at the junction of the paths leading to the two major valleys of the Theban Necropolis and frowned down into the nearest valley. It was impossible to see anything of any importance from that vantage point; the place where the workmen had set up a temporary camp to serve them during their ten days' stint working in the Valleys was completely hidden. He had been standing there just that morning and heard screams that made his blood run cold. He had seized his spear and gone pelting out along the path only to find that one of the workmen had been experiencing problems with a loose sandal and a sharp rock.

Amusing, maybe, but not when you really thought things through. He had volunteered to protect the workmen, and it was hard to do that when you couldn't see them properly.

What should he do? He had some ideas, but a good heart and a willingness to make sacrifices, while laudable, was not very effective without any skill to back them up. He thought he might go to the Necropolis police for their advice. Maybe they could suggest something? Or perhaps they would step in and widen their patrols to include the town? He could ask.

He sighed and frowned at the loose scree pouring down the hillside, and thought, not for the first time in the past day, of the things that needed to be done to improve matters. There was so much to do, and he thought there might be little time in which to do it. There had to be a secure vantage point where the defenders could see the workers. If only he could find someone to advise him!

He leaned on his spear, feeling the sturdy shaft within his hands, wishing he knew how to use it. His gaze traveled along the path to the Valley of the Queens. He would do a circuit, he thought. It might be afoot, but at least he would be present and ready to serve. He straightened, shifted his grip on the spear, and then turned as someone called his name.

His expression lightened as he saw Master Neferhotep striding toward him followed by a tall, strongly built man just past middle age with the look of a warrior about him. The newcomer was gazing around with the touch of a frown, but the expression eased as they approached.

"This is Sa-Ramses," Neferhotep said. "He came to offer his services as a scribe. I can certainly attest to his quality, but he tells me that he has seen some fighting. Based on what you have told me, Djedi, we have a greater need for fighters at the moment than scribes."

The other man stood silently as Neferhotep gave his credentials and bowed to Djedi when he had finished.

Neferhotep looked up at Sa-Ramses. "Djedi came to the town fathers and offered to start a corps of guards. You are his first recruit-if it pleases you."

Sa-Ramses smiled faintly. The faintness warmed as Neferhotep took his leave, saying that he would see to assigning quarters.

They watched the foreman head down into the Valley of the Kings.

"Do you have a tomb underway?" Sa-Ramses asked.

"His majesty's," Djedi said. "It is continuing now. There had been a delay recently."

Sa-Ramses nodded. "I imagine things are at the whim of the nobles."

"That's fair to say," Djedi agreed. "Though they are paying us to do this, so I can't complain." He mulled over that thought for a time and then said, "You might as well see what we're dealing with. Nothing like this has happened until this year."

**   **   **

Is there any pattern to the attacks?" Sa-Ramses asked later as they walked along the path.

"None that I can find," Djedi said. "They started just before His Majesty came here to see to his son's tomb. There have been two more since then."

"What was the most recent?" Sa-Ramses asked.

Djedi shook his head. "There's shade here, you learn to cherish it. Let's sit down and drink some water. Then we can circle back." After they had done so he said, "Most recently? It was yesterday, late. One of our elders was assaulted up within sight of the town. Unfortunately, no one was about. They took some things. Not much-little of value. Then they started abusing him. I heard the sounds and came at a run."

"You? Alone?"

"Who else? There was no one else to come with me-and I couldn't just leave him at their mercy. I had a walking stick, and I lit into them."

Sa-Ramses was eyeing him with a thoughtful frown. "That was brave of you."

"What else could I do? Another tried earlier, but he was pushed. He fell and struck his head. He died as I held him. That was the evening after Master Kenamun left. I said we needed a force to protect us, and when they told me I had to wait for him to return. I…" He fell silent.

Sa-Ramses seemed to be smiling. "You…what?"

Djedi frowned. "I said that I would be their guard until others could be found. I kept thinking of old Akhti. He is shaky and was afraid to leave his house this morning. Some of the men spoke with him, offered him protection."

"Is he all right now?"

"More or less," Djedi replied. "As much as you can expect. He is fearful and sore. Such an inoffensive old man!"

"Predators are not concerned with the gentleness of their victims," Sa-Ramses said with an ironic smile. "Only with the ease of their endeavors. Of course they would select that old man as a target."

Djedi looked at the man. He had stood and was scanning the heights, narrow-eyed, gauging the path, looking at the various shelters. "I had gone to the foremen a week before that," he said diffidently. He also stood up, dusting his hands.

Sa-Ramses waited until he was beside him and then turned to follow him along the path. The day was warming rapidly, soon it would be very hot indeed.

"After the second attack I had said that we should see about setting up a group of guards for the village," Djedi continued. "Last night, with old Akhti bloodied and sobbing, I went straight to Neferhotep and said we had to do something. When he said we should wait for Kenamun's return, I said I'd be a guard if they would take no other steps."

Sa-Ramses looked thoughtful. "Is there no one with you, then?" he asked.

"Not yet," Djedi answered. "It just happened last night. I am hoping... Well, actually there *is* you, isn't there?" He paused, saw Sa-Ramses' smile, and continued. "I am strong enough for now. Besides, I am alone now-no family now that my mother and father are gone-and if I am hurt no one will be the worse. Someone had to do something, and I thought it might as well be me."

Sa-Ramses' expression was hard to read. "So, this was your idea?"

"Something needed to be done," Djedi said. "I couldn't let things just-just sit. Oh, they said that they would speak with

Master Kenamun, when he came back, but that wouldn't be for days. And my old master was so frightened. He was like a father to me-him and Kenamun-when my parents died."

Sa-Ramses' expression had shifted to a thoughtful frown. "It seems as though you are doing your best," he said. "And you are not a trained soldier. Not yet. No one could fault you for that old man's suffering."

"But still..." Djedi looked down. "I did ask him to forgive me this morning as the physician was tending him. He told me not to be a fool. The physician agreed."

"This town has at least two sensible men, "Sa-Ramses said, but added nothing further.

Djedi paused and then said diffidently, "Master Neferhotep says that you've seen some fighting?"

Sa-Ramses nodded. "I have," he said. He added "Sir."

"By the look of you, you're not from around here. Royal army, maybe?" Djedi allowed himself to sound, as he felt, hopeful.

Sa-Ramses' eyes narrowed a little in the hint of a smile. "That is right, sir," he said. "I served in the armies for... For some years, under Horemheb, then His Late Majesty, and then His Majesty most recently. I am on a leave of absence at the moment."

"You saw them, then?"

Sa-Ramses' expression was still somehow amused. "As close as I am to you," he said.

"No! His Majesty? Did he see you, to speak with you? Or... did he ignore you? Great lords do."

Sa-Ramses shook his head. "His Majesty comes from an old army family. He tries not to be rude to anyone."

"Oh, I know that," Djedi said. "We all do. He came to his son's tomb recently, and he spoke everyone fair, though Kenamun said that he seemed heartbroken."

Sa-Ramses was eyeing his feet. "Why would he be heartbroken?" His voice was suddenly weary.

"Haven't you heard? His son was killed in some fighting. In Palestine, I think. His Majesty got back to learn that his son was already buried. It must have been terribly hard. He came here to visit the tomb."

He looked over at Sa-Ramses and spoke impulsively. "Why, you're exhausted! I am sorry, twittering along when you're tired. It takes time to get used to this area when you're not from here. Let's sit down here. This bit of shade will deepen this afternoon, and it's comfortable now.

Sa-Ramses' color had started to return. "I will be fine," he said.

"No," Djedi said. "We can rest here. There's nothing awaiting us. You're new, and there are things to see. Did you see foreign fighting? Against the Hittites? His Majesty captured Kadesh, I know. I saw the carvings underway at Opet when I went there with Master Kenamun."

Sa-Ramses smiled, though his eyes were shuttered. "They are a powerful nation," he said. He extended his arm, pushing the sleeve of his tunic above his elbow. "I got this in some hand-to-hand fighting."

Djedi eyed the scar and whistled. It was obviously from a sword or knife. "How did the other fare?"

Sa-Ramses shook his head as he pulled his sleeve down. "He lived to fight again, most likely," he said. "Though I suspect it took some time."

Djedi looked at the scar again, then raised his eyes to Sa-Ramses' face. "How long were you in the armies?" he asked.

Sa-Ramses was frowning into space, as though he were remembering a time and place lost, never to be recovered. "It was..." he paused. "Thirty years. All of it."

"You started young, then," Djedi said, sparking a suppressed smile from Sa-Ramses. "And you're here? Why?"

Sa-Ramses raised his head and looked at Djedi. "It seemed the best place to be, at least for now."

Djedi heard the words, but he also heard the tone. He nodded and said, "And you are willing to take service here?"

"I am."

"Then welcome. I think we need you. You may save our lives."

Sa-Ramses looked him over with a frown. "You're taking a lot on faith," he said.

"Sometimes faith is enough," Djedi said.

** ** **

Some time later Seti looked around the house that had been assigned him, a tribute, if he had known it, to Neferhotep's determination. It was pleasant enough, with a main room opening off the street, followed by a second room with a cellar, then a kitchen and a third room for a bedroom. Steps beyond that room led to the roof, and beyond them a kitchen with another cellar.

He set his small pack down. Compared with his Spartan provisions, the bedroom was ornate. He could send for goods, perhaps. *Yes, but how would I pay for them?* The thought made him hesitate just as a fist thudded on the door twice.

He opened it to find a parade of villagers with gifts of food, of clothing.

He stood aside, startled, as they came in, set things up, moved things to more comfortable positions, loaded his pantry and then, smiling, bowed and left, with one couple lingering by the door. They offered supper.

He was startled, touched, and pleased to accept.

XXIX
Memphis

The arrival of any of the big ships was always a cause for celebration at the Port of Peru-Nefer; who knew who might be aboard, or what might be coming to the city? The docks thronged with spectators waiting for a glimpse of the ship. The sunlight picked out details of color, collars of flowers, faience necklaces, gold and carnelian on the wealthier people.

Prince Ramesses was waiting on the docks. He had received word that a big ship had been sighted, but the runner had not been sure which ship it was. Ramesses had done some thinking after posing some pointed questions and came to a conclusion that he fervently hoped was correct.

Here she comes!

Ramesses turned and gazed north toward the bend of the Nile. As he watched, a high-rearing prow moved through the curtaining border of reeds; he could see the sail now, marked with Pharaoh's names. *Prince of the Winds*, as he had hoped. She navigated the curve in the river and was sailing straight at him, the waters of the river rippling to either side of the bronze-clad prow.

She was coming swiftly now; the sail was reefed and furled. A bank of oars emerged from their ports, dipping and flashing in the water. Now that her bulk was beyond the bend, Ramesses watched the white-sailed escort of smaller ships following her like a bevy of goslings.

Ramesses caught himself standing on tip-toe, craning his neck for a view of the captain. After a moment his face relaxed in a smile, and he waved to the man standing at the bow.

The ship was nearly upon them, the light flashing from the great beams of cedar that formed her hull. The oars dipped once more and then raised upright and held there as the ship glided in to her berth and was made fast.

Ramesses straightened, his face lit by a wide smile as the gangplank thudded to the quay. The man at the bow saw him, raised a hand in salute, and strode down the gangplank.

Ramesses hurried forward, his hands outstretched. "Khonsu!" he cried.

The Admiral of the Memphis trading fleet stopped before him, gripped his shoulders, and pulled him into a quick embrace. He was a dark-eyed man in his early fifties, with quirky brows and a mouth bracketed by lines of laughter. "Ramessu!" he said. "It's good to see you here!"

Ramesses smiled down at him. "Welcome back, Khonsu," he said.

The admiral's expression changed as he took in the royal circlet and sidelock. "What's this?" he asked.

Ramesses lowered his eyes. "I am Crown Prince now," he said quietly.

"Nakhtamun?"

"Killed." The word was softly spoken, but the clangor about them seemed to dim.

Khonsu met his gaze for a moment and then nodded. "Let's go to His Holiness," he said. "We can speak in private there." He added, "I am so sorry, Ramesses."

"That's another thing," Ramesses said.

Khonsu lifted his eyebrows.

"Wait till you see..."

**   **   **

"*What!*" Khonsu demanded.

"I thought I spoke clearly," Nebamun said.

"Vizier of the North!" Khonsu exclaimed. "How did Seti dupe you into it after all this time?"

"His Majesty did not 'dupe' me into' anything," Nebamun replied. "He sent me a direct order. I had no option but to obey."

Khonsu frowned thoughtfully. "That isn't like him," he said. "He never throws his weight around like that. Unless..." He paused, considering. "Unless he thought the risks were high enough to merit it."

"That is probably the case," Nebamun sighed. "He left Egypt in Ramesses' hands."

"Ramesses!"

"He is an impressive young man," Nebamun said. "You will see. But his father feels he needs some guidance." He shook his head. "If he had only asked me. There was no need to stir up old phantoms..."

Khonsu smiled at his father-in-law. "Perhaps he sought to let in the light and lay the old phantoms," he said. "How did this happen?"

Nebamun folded his hands in his lap. "It is a hard, sad story to tell," he said. He frowned. "And I must hold an audience as Vizier tomorrow. I hope there are no ghosts there..."

XXX

The audience chamber of the Vizier's palace was filled with murmuring people. White-robed priests with shaved heads spoke earnestly together. Officers armed with sickle-shaped swords spoke with bureaucrats under the light that filtered down through the clerestory windows. The frescoed walls, inlaid with faience tiles and bordered with golden dadoes, glinted in the light.

Voices were furtive amid the magnificence of gilded inscriptions and inlaid decorations.

"This has come too suddenly..."

Perineb, who was representing the Temple of Ptah, turned from his conversation to look inquiringly at one of the soldiers. "What do you mean by that, Captain?"

"There was no word at all, Your Grace," the officer said. "We only learned of this measure within the last few days, from a courier who told us that His Majesty commanded it. We hear now that Count Pasenhor has left without a word to anyone. Lord Nebamun has announced he will govern the Faiyyum. I don't know..."

"Are you saying that His Holiness would lie, then?" Perineb asked mildly.

The officer blinked. "Well, naturally I am not," he stammered.

Perineb smiled. "I thought not. His Holiness' years in Pharaoh's service have been untouched by scandal. Those who enjoy spreading vicious rumors would do well to remember it."

His voice had been clear. People stared at him. He resumed his conversation with the others near him, seemingly oblivious to the speculative glances he was getting and the rising murmurs.

Eyes turned toward the high cedar doors closing the audience hall from the Vizier's private rooms. They remained closed.

Admiral Khonsu had been listening to the talk around him and looking grim. His expression lightened and he brought his left fist to his right shoulder and bowed profoundly as the tall cedar doors opened. Armored guardsmen strode into the gathering, fanning out to either side of the doors.

After a moment of silence they heard the rustle of fine cloth and the jingle of golden ornaments as Nebamun, High

Priest of Ptah and now Vizier of Northern Egypt, came briskly up the aisle toward the dais, followed by two fan-bearers.

He was wearing the plain garments of a non-royal official. He ascended the ramp of the dais, inclined his head to the gathering, bowed to the empty throne that sat in the center of the dais, and sat in the smaller chair to the left of the throne, propping his sandaled feet on the footstool before him.

He nodded to the Palace Marshall, who rapped his staff three times on the floor. When the room was silent he said, "Let all present know that I speak with the voice of the Lord of the Two Lands." His voice quivered for a moment and then steadied and grew stronger. "I am here to judge any disputes that have arisen, and I will consider any petitions that may be brought today. Speak and His Majesty will hear you through me."

The room murmured into an uproar. Disjointed sentences, exclamations. The guards on the perimeter fingered their thrusting spears and looked at each other.

The Marshal's staff crashed against the floor three times. "This audience is in session!" he cried.

"Let the first petitioner come forward," Nebamun said grimly.

Time passed slowly. The audience was notable for its severe propriety, petitions presented, evidence given, decisions rendered by Nebamun in rigid conformity to Pharaoh's commands. Khonsu, quietly observing the proceedings, concluded that everyone had forgotten the initial unease after the first moments. People were beginning to relax.

A question arose regarding the disposition of troops in the delta. It had been referred to the Vizier's court in Pharaoh's absence. Nebamun sat forward to listen and ask questions of the officers who had come to present the situation. The question interested him; he had grown less rigid in the course of the audience and was smiling.

"Well done," he said. "I could not have expected any better result. It is my judgment, acting in His Majesty's behalf—"

"Who named you Vizier, My Lord?" The words were shouted from the back. A murmuring commotion rippled through the hall. People looked around, but no one came forward.

Lord Nebamun raised his head and spoke clearly. "*Who* named me? The King of Upper and Lower Egypt, Lord of the Two Lands, The Son of Re, Men-Maat-Re Seti Merneptah, sent word to me, in his own hand, by express messenger from Thebes, commanding that I assume the position of Vizier of the North until he was able to appoint someone permanently. I am obeying his command as I must do."

Sound began to build in the room. The comments were now spoken higher than a whisper, but not loudly enough to be clearly heard. Khonsu could catch the trailing ends of hissed arguments.

Nebamun's face was set and grim, but his voice was calm as he called the meeting to order. "We are not here to argue with His Majesty's wishes," he began.

"*No!*" another voice shouted. "We are here instead to see a Prince of the old line try to usurp His Majesty's place!"

The sounds built to a crescendo, people speaking more loudly, turning to one another, trying to find the speaker; Khonsu caught a glimpse of the man, moving swiftly and yet stealthily through the crowd. Khonsu started toward the movement, intent on cutting off the man's path toward the throne.

Lord Nebamun rose to his feet and strode to the end of the dais. To Khonsu's eyes Nebamun's composure, rigidly maintained in the face of ongoing accusations, was starting to crack. Khonsu doubled his efforts to intercept the inciter.

"His Majesty ordered that I assume this office," Nebamun said over the increasing noise. "I am here in obedience to his command. Speculation is useless. I have been the servant of His Majesty, of His late Majesty, of Pharaoh Horemheb, and of Ay, all my life. I want nothing more than to see Pharaoh back in his rightful place, well in heart and body."

A shout came back. "You lie, My Lord!" The next moment Nebamun had thrown up his arm and dodged to the side as a rock hurtled past him.

The room burst into an uproar, people looking for the speaker, yelling one another down, at the edge of a riot, moving closer to the dais.

Nebamun, white-faced and rigid, drew breath to speak, to try to stop the chaos when a clear voice rose over his like a trumpet, cutting through the cacophony like a sword.

"I have never heard such nonsense in my life!"

The shouting stopped; that voice was familiar to all in the room. People looked around craned their necks as a commotion began near the door. Prince Ramesses strode up the walkway to the dais. He inclined his head to the Vizier and turned to face the crowd.

"From what I have heard during this entire appalling session, certain among the people gathered here insist that His Holiness, the High Priest of Ptah, is to be insulted by witless innuendos gabbled by people who have heard tales of the bad old times and wish to blame His Holiness for them since he is the son of one of the greatest men of that time!" His eyes flashed as he gazed down along the avenue of frescoed captives toward the edge of the crowd. A detachment of soldiers moved into the room to ring the crowd.

"Take heed, all of you!" Ramesses said. "You see before you Ramesses, son of Seti, son of Ramesses, Regent of this land in the absence of His Majesty by His Majesty's command! Do you dare say that I am a pawn in this fictitious intrigue that you have concocted for reasons that you do not wish me to assign to you? His Holiness was appointed to the northern Vizierate by His Majesty in a time of urgent need, with the appointment confirmed by public and private letters in His Majesty's own hand. The appointment is satisfactory to me; I do not choose to countermand it!"

Silence surged back on the echo of those words.

"Well?" Ramesses demanded. "Speak up! I've heard the whispers and the insinuations, and it is time to clear them out!"

His lip curled at the continuing silence. "You trouble-making cowards! You know who you are and so do I! And what was said outside these walls! Yes, I do. Get back to your properties and hold yourselves there! You are under house arrest until I have decreed otherwise! I have spoken; don't make me amend what I have said!"

He looked around the room, the glare gone. "As to the rest of the people assembled here," he said in a quieter voice, "We will be changing some things. Those of you carrying weapons will surrender them to the guards who will be moving through this room. Those who refuse will be escorted to their homes. They will be questioned further. This is an audience, not a venue for a brawl."

Khonsu, standing at the side of the audience chamber, hid a smile. *Bravo, Ramessu!* he thought. *Very impressive!* He watched Ramesses turn and go back to the center of the dais.

The Crown Prince turned, bowed to Pharaoh's empty throne, and took his seat in the smaller throne to the right. "This audience will continue," he said. "Those with concerns to place before the Vizier are invited to come forward to present their cases. I, too, will listen and, if His Lordship permits me, will add any insights I may have."

XXXI

"I watched you," Khonsu said. "You were shaken at the beginning, but you recovered. And then when the commotion began... You're not usually at a loss."

Nebamun looked down at his hands which were uncharacteristically folded together before him. "Old phantoms, as I had feared."

Khonsu looked up at him, a slight frown creasing his forehead. "The phantoms you mentioned before?"

Nebamun lifted his cup of beer and looked into it as though gazing through it to another time. "I was at an audience my father held in Thebes during the second year of Tutankhamun's reign. Akhenaten had been dead for some years, and the disintegration of the empire was being assessed. People wanted to assign blame. A man of my father's stature, who was not, himself, interested in hunting down bunglers, was a natural target.

"My father was sometimes too princely. He continued as he had, doing what he could to preserve this land, taking upon himself, unnecessarily, I think, the blame for shortfalls. This was the time that Tutankhamun was falling under the influence of those who had always stood against my father. It was a bad time, but he had hope.

"And then he held an audience in Thebes-he was Vizier of the land, both north and south. I was there. He was careworn, but his voice and bearing were unchanged from the man I had known and loved all my life. I remember that day. I was there, as I said. Watching him, so proud of him. He truly was a magnificent man. But that day was different.

"The audiences were always conducted with propriety. The petitioners had their say and my father questioned them, considered, and answered thoughtfully. Though he was a Kinsman, a Prince and one of Akhenaten's friends, no one had ever doubted his own integrity.

"He heard cases, pronounced judgment, dealt with all as he had always done. But then, late into the audience, as he turned to review a document, a voice shrieked, *'You lie, My Lord!'*

"He was shaken, but he straightened and said 'Who complains of me? Come forward and bring your charges!'."

"A stone came arcing up through the crowd. The stone-thrower was not a soldier-it was poorly thrown, but it hit my father and drew blood.

"The crowd roared and surged forward. My father stood alone before them, blood streaming down his forehead, and ordered them to disperse."

Nebamun eyed his folded hands. "They did." He finally looked up at Khonsu. "That moment was the beginning of the terrible times. I knew it as such in later years, and to see it come to me and know that it was starting again, that I had not escaped my doom, that it would be for me as it had been for my father..." His voice dropped. "And I would not be able to escape."

"But you recovered, Father. And it went well."

Nebamun smiled and shook his head. "How could I not recover with that clarion-voiced son of Seti's speaking for me? I felt as though a division of chariotry had been sent to my rescue. I had an ally, I had hope..."

His eyes narrowed as he gazed ahead of him. "I might, perhaps, have recovered better than my father. He was a great man, but he was fortune's darling for most of his life. He did what was right and was content in his life. I have tried to do as he did, but unlike him I became cynical. Sometimes that helps to armor you. And sometimes it makes you inflexible. I am older than he was at his death. I don't know. I don't know."

"Must you continue?"

"I refuse to retreat from ghosts at my age, Khonsu. I only pray it doesn't kill me."

They both looked up at a commotion at the door. Prince Ramesses came briskly into the room, waved them to their chairs and settled himself on the edge of the pond. "It went very well!" he said. "After that one difficult moment. Idiots! Some of them have been released, the others are being questioned." He looked at the lift of Khonsu's eyebrows. "Gently," he said. "I just want them to learn a lesson."

"Well done, Ramessu," Khonsu said. "Your father would have loved to hear you."

Ramesses smiled and shook his head. After a moment he spoke quietly. "I heard you in that audience hall, My Lord," he said. "You were at a complete loss..."

Nebamun lowered his eyes.

Ramesses knelt beside the High Priest's chair. "My father appointed you Vizier because you are courageous, and because you are incorruptible." He took Nebamun's hand between his. "But my father would never want to cause you any heartache. This has touched you closely. You may resign, if you choose."

Nebamun smiled wearily. "With your support, Ramessu," he said, "I can fulfill the position as long as I am needed." He tightened his grip on Ramesses' hands. "I was happy to see you striding up that aisle. Where were you?"

"I had gone in and stayed by the door. I thought we might see some trouble, so I made myself inconspicuous."

Khonsu eyed him with a touch of irony. "And no one saw you?"

Ramesses' mouth tipped for a moment and then righted. "I was holding my diadem and sidelock in my hand. I was one with the crowd."

"Were you, perhaps, squatting on the floor?" Khonsu murmured.

"Not at all, Admiral. I was resting on one knee. Well," he continued, "I do think they will behave themselves now, especially since I know now who to watch." He smiled at Nebamun. "I have been thinking things over, Holiness. You learned from a great man, and you, yourself, are a great man- no, don't bow! It appears that I am, willy-nilly, destined to have a hand in governing Egypt in times to come. Could I, perhaps, come to your audiences during this time and learn from you?"

His bland smile did not alter as Khonsu and Nebamun directed suddenly intent stares at him. "It would be good for my children, as well, to become accustomed to being in crowds," he said. His expression warmed and he released Nebamun's hand. "My dearest Lord," he said in a quieter voice. "If it *must* be done, then it *can* be done. And I will be with you to see that it is so."

XXXII
Deir El Medineh

Evening had fallen and the village lay silent in the gathering dark. Seti was sitting in the courtyard of one of the tombs high along the hillside overlooking the town. The small, steep-sided pyramid behind him marked the tomb chamber itself; the stone slab lay beside him, and he had placed some of his supper there as an offering.

A trace of sunset's pink lingered at the horizon, but the stars had broken through the darkening sky. He sat with his back against the wall, his face tilted toward the stars, cool and serene after the bustle of the day.

Well... perhaps not 'bustle', he thought, reviewing things. *But Ye Gods, I am tired!*

It had been the start of his second week serving as a guard for the workmen, and he had a lot to think about. Djedi had been delighted to introduce him to the various people of the town, and he had been the object of a good deal of covert curiosity.

He had gone with Djedi to the Tomb of His Majesty, walking along the major path from the village, which headed north from the western foothills along the top of the cliffs surrounding the mortuary temples of Hatshepsut and Mentuhotep at Deir el Bahari to the workmen's encampment that housed them during the stretch of days that they worked on the tombs. From there the path went north and east before it descended to the Valley of the Kings.

It was a beautiful walk, he had to admit, with wonderful views of the Nile from time to time. The view of Deir el Bahari from the heights was splendid, but the splendor was overlaid in his mind by surprised dismay. Foremost among the reasons for his unease was the number of people who were guarding the workers, the town, the cemeteries and the tombs. Two, to be precise: Djedi and himself.

He leaned his head back and stared up at the river of stars that formed the 'Passage of the Crocodile', and then closed his eyes. Two men to guard the tombs, one of them terribly inexperienced.

"I am a painter," Djedi had told him during a pause when they took to some shade and ate the lunch they had brought from the village. "But I am pretty active, and I am a swift runner."

A swift runner... Seti opened his eyes again, pictured the town, lying open and vulnerable in its bowl of cliffs, and then, with the bend of an ironic smile, led an attack on the town at the head of a division of chariots.

They would circle on the spine of the hills overlooking the necropolis, coming in from the desert. If he recalled correctly from the times he had visited the great mortuary temples along the Nile, a respectable path ran northeast past them, joining another that ran north-northwest along the backs of the hills, leading straight into the Valley of the Kings. From there it was an easy march to Deir el Medineh itself and then the Valley of the Queens.

He pictured the lines of chariots moving along the cliff-top pathways, made passable from generations of workmen's' feet, at a smart trot, picking up speed as they drove west-southwest, skirting the valley with Deir el Bahari and then tore into the village at a gallop, bows ready, spears in hand.

The villagers would be milling around, screaming, some of them trying to fight, others turning to flee. Fight or flight made no difference; women were scooped up, the older, ailing men and women were speared and left to die as the attackers systematically looted the town, taking valuables, provisions, the precious materials used by the artists.

They would try to run for the small temples; Seti imagined the ease with which he could take those buildings with a squadron of infantry. He could imagine the people hiding in the sanctuary, the grate of metal upon bone, the reek of blood...

He had come upon the aftermath of such attacks. It took little imagination to picture what had gone before. The children running up the hillsides, screaming. Some of them, trying to hide among the tombs, would be cornered and put to the sword. Others, running for the mortuary temples, would be trampled. The raiders would go after the women. Presently the dark night would ring with screams that would echo through the empty, reddened streets.

He opened his eyes and gazed up at the stars again.

"Not this time," he said quietly, and rose to his feet. He looked down at the offering slab. "'A thousand of bread and of beer, a thousand of geese and oxen, of linen and alabaster, of sweets and of all good and pure things," he said softly, the prayer of abundance for the dead, and left the enclosure.

**   **   **

He was frowning as he descended the path to the main street of the village. Children ran up to greet him; he smiled even as his heart turned over when dark eyes raised to his with the shadow of a familiar smile. One took his scribe's kit, another offered to carry at leasrhis dagger. "Be careful with it," he said. "It's sharp."

He found Djedi waiting at his house with Neferhotep and another, older man who had a familiar look to him. It took him a moment to remember where he had seen him.

"Here you are, good Sa-Ramses!" Neferhotep said. "I wanted to present you to my uncle." He turned to the man beside him. "This is Sa-Ramses, Kenamun. He came to me two sevendays ago, seeking work. He is an excellent scribe. I can attest to that, but he has been a soldier, as well." He beamed as Seti bowed, keeping his head lowered. "My uncle is the Senior Foreman here. He had to travel south to inspect some work our men did for the governor of Djeba."

"I am sorry I was not here to greet you when you first came," Kenamun said. "We have had reason to seek soldiers, and Djedi describes your arrival as a godsend."

"It is!" Djedi said, beaming.

"Your Honor is too kind," Seti said. He straightened to find Kenamun eyeing him with a touch of puzzlement. The expression was smoothed after a moment. Seti wondered if the man might try to say something. A good attack was the best defense, he thought, meeting the look straight on.

Kenamun blinked and then lowered his eyes. "I beg your pardon, Master Sa-Ramses," he said. "I did not mean to stare. You have a familiar look to me; the likeness is elusive..."

"My family comes from the north, Master Foreman. There are many there who could easily be close kin." He paused to allow the words to be heard and then bowed. "I beg your forgiveness. I have things that must be done this evening."

Neferhotep stretched out a hand to forestall him. "Please. Wait," he said. "We need to speak with you."

Seti hesitated and then nodded. "Come in, then," he said, and motioned for them to go before him.

Djedi lingered at the door. "I have to go," he said. "A dinner... If you think I should stay...?"

"I will report on our conversation tomorrow," Seti said with another bow. "If that is satisfactory."

Djedi smiled, nodded and left. Seti, watching him move off with a brisk gait, thought of Ramesses and smiled.

He went into the house to find that Neferhotep had taken one of the stools. Kenamun was standing, leaving the other stool empty.

"I might suggest, when I leave, that you need another chair or stool," Kenamun said.

"I need no extra stool, sir."

Kenamun smiled and settled himself on the floor. "Possibly. But it would be good to make your position on the floor a matter of choice rather than necessity, as I do. Do sit down, sir."

Seti suppressed the flash of a grin too late to hide it from Kenamun.

"You've heard of the problems we've been having off and on," Neferhotep said. "I understand you've been through our settlement, as well. Djedi has had nothing but praise for you." He stopped as Seti smiled.

"Master Djedi is a good man," Seti said, "But I have done nothing other than to follow him and listen to what he has to say." He considered for a moment and then added, "Indeed, I am surprised at the trust you have shown me, a stranger, in the short time I have been here."

"Djedi found you acceptable," Kenamun said slowly, the shade of puzzlement still in his eyes. "He is young and sometimes a bit of a rascal, but his mind is sound and his heart is good. He feels that you should perhaps lead the guards of this village, since you obviously have a great deal of experience."

Seti looked up. His startled expression eased to a smile. "You are being over-hasty, sir," he said. "For all you know, I am some sort of scoundrel trying to take this village for all it is worth."

"I don't think so," Neferhotep said. "You don't feel foul to me."

Seti lifted his eyebrows. "You are placing a great deal of trust on feelings," he said.

"They're good to trust, within reason," Kenamun said.

"Then there is this small thing to consider, as well. The corps of guards for Deir el Medineh currently consists of two men; Master Djedi and myself."

"But do we need more?" Neferhotep asked. "It could be difficult to get any men to work here."

Seti schooled his voice to meekness. "It must be as the masters of this village decide," he said. "What is the alternative?"

"We could train our men in fighting," Neferhotep said. "Couldn't we?"

"That may take some time," Seti said. "The question is whether you have time." He paused to allow them to consider this, then continued. "Could we review what you know of the attacks?" At Neferhotep's nod he continued. "I have heard that ruffians came through. Djedi was there, but as one who was in the thick of things, his recollection is more emotional than factual. Perhaps you can tell me more?"

Neferhotep started.

Kenamun nodded. "I was away from this village until this morning, Master Sa-Ramses," he said. "Neferhotep can answer your questions."

Seti inclined his head with the air of one admitting a point. "Then, if you do not object: how did they proceed? Afoot? Mounted? What sort of weapons did they use?"

"They came all at once," Neferhotep said, "We had no chance to take stock."

"Arrows? Knives? Slingshots? Spears?"

"It happened so swiftly , " Neferhotep said with the sudden feeling that he was trying to dodge a volley of arrows.

"How many were there? Don't you even *know*?" Seti's voice, which had grown clipped and harsh, gentled suddenly. "I apologize, masters. I forget the courteous usages after years of other concerns." He let the words echo for a moment. "Please: tell me what happened these other times. How many attacks were there?"

Neferhotep looked down. "There were two times," he said. "Two?"

"Well..."

"More than two?"

"I was told there were three," Kenamun said. "The first time, an old man was waylaid upon the cliff path. The other times, I am told, were different."

"And what happened?"

"They came from behind the hills. We had no warning."

"How many people?"

"More than three," Neferhotep said.

[126]

"And what happened?"

Neferhotep cleared his throat. "They came into the town."

Seti was frowning. "How did they get past your lookouts?" he asked.

"They—"

Kenamun interrupted Neferhotep. "We have no lookouts."

Seti raised his eyebrows.

"We think they climbed the wall," Neferhotep said.

"They... climbed the wall," Seti repeated, drawing out the words without expression. "And then what?"

"They went to one of our elders and demanded treasure. They struck him." Neferhotep paused as Seti growled a curse. "He was terrified, and he obeyed..."

"One of our young men tried to intervene. He was pushed and struck his head on the corner of a step. He died several heartbeats later. Djedi, I understand, was holding him."

"And then?"

"I understand that they came once more, but Djedi drove them off."

Neferhotep cleared his throat. "That was the eve of your arrival."

Seti's frown eased and he nodded. "I see. I am sorry to hear of the one man's death, and of the elders who were terrorized. Such an experience can sometimes destroy one who has lived in security and safety all his life."

"They have been taken in hand by one of the priests here," Neferhotep said. "They are recovering."

"That, at least, is good," Seti said.

Kenamun and Neferhotep traded looks.

Seti's gaze shifted, as though he were watching something just beyond them. "Do you know what will happen?" he asked. "What will *really* happen, divorced from tales told by those who believe in happy endings? Let me tell you.

"You have been attacked by a small group of ruffians. The group will not be small for long. News of an easy target will always spread. The ruffians will be killed or assimilated by a worse group, which will step in to do things correctly.

"They will come against you in numbers. They will come from the west, which is your blind spot. You will listen to your point riders who report to you-for by this time you *will* have them-and realize that there is little time to spare. You tell the townsfolk to head for the hills or the river. They will mill around, screaming about their belongings even as you shout to

[127]

them that danger is coming at a gallop. They shout, squabble, arguments escalate, and you want to wash your hands of them, knowing that some will be lost, and praying that it will not happen. But you can't leave them to their fates, so you remain because they are your charges and you are responsible for their welfare."

Neferhotep's mouth had fallen open. He closed it and swallowed.

Seti eyed his expression and continued. "Desperate for help, you send what men you can spare to the great mortuary temples, shouting a warning. They may bestir themselves... Maybe. Serving the dead tends to make the servants lazy."

"But if they took shelter in the village temple..." Neferhotep said.

Seti directed a look at him. "I could storm that structure with five men," he said. "Afoot." When Neferhotep made no response he continued. "Back at the town, the escape routes will be blocked with fleeing villagers and their belongings.

"The raiders have been sighted; you hear people screaming, praying as the road between Deir el Medineh and safety becomes impassable.

"You shout to them to listen to you. You try to say something compelling, something that may save them. And then you turn to fight as well as you can with the few men that you have, but mallets and clubs are not very effective against arrows and edged weapons.

"The roadway is choked with dead and wounded when the fighting is over. You are among them, looking sightlessly up at a darkening sky as the town is put to the sword and the night is filled with the screams of the women who have been captured."

He added, "The people you appealed to for help will make long speeches about your valor and gallantry as your unburied bones whiten in the sun, picked clean by vultures and hyenas."

The two foremen had drawn together, silent and enormous-eyed.

"Is that what you want?" Seti asked. "For that is what you will get if you continue as you are. Doing what is necessary will cause some hardship and inconvenience, but it is time for the governors of this town to make a decision: do you want to protect these people who are trusting you? Or do you want to be popular? You will have to make a choice at some point."

Silence crashed back. Kenamun swallowed, looked over at Neferhotep, who was also frozen with shock. "Plain speaking, Master Sa-Ramses," he said.

"I can tell you nothing but the truth, good Foreman," Seti said. "It is not pretty, but it may save lives here." He folded his arms and looked directly at them.

"I thank you for your honesty," Neferhotep said, his voice shaking. "You have... fought these people?"

"Time and again."

"Your candor is difficult to hear," Kenamun said. "But I think it is a greater gift than fair-sounding lies."

"I thank you, good Foreman," Seti said with a bow.

There was nothing more to say. Neferhotep and Kenamun left to return to their own homes, each knowing that sleep would be nonexistent that night.

XXXIII

The night wind pushes its way through the narrow windows of Foreman Kenamun's house. It bears the scent of the Nile, of open fields and fish frying in the evening.

The man lying on his bed does not catch the scent; he lies rigidly quiet, his head propped on his headrest, but his mouth tight with fear.

Images are forming behind his closed eyelids. The King's tomb in a fitful night, the outlined drawings, ready for his chisel, flickering in the torchlight.

He takes his chisel and alters the outline of the King; looking up into the carved eyes, he sees that they are almost alive, fixed on him with an expression of warning.

Crashes from outside; looking up the long stairway he sees the night sky dark red and flickering.

The tomb is empty; where is everyone?

He pushes to his feet, runs to the doorway.

Screams, shuddering through the night.

What can he do?

More cries; he can hear children. His knees give way under him and he collapses against the ground, hands clutched at his chest. It is just as Sa-Ramses described.

Motion behind him. He turns and sees that the drawing of the King is shifting, altering, becoming flesh. It solidifies as he watches, pushing away from the wall, stepping down onto the carved stone.

"Wait!" he cries.

The King turns to look at him with wide, carved eyes. He can see the shine of tears running down his cheeks.

"The attackers! They're destroying the village!"

The King's eyes warm into living flesh. "I thank you, good foreman," he says with a bow, and moves purposefully into the scream-filled night.

** ** **

Kenamun sat up, his heart pounding.

I thank you, good foreman

Why had the words sent him spinning into wakefulness?

He drew a shuddering breath, remembering. He did not sleep again.

** ** **

Djedi settled on the smooth rock by the path and stretched out his legs. He had passed a busy and tiring morning. Sa-Ramses was astonishingly energetic for a man old enough to be Djedi's father. He seemed as fresh after all that time as he had been when they set out. Djedi had decided it was time to take a rest. "No, I'm tired, morning is passing and it's turning into a hot day. Let's just sit down and drink some water. It isn't as though I'm being attacked this very monent!"

Sa-Ramses propped his foot on the side of the rock and eyed Djedi. "Drink, then," he said, and watched with a dark smile as Djedi unstoppered his skin and raised it to his lips–

Sa-Ramses knocked it out of his hands.

"Hey! What are you *doing*?" Djedi reached for the water skin and stopped as the point of Sa-Ramses' knife pricked his jaw.

"Tell us where the treasure is, boy-or we'll gut you right here!"

"What?"

"Where is it?" Sa-Ramses' dark eyes narrowed. "Not talking, are you? We'll make you. Haul him upright, you-hold him! Now, boy, you're going to be very informative, or very dead!"

Djedi backed away from the knife. "What are you doing?" The point followed him. "You're joking, aren't you?"

Sa-Ramses showed his teeth. "Am I? I'm getting impatient, boy. Shall we bash your head in and look for ourselves?"

"Who are you talking to?"

"Chatty, isn't he? Less talk or you will be very sorry!"

Djedi's brows drove together. "This isn't amusing!"

"I think it is, and when we have your treasure, you will too!"

Djedi took one swift step backward, fists bunched, kicked Sa-Ramses' knife hand aside, and tried to close with him.

"That's better," Sa-Ramses said, blocking a blow with his forearm and countering with an uppercut that Djedi barely dodged. "Try hitting me again!"

"Gladly!"

Sa-Ramses was laughing now. "Ah! I've made you mad! Come on, fight! You're doing well for an inexperienced fellow!"

Djedi stepped backward and lowered his fists, eyeing Sa-Ramses. When there was no further attempt to fight, he dropped to the ground and drew his knees up. "I think I get your point," he said.

"That being-?"

"That being that we need to practice. Or I do."

"You don't need to practice much," Sa-Ramses said. "You have good instincts, but your temper tends to get in your way."

"What were you doing?"

"I was pretending to be one of those intruders. You said they came unexpectedly. There's no reason to think they might not have come upon us here, sitting and guzzling water. This is war, and a warrior has to be prepared."

"I'm not a warrior."

"You can be, Djedi. A good one."

Djedi looked up at Sa-Ramses. The sun was behind the man's shoulders, blinding him. "Do you really think so?"

The voice came from the sun, tinged with a smile. "You will be, Djedi. You have the heart and the courage now. I'd have you in my army in a heartbeat."

"Your army?"

"I was speaking in parables," Sa-Ramses said. "I'll retrieve your water, and we can talk some more."

XXXIV

Kenamun shook out his robe. The morning's meeting with the Vizier had been brief. His Excellency had seemed preoccupied, though he had listened kindly to Kenamun's concerns-supplies, some men to help protect the village-and had promised to look into matters. Kenamun's experience with Lord Intef had given him some confidence. The man, who had spent years in the Royal Army, kept his promises.

He nodded to everyone, commented on the work being done, and then approached Sa-Ramses, who was standing quietly, his weight resting on the shaft of a spear, gazing through narrowed eyes across the shimmering landscape to the distant sparkle of the Nile. He straightened and bowed as Kenamun approached him.

"Good evening, Master Sa-Ramses," Kenamun said. "I had a chance to give some thought to what you told us last night. I have some concerns. I will call upon you this evening to discuss them."

Sa-Ramses' brows drew together fractionally, but he bowed again. "I am at the Foreman's service," he said.

Neferhotep was frowning. "Should I be there?" he asked.

Sa-Ramses turned his dark gaze on the man.

"No," said Kenamun. "I thought about the things Master Sa-Ramses told us and had some questions.." He smiled at Sa-Ramses. "I will look forward to speaking with you this evening."

** ** **

"This is good wine," Kenamun said, looking into his cup with his eyebrows raised.

Sa-Ramses sat back against the wall and raised his cup with the hint of an ironic smile. "It was a gift from one of the townsfolk," he said. "They have been generous to a newcomer."

Kenamun sipped. "I wish I could be the beneficiary of such generosity," he said with a smile. He looked around the reception room with new eyes. The villagers had shared furniture and food. It was spare but comfortable. "They can be generous when they've taken someone to their heart," he said. The lurking smile in Sa-Ramses' eyes made him smile back.

"You are very kind," Sa-Ramses said. "But you spoke of some concerns this afternoon. You addressed me, specifically,

[133]

without including Commander Djedi. Do your concerns involve me, personally?"

Direct speaking, Kenamun thought. He raised his cup in a half-toast, sipped, then set it down. "This situation does not involve Djedi."

Sa-Ramses bowed. "I understand," he said. "I will not interrupt you any further."

"It was no interruption," Kenamun said. "I have some concerns regarding someone in this village who is other than he originally seemed." He paused as Sa-Ramses frowned. "No, I do not mean in any dishonest fashion. But it is clear to me that we are dealing with someone who has misrepresented himself to the town."

Sa-Ramses set his cup down. "Who is this man? Is he someone I have encountered?"

"You have dealt with everyone in this town, Master Sa-Ramses, including this man. He has been given a position of trust and of honor. The townsfolk have taken him to their hearts, and I think he feels kindly toward them in his turn."

Sa-Ramses' gaze was very direct. "And do you fear that this impostor poses any threat to the town?"

"Not at all."

"Then there is no need to take any action. Unless you wish me to keep my eye on him. Can you tell me who he is?"

Kenamun shook his head slowly. "I don't think I should," he said. He was silent for a long moment, frowning, as Sa-Ramses watched him.

He raised his head, flashed a glance at the pendant at Sa-Ramses' neck, then looked directly into his face. "Let me tell you a story, instead. Are you willing to listen?"

Sa-Ramses' smile edged into irony. "I am, of course, at the Foreman's service," he said.

"Well, then. There was a man once whose son died tragically. He received the news late, long after his son had been placed in his tomb. The news itself was given to him suddenly, with no warning. He had no chance to compose himself. He was unable to mourn his son properly and heal his own grief.

"He made the journey to the tomb bearing offerings that were important to him, only to find that the tomb was closed and sealed. He had to delay his visit and the offerings while the tomb was opened. He was able to make the offering at last and ease his heart in that manner, but he was at loose ends, lost, as any father might be. To add to his grief, this man was highly placed, with little privacy."

Kenamun paused and then continued gently, "A broken heart is a terrible wound to bear privately. To be forced to do so publicly must be intolerable."

Sa-Ramses lowered his head.

"This is important, Master Sa-Ramses," Kenamun said. "You must understand that I am a sculptor. I can see the skull beneath the flesh, and I can remember what I see and recognize that line of bone, even if it is no longer disguised by garments, or other such devices. I saw that man when he came to his son's tomb. I recognized him when I saw him again."

Sa-Ramses looked straight at him. "And that man is the impostor?"

"Yes."

Sa-Ramses was frowning. "But if you feel that he poses no threat to the town—"

Kenamun interrupted him. "I have fears for *his* safety," he said. "Not from this town, for they love him as I have said, but perhaps from concerns outside this town, concerns in this land. I do not wish this impostor to be at risk, and I fear that we may not be able to protect him if danger does come."

Sa-Ramses' eyes creased a little at the corners. "I suspect I know who this man is," he said. "If I am correct, then I am intimately acquainted with him. You need have no fear for him, Master Foreman. He can summon supporters at very short notice, and he knows how to fight. Nor is he foolish enough to ignore the goodwill of this town. He would come to the town fathers at need and present his credentials."

"That is good to know," Kenamun said. "I hope he knows that I, Kenamun, would give all the assistance I could if it comes to that." He added quietly, "As would all the people of this village, though they do not know who or what this impostor is. He has become one of us."

Sa-Ramses did not look up. "I must ask one question," he said. "Is it possible that this impostor may bring danger to the town?"

"Absolutely not. In my judgment his presence is a blessing to all, and, I think, to himself. He is welcome here."

Sa-Ramses raised his eyes. "It is settled, then?"

"Yes, Master Sa-Ramses."

Sa-Ramses looked up at him. "I understand that you lost a child tragically," he said. "Your own eldest son. I am sorry."

XXXV
Memphis

Egypt had settled back into its usual serenity after its initial astonishment at the news of His Majesty's disappearance. The astonishment had reawakened when two of Memphis' prominent nobles left the city suddenly, and without explanation, to take up residence on their estates. Talk had spiraled into conjecture, accusations and near-hysteria, but the daily presence of Lord Nebamun, acting as Vizier of the North by Pharaoh's command and attended by the Crown Prince Ramesses, eased the misgivings of all but the most suspicious citizens. The Southern Vizier, Intef, communicated closely with Nebamun. The continuing presence of Prince Ramesses, who was often seen in public with his children, giving audiences, greeting the citizens during the Vizier's audiences, did much to reassure the populace, who concluded, by and large, that His Majesty, having suffered a terrible blow in the death of his eldest son, had most likely decided to rest and recover from his various hurts.

It was only reasonable, the people said. Surely one could excuse a desire for privacy by one so bereaved. And so prayers were offered in the various temples, and in the various homes, throughout Egypt for the safety and good heart of His Majesty.

There were some, however, who were not satisfied with that conclusion...

** ** **

Nebamun straightened his cramped spine, brought his hands before him and gripped them tightly. Stretching his arms straight out in front of him, he brought his clasped hands up over his head, bent his elbows and stretched his arms down behind his neck, finishing with a sound between a grunt and a yawn. That was better.

"That's that lot for today." He cocked an eyebrow at his personal scribe, who was grinning. "If I can't get to the archery course, or get some decent exercise," he said, "At least this helps."

"It has been a long day, Holiness," the scribe said, gathering his brushes and setting them in the slot in his scribe's palette before closing it. "Nearly over, praise Ptah!"

Lord Nebamun rose. "And to think I once enjoyed watching my father at his work..." He stretched again. "Go home, Nepri," he said. "And thank you. Give my best greetings to your family and tell—"

A sharp rap on the door made him stop and trade stares with Nepri, who got to his feet and went to the door. He opened it; Nebamun heard a murmur of voices. Nepri turned, "The Princesses Iset and Tia, and Count Tiyah, wish to speak with Your Holiness," he said, and stepped to one side.

Princess Tia swept into the room. She was a woman in her late twenties, Pharaoh's second daughter. As the reigning toast of Memphis during her father's tenure as Vizier of the North, she had made a love match with a royal official who had the same name. Passing years and two children had not dimmed her beauty, but the indulgence of an imperious will had turned her sharpness to harshness.

She gave Nebamun a perfunctory bow. "I have come to speak with you, My Lord!" she said, locating a chair and positioning herself in it without waiting for an invitation. Her husband, a quiet man with what Nebamun had discovered was a lurking twinkle, raised his eyebrows for permission and drew another chair forward for Princess Iset.

"You are welcome here, Princess," Nebamun said, but with a silent sigh. He traded smiles with Iset, Pharaoh's eldest child, and with Lord Tiyah. "How may I be of service?"

Tia disposed her shawl around her shoulders and lifted her head. "It has been some weeks since we had word from my father. I have grown concerned. Where is he?"

Iset started and stared at her sister.

Tia ignored her and smiled fixedly at Nebamun.

"Word has been released that His Majesty is in good health and spirits," Nebamun said.

"Yes, yes," Tia said. "We have all heard *that*. I wish to know specifics. Where is he? How can I reach him?"

Nebamun inclined his head to Tia. "I regret, Highness, that His Majesty will not allow me to discuss his whereabouts," he said. "Except to say that he is well and safe."

"Pooh!" Tia said. "Not permitted! Where is he?"

"His Majesty will not allow me to discuss the subject," Nebamun repeated. He smiled at her and added gently, "Even with you. I am permitted to say that His Majesty is in good health and spirits."

"That is ridiculous!"

[137]

"It is, nevertheless, His Majesty's strict orders."

"I don't believe you," Tia said. "When did he tell you this?"

Count Tiyah cleared his throat.

"Quiet!" Tia snapped. "Well, My Lord?"

"He gave me the instructions in writing, by his own hand, sent from Thebes. A separate letter was sent to Prince Ramesses."

"Then he is in Thebes!"

Nebamun's smile grew steely. "His Majesty's orders have not changed," he said. "I cannot disobey my King. I am forbidden to discuss his whereabouts, as I told you, even with those he lov—"

"I am his daughter! You may tell *me* where my father is!"

Nebamun met her stare. "I am forbidden," he said.

Tia revealed a formidable scowl. "Don't be difficult, My Lord!"

Nebamun's smile widened. "Don't be obtuse, Highness," he said.

Tia rose to her feet and pointed a relentlessly straight finger right at his chest. "You mannerless *upstart!*" she said slowly and deliberately, enunciating every syllable.

Nebamun pushed himself to his feet and took a step toward her. "I *beg* your pardon?" he said.

Iset had risen and laid an urgent hand on his arm. "Please, my dear lord!" she said. "I beg you—! Tia, are you *mad?*"

"Don't be an idiot!" Tia said through her teeth. "He has been dodging and prevaricating!"

"Dodging and prevaricating?" Iset repeated. "He told you that Father forbade giving any information on his whereabouts!"

"That is beside the point!"

Iset turned to Nebamun with a helpless motion. "I am so sorry, My Lord!" she said. "Mother told me that she was dropped on her head as a baby."

Count Tiyah steepled his fingers together. "I...do believe that His Holiness' maternal grandsire was Amenhotep the Great," he said. "And he is a direct descendant on both sides, in the primary male line, of Thutmose the Great..."

Tia glared at her husband.

Nebamun lifted an eyebrow and patted Iset's hand. He backed a step and sat back in his chair, his arms folded before him.

"Hold your tongue!" Tia snapped. "His manners—"

"Border on saintliness!" Iset said. "He is too great a gentleman to throttle you as you deserve! Or perhaps he feels it beneath him to kill a lunatic!"

"*Lunatic*! Tia shrieked.

"You have the manners of a fishwife! For that matter, *Your Highness*, your title reaches back only five years, to when Grandsire became Pharaoh!"

"What does that say about you?" Tia retorted.

"I've never deluded myself about my own worth," Iset said. She turned back to Nebamun, who was sitting back and watching with the hint of a smile.

She relaxed. "Oh, my dearest lord," she said. "I beg you to believe that I had no part in this!"

Nebamun smiled, drew breath -

A voice rang out behind them. "No one expects *you* to be such an idiot!"

Nebamun lifted his eyebrows. He had opened his mouth to speak, but the clear baritone that rang through the hall was not his voice.

Ramesses strode into the room and scowled at his sister. "Why are you annoying His Holiness with your impertinence?" he demanded. "You may thank all the gods he didn't lay you out as you deserved!"

"It is beneath His Holiness to fight with half-wits," Count Tiyah murmured.

"*What* did you just say?" Tia gasped.

Her husband looked at her with raised eyebrows.

"He was rude to me!"

Ramesses stared at her.

Count Tiyah cleared his throat. "His 'rude' words were, 'I regret, Highness, that His Majesty will not allow me to discuss his whereabouts, except to say that he is well and safe.'" He added judiciously, "I think he bowed to her as he said it, but I can't swear to it."

Ramesses raised his eyebrows at his eldest sister.

Iset smiled at him. "He is right, Ramessu," she said. "That is what His Holiness said. Tia told him he was a 'mannerless upstart'."

"So His Holiness' 'rudeness' consisted of not knuckling under to you," Ramesses said. He went to the state chair and sat down in it, placing his feet neatly on the footstool. "Listen to me, Tia," he said. "I don't want to have to repeat it. His

[139]

Holiness has been a good friend and counselor for our family at all times, but especially in this time of grief. For such a man to be so thoroughly annoyed and insulted by your arrogance and impertinence is intolerable! I am Crown Prince of this land. If you have something troubling you, then come to me! Be warned: unlike His Holiness, I *am* from an upstart family, and my manners have been known to slip! Am I understood?"

"There's no need to take that—"

"*Am I understood?*" Ramesses spoke slowly and clearly.

Iset dimpled, a surprisingly impish expression for one of her stately manner.

"*Tia?*"

Tia was scowling. "Yes..." she started. "But I—" Her brother's continuing, hard stare made her lower her eyes. "I understand Your Royal Highness," she said.

"Excellent," Ramesses said. "I don't want to have to explain it further. You may go."

He watched his sister sweep from the room, followed by her husband. Count Tiyah paused at the door to bow to Ramesses and then Lord Nebamun before following his wife.

Iset smiled again. "Well done, Brother," she said. Her smile deepened as she went to Nebamun and took his hand between hers. "I am so sorry, My Lord," she said. "If I had known what she had planned..." His expression made her dimple again and she leaned forward to kiss his cheek before departing.

"Well, that's that," Ramesses said as Nepri closed the door behind the group and then bowed himself out. "It's a good thing I arrived when I did."

"You saved your sister a tongue-lashing," Nebamun said. "I was looking forward to it."

"Pity," Ramesses said. He looked around the room. "It's late," he said. "Were you ready to return to your quarters?"

"I was," Nebamun said. "There was an interruption, as you saw. Come with me; Her Ladyship hasn't seen you in some time, and she was asking about you."

Ramesses looked thoughtful. "I must apologize," he said. "I always brought the children over, but then Nakhtamun..." He paused. "I thought the world had changed forever, but it's odd to see that, actually, life moves on even after something like this."

"It does," Nebamun said. He rose and stretched, then smiled up at Ramesses. "Come along. You're welcome even without the children."

** ** **

"What did she call you?" Lady Mayet demanded. "How dare she!" She was sitting in the evening twilight with a spindle in her hands, spinning fine linen thread. She wrapped the spun thread around the shaft of the spindle and set it aside. "I trust you spoke to the point!"

"I didn't have to," Nebamun said. "This young hero came to my rescue."

"I don't think you needed to be rescued, My Lord," Ramesses said. He raised his eyes to the garden pond. "Can we sit and watch the sun on the water?" he asked.

Lady Mayet smiled at him. "Of course!" she said. She pushed herself to her feet and reached for her cane.

Ramesses put out a hand. "Please, My Lady," he said. "Allow me!"

Before she could protest he went to one knee, took her hand and set it around his neck. The other arm scooped her up and he pushed to his feet.

"Put me down, you silly boy!" Mayet laughed.

"I will when I get you to your seat" he said, easily carrying her to the small table and chair by the pond.

He started to straighten, but she halted him with a hand to his cheek. "Thank you," she said, and kissed him.

He raised his hand to cover hers, turned and kissed it, and then stood.

"I came to ask His Holiness whether he had received any news from my father," he said.

Nebamun hid a smile. "I have," he said. "He is among friends, well and healthy. Happy? I am not sure, but happiness is not easily found in times such as this."

"No," Ramesses said. "The blow was very recent. I wish he had received my letter when I sent it..."

"If wishes were horses," Nebamun quoted, "Beggars would drive chariots. We do our best. As it is, your father has friends around him, is being useful and liked, and I think all will be well."

Ramesses nodded. "That is good. May I send a message in your pouch when next you send one?"

[141]

XXXVI

The arrow hissed from its quiver. Hazel eyes gazed along the shaft. A nod; leather-clad fingers fitted the nock to the bowstring. The archer raised the bow in one smooth motion. A fluid release of the draw hand, the draw arm and bow arm remaining stationary as the arrow sped to the butt, to sink up to its shaft right in the center of the target.

The archer held the position for a moment before lowering his bow.

"Right on target!" The Governor of Memphis clapped his father-in-law on the shoulder. "I shouldn't be surprised!"

"Meaning that you *were* surprised, Nesuptah?" Lord Nebamun said dryly.

His son-in-law only smiled and shook his head. "You won't get me to quarrel with you, my father," he said. "You're a fine archer and a finer fighter. I am not your match."

"You disappoint me," Nebamun said. "Another shot, I think..." He let fly another arrow and then nodded.

"You amaze me," Nesuptah said. "If I were half as good an archer at my age as you are at yours, I would be in heaven!"

"Better and better," Nebamun said through the edge of a grin. "With one foot in my tomb I can still shoot arrows."

"I said we wouldn't exchange words."

"Pity," Nebamun said. "I enjoy our quarrels. Do you want to shoot?" He offered his bow.

Nesuptah raised his eyebrows, hesitating. He was a man in his forties. A decade of governing had left him a little softer than he wished to be. He eyed his father-in-law's strong shoulders and nodded. "A lesson with a master archer!" he said. "I'd be a fool to refuse."

Nebamun smiled and shook his head. "You can always ask, Nesuptah," he said. "You know I would not refuse." He handed his son-in-law the bow. "There. Now, hold your arm forward, like that. Yes. Draw back, slowly. Can you feel the pull in your shoulder? Sight along the shaft. Steady...steady... steady... Now!"

Nesuptah held the pose for a moment, and then released the string, flinching as it struck his inner arm. The arrow flew a little wide of center, but still landed in the butt. He lowered the bow, "Not a good showing," he murmured.

"I would say it was a good showing; when was the last time you drew a bow? Years, I am sure. You did well, after such a long time."

"Just as you're doing well as Vizier," Nesuptah said, surreptitiously rubbing his shoulder. "I know you weren't happy originally."

"I am still not happy," Nebamun said. "But I am resigned now."

Nesuptah took another arrow and nocked it.

"Not so fast," Nebamun said. "You just shot an arrow from a powerful bow. You need to rest."

"Just one shot!" Nesuptah objected.

"Nevertheless," said Nebamun. "An archer needs to relax after each shot to allow his muscles to recover from the effort of shooting. Especially if he is out of practice." He smiled at Nesuptah's expression. "It needn't be long, but it must be done. If you don't allow for time between shots, you will tire rapidly, and you will be sore the next day. Tired muscles don't perform well. And exhausted minds tend to blur. Sit down and have some beer."

The Governor nodded and set the bow aside. He took a cup of beer from Nebamun and sipped carefully.

"You didn't come to me just to pick a fight and tell me I am a doddering fool, Nesu. There was a reason. There always *is* with you. Tell me."

"Am I so transparent?" Nesuptah demanded.

"You are with me. What is wrong?"

Nesuptah took the bow again, toed a line in the sand, nocked and drew an arrow.

"You will have to answer me eventually," Nebamun said.

The Governor let fly, swore as the arrow went wide, and turned.

"You lowered your arms too soon," Nebamun said. "It threw off the arrow's trajectory."

"Do you *only* talk of archery?"

"It's better than silence," Nebamun said. "And you are shooting at a target in an archery range. Come on. If I hadn't thought you a fine man I would never have let you marry my daughter. What is wrong?"

Nesuptah raised his eyes and looked straight at his father-in-law. "Where is His Majesty?" he asked.

Nebamun's smile edged into irony. "I can't tell you."

"Can't? No, that's wrong!"

"I am sorry, but it's quite correct."

"You can't tell me!"

"I believe that's what I said."

"Why not?"

"Because I am forbidden to."

"Forbidden? By whom?"

Nebamun sat back and steepled his fingers. "Just see if you can guess, Nesu."

"This is not amusing!"

"Did I say it was?"

"It's outrageous!"

"That's what I thought when I received the order."

"Order? From whom?"

"Whom do you think? Honestly, Nesuptah, I am beginning to think that my grandchildren were sired by a half-wit."

"This isn't a laughing matter!"

"Do you hear me laughing?" Nebamun countered. "Sit down and toss off your beer. It will help settle you—and let us talk seriously.

"Ye gods! Direct speaking!"

"Wait and see." Nebamun eyed his son-in-law. "Why has the question come up—apart from the rather unhealthy curiosity the populace seems to have for anything involving His Majesty? Do they think he has been foully murdered?"

The Governor's brows drew together fractionally and then relaxed. "Your sense of humor, sir, is sometimes rather odd," he said. "No, I don't think anyone suspects murder, though there are some among the regional governors who revel in innuendo and conjecture. You, sir, are not suspected."

"You have no idea how thoroughly you have set my heart at rest," Nebamun said as he settled his arrows in their quiver and polished the wood of his bow.

"Don't be sarcastic," Nesuptah said. "It is a profound compliment. Your actions as Vizier have been intelligent and beyond criticism. Everyone respects you. Some are surprised that they do, I might add."

"Those who had to relinquish my family's holdings when I was brought back from the dead, perhaps?"

The Governor shook his head. "Don't try to divert me. No one has heard from His Majesty in several weeks." He frowned and looked up at Lord Nebamun. "Some people are getting very worried. Where is he?"

"I told you, Nesu: I am forbidden to say. But I can tell you that he is safe and my hand is over him. Is that sufficient?"

Nesuptah frowned. "For me, certainly. But for the others... I am not sure..."

Nebamun considered for a moment. "I may be able to remedy that," he said.

"How?" Nesuptah asked.

"I am sending a bodyguard and making discreet arrangements for His Majesty's safety." He looked thoughtful. "It may be difficult," he said. "I don't want to expose him to danger." He paused as Nesuptah snorted. "Don't be a fool," he said. "There *is* danger involved, and I am very much aware of the care that is needed. I have one chosen."

Nesuptah frowned, judged the answer appropriate, and dropped the topic. "But you say you aren't happy as Vizier," he said.

Nebamun did not react to the change of subject. "Not at all," he said. "I am not suited for it. I was afraid at first. No, don't stare. You know what I mean. Now it isn't so difficult. But it is not what I was born to do, and it is not my skill. I will hand the title over with a glad heart when one is found to take it. Poor man."

"You say this," Nesuptah said. "And you say that it was not what you were born to do, even though your father was perhaps the greatest Vizier Egypt ever had. Forgive me, My Father, but what is it that you think you were born to do?"

"Me?" Nebamun said with the hint of a smile. "I was born to be an officer of archers. Perhaps rising as high as Commander of Five Thousand, like Achtoy." His smile deepened. "It was not to be, of course, and matters took the course they did. I would not exchange one moment of what was for what might have been. Would I have met my wife? Possibly not... Well. For all that I don't think I did what I was born to do, I do believe I did what I was *meant* to do, and that is what is most important."

**   **   **

Nebamun remained at the archery course after the Governor left. He spent a long time firing arrow after arrow after arrow into a row of targets. By the time he was finished a line of murmuring guardsmen and Royal Army soldiers stood behind him. They applauded as the last arrow buried itself into the target.

He lowered his bow after the last shot, smiled at the crowd and bowed.

Shortly after his return, Nebamun sat back in his chair and frowned at a sheet of papyrus that he had filled with writing. His mouth bent in an ironic smile and he laughed aloud at the final sentence. *Yes*, he thought, *that should get a reaction!*

A tap at the doorway; he raised his head. "Come in, Ptahu," he said.

Commander Ptahemhat strode into the room and started to drop to his knees. He intercepted a look from Nebamun and straightened. "I am here, Father," he said with a smile.

Nebamun returned the smile. "It is good of you to come so quickly," he said as he rolled the sheet of papyrus and flattened it. "You didn't have to drop everything." He folded the flattened roll three times, tied it with twine, and sealed it with a pinch of clay and his own seal. "I have a message for you to take south to Thebes," he said. "You are to go to Deir el Medineh-the city of necropolis workmen there-and hand it over to the fellow whose name is on the message."

'And who would that be?" Ptahemhat asked.

"The name is on the message," Nebamun said gently. He smiled and handed him the note. "If at all possible, remain with him while he reads it. You might find it amusing. Incidentally, the message contains a command from me with all the weight of Pharaoh's power to it. It cannot be countermanded, no matter who tries. The recipient is well aware of this, and you should be, as well, in case the recipient tries to argue."

Ptahemhat looked at the superscription. "Sa-Ramses?" he asked. "Who is he?"

"Don't ask questions I can't answer," Nebamun said. And smiled at Ptahemhat's startled expression.

XXXVII
Deir El Medineh

The setting sun was sparking a red glow along the shoulders of the encircling cliffs. The outlying paths were cooler now; with nightfall they would be cold. The tomb workers were returning to their houses, some in the temporary camp set up midway between the village and the Valley of the Kings, the rest trudging home for four days' rest. Seti was walking with them, quietly listening to the conversation around him, smiling when someone spoke to him.

He reached the well, set just outside the village's circling wall. Water was brought in from the river every week and poured into the well, to be used by the townsfolk. His canteen was nearly empty. He paused to refill it. People were laughing and chattering in the evening coolness. One of the town women saw him, took his canteen and filled it for him with a bright smile that widened as he took it from her with a bow made courtly by years of serving as Vizier.

Children, running underfoot, stopped to smile up at him and cry his name. They crowded around him, laughing and chattering about their day's activities.

He dropped to one knee to be at eye level with the smallest. They were wide-eyed and friendly, and he felt his smile growing unsteady as he remembered past years and children now grown with their own children. Where had the years gone? And what had they left him, all those days? Nothing but memories. But what else was there that lasted?

A little boy climbed on his knee; he settled on the ground and lifted the tot on his lap, receiving a smacking kiss from the boy as others crowded around, clamoring for a place in the circle of his arms. He pondered the question as he lowered his cheek against the cluster of heads, inhaling the scent of healthy children, hearing their chatter.

What else? When time had passed and you were alone, what did you have?

Memories? But memory could fade. And if the memories departed, never to return?

His eyes blurred and he pushed to his feet, pleading fatigue. Smiles, a hand clasping his briefly, a wide-eyed smile cast over a shoulder, a kiss blown and caught, before the children ran off, leaving him to gaze after them, curiously breathless.

He felt eyes on him and turned. A woman was standing quietly, a water jar at her feet. She had been watching him. She was tall and straight, not in her first youth. Her eyes lingered on his face and softened, but she bowed and moved away from the well.

** ** **

Djedi leaned on his spear and sighed. Weeks had passed since Sa-Ramses' arrival. He had learned more in those weeks than he had in his entire life. How to fight—he had been pronounced talented but in need of practice and training at single-stick, archery and swordplay. The training had begun immediately: morning sessions outside the town. Some of the men of the village had started coming by to watch. Sa-Ramses included them in the lessons, pairing them off and watching them.

"Not so bad," he had said. "It might take some effort to beat you..." The pupils had eyed each other and grinned.

Djedi had been treated to some fascinating discussions on strategy, and he was beginning to understand what it meant to be a commander of men. It was not just being ready to fight; it was complicated, involving more than a strong body.

He had thought himself fit. He had learned that proper fighting required more strength than he had realized. He thanked the gods he had been active, otherwise he wondered if he could have risen in the morning. As it was, he was learning.

** ** **

"Hit me," Sa-Ramses said.

"Hit *you*?"

"Yes."

"But I—"

"Pretend I'm one of those who struck your old master. Come on. Don't be shy."

Djedi eyed him, cleared his throat, cocked his fist, and then lowered it. "No. I can't. It's—"

"It's what?"

"Wrong."

Sa-Ramses shook his head with a sigh. "You had no trouble hitting me when I pretended to be a marauder. Imagine that my hair is black or that I am the young apprentice who elbowed your ribs and made rude remarks about you in front of the girl you fancied."

[148]

Djedi frowned, balled his fist, launched a blow, and gaped up at Sa-Ramses standing above him.

"Not bad. You need to make a fist differently, or you'll dislocate your thumb."

"But what happened?"

"You tried an overhand blow," Sa-Ramses said. "Not badly done, actually. But going at an enemy from above can be risky, since you are going over your center of balance. I ducked under you, used your arm and your weight as a lever, and threw you over my shoulder."

"But—"

"I was gentle with you – I'm training you, after all, but you made a dangerous move, and I was able to take advantage of it."

"I've knocked people over with that movement."

"They aren't trained fighters," Sa-Ramses said. "But you will be." He gripped Djedi's hand and pulled him to his feet. "We'll try that again – slowly this time – and you can see what I mean. Then I'll show you an underhand blow that is hard to counter."

** ** **

Djedi sat on the heights with Sa-Ramses later that afternoon, and he mentioned, shyly, that maybe Sa-Ramses should be the commander, and not him.

"Now why did you say that?" Sa-Ramses asked.

"Well..." Djedi had paused. "Well, you're obviously so much more experienced than I am... And some of the others did serve in Horemheb's army for a time, when they were pressed into service during an emergency."

Sa-Ramses snorted.

"I am serious. A more experienced commander could make us ready to fight. Better than I could."

Sa-Ramses un-stoppered his water skin and took a swallow. "Yes," he said, tapping the stopper back with the heel of his hand. "I can see how eagerly they are queuing up to offer their vast experience." He looked up at Djedi. "Based on my assessment, right now they would be what we call 'the awkward division' in my army."

"But you—"

"I am standing behind you and teaching you," Sa-Ramses said. "Isn't that enough? You will learn, Djedi, that you may well command people who are smarter, more experienced or better fighters than you are." Sa-Ramses set the water skin beside him.

"But won't that make them resent me?"

"And if it does, why should you care? You are the commander, not everyone's best friend." He eyed Djedi's expression and said more mildly, "It isn't likely, though it has happened. But you are the commander, and they are your subordinates. You have the final say in what is done and how. They had better understand that. You guide them and protect them, and take the blame, as well, when you meet with failure."

Djedi thought this over.

Sa-Ramses watched his expression and then said, "You listen to what they say and then make your own decision, which they have to follow. If you succeed, you get the glory. If you fail, you get the blame." He tipped an ironic smile and said, "Though there is nothing to stop you from blistering an erring subordinate in private."

Djedi began to grin. "I think I understand," he said.

"Good," said Sa-Ramses. "Let us try an illustration. We will pretend that there is a group of armed, unfriendly men coming along that path that we can see. What do you do?"

Djedi frowned. "I would say, 'Sa-Ramses, make your report.' I'd listen and make my decision." He hesitated. "What *would* you recommend?"

Sa-Ramses frowned. "Very well, Commander. I suggest that we make our way east of here, parallel to their path. Then, past the roughness of this terrain, swing down and engage them."

Djedi nodded.

"Well?"

"I wouldn't do it," Djedi said.

"Why not?"

Djedi wavered, took a breath, and said, "I happen to know this area. Where you want to hit them is bad footing. But if we let them get closer to the town there's another path that intersects the one they're taking, and if we can get there quickly and spring the surprise on them, they won't have anywhere to go."

Sa-Ramses directed a frown at Djedi. "You are wasting time. They are coming quickly and we need to strike at them. If we take that parallel path, we can hit them hard and destroy them."

[150]

Djedi returned the frown. "No," he said. "I tell you I know that area. The ground is crumbling-we would fall and they would kill us all. It might be faster to strike them there, but success is more certain if you do what I tell you!"

Sa-Ramses folded his arms and frowned at Djedi, who met the stare.

Sa-Ramses smiled suddenly. "Well done!" he said. "That is exactly what you should be doing. Get advice, consider it, and then make your own decision."

"But you weren't offended that I didn't take yours?"

"I am not such a fool. You had some knowledge I didn't."

Djedi was beaming. The smile faded after a moment. "If only we had a few more people."

Sa-Ramses nodded. "You need men," he said. "Men aren't volunteering. Maybe it is time to volunteer them."

"'Volunteer' them?" Djedi repeated. "What do you mean?" His expression was startled as Sa-Ramses spoke. As he listened, Djedi began to smile.

XXXVIII

That evening Djedi moved briskly down the main street of Deir el Medineh. He had a knife at his belt and a wavering smile on his face. Sa-Ramses followed him, carrying his scribal kit.

They paused before a door. "This is Harmose's house," Djedi said. "He's a stonemason."

Sa-Ramses nodded. "Excellent. He should be a good, strong fellow, then."

Djedi moistened his lips, took a deep breath and looked at Sa-Ramses, who was standing with his arms folded. At a nod, he tapped on the door. There was no response.

Sa-Ramses cocked an eyebrow at him, stepped forward and rapped smartly with his fist, then stepped back and waited with poised brush and modestly lowered eyes as it opened to a chorus of outraged oaths.

** ** **

"Right as we were eating our dinners!" Harmose said. He was sitting cross-legged on town wall and drinking a cup of beer. It was mid-morning, and the off-duty contingent of tomb workers had gathered to drink some beer and exchange gossip.

"I heard a tap and thought it was next door," Harmose said. "Next thing, the door was shaking as though someone was kicking it, and I opened it to find Djedi standing there looking at me like he wanted something. He certainly did!"

"Join a corps of guards for this town?" Benetamun, the town's Master Outline Scribe suggested.

"He got you, too?" Harmose asked.

Nods all around.

"He made a speech about how we needed to get together and take care of ourselves after the last few raids," Haru, a sculptor, said. "Well, I didn't think it was a bad idea. Piay was my friend, and he was killed, but when he started talking about what was involved I had some misgivings. Damn it, we just finished our ten-day stint in that god-cursed tomb we're carving!"

"Did you say that?" Benetamun asked.

"I did. That fellow Sa-Ramses shot me a look that made me feel as though I were trying to present a case at the Vizier's court."

"Did he say anything to you?"

[152]

"No," said Haru. "He just folded his arms and looked at me."

"He did to me!" Harmose said. "Djedi said that everyone was working on His Majesty's tomb, and everyone was going to be asked. I told him to forget it. Sa-Ramses coughed politely and then asked if I'd seen what they did to poor Paweru and how I'd like it if they did that to my father."

Haru grinned. He knew Harmose's father. "What did you say?"

"I said my father was a stonemason like me and knew how to swing a maul, at which point Sa-Ramses said that it might be best to join with my father and show the rest of the group how to swing mauls against the heads of attackers."

"He said that to you?"

"He sure did. And he said it so...so meekly, I found myself agreeing with him."

"He spoke to me, too," Benetamun said. "It was all very polite and proper, with him looking to Djedi for permission to open his mouth." He grinned as Harmose snorted. "Well, yes," he said. "He had a brush in his hand, but I received the impression that he could take me out if he wanted to."

Haru said, "*I* said that we shouldn't have to fight, that His Majesty should have sent soldiers to protect us. He just looked at me and said that maybe no one had told His Majesty about it and perhaps they should. He also pointed out that it would only be for a short time in the evening, according to Captain Djedi, and we wouldn't be working on that 'god-cursed tomb' for 'that fool of a King'."

"*Fool?*" Benetamun exclaimed.

"I said I wouldn't stand for anyone talking about His Majesty that way," Haru said. "He withdrew the comment, but he was smiling. Then he turned to Djedi and... And stepped into the background again."

"He was that way with me," said Benetamun. "Oh, so polite, and I found myself signing up. He's very smooth."

"Who is he? He looks familiar. Djedi's the commander, isn't he? But this fellow—"

"Defers to him," Harmose supplied. "In all things."

"Well, then, if we're dealing with Djedi, why did we join?"

Haru looked thoughtful. "I got the impression that Sa-Ramses could probably hurt me rather badly. He has a stare like an auger. But have you noticed that Djedi's different now? More... more resolute. Or maybe more responsible... Impressive, in fact. But still, why isn't Sa-Ramses commanding?"

**   **   **

The question was asked time and again during the week that followed. The townsfolk finally approached Kenamun with the question. His response made the speculation die.

"I looked into him very thoroughly," he said. "And I finished by approaching him, myself, and speaking very frankly with him. I am satisfied with him. He is a good man: I have found no reason to be worried about or afraid of him. He is happy to serve under Djedi. He says, in fact, that Djedi is shaping up to be a fine officer. We're fortunate to have him here. In fact," he said with the hint of a smile, "We could trust him with our lives."

XXXIX

Seti moved quietly into the life of the village after that day, accepted as one of them, Master Sa-Ramses, welcome in their homes, trusted with their children.

That surprised him. He concluded that they were an intuitive group, perhaps. At any rate, for all of him, their intuition was correct. He had always loved children, he the warrior. And now it was as though he had never become King and was still free to drop to his knees to watch a game of bowls or admire an amazingly ugly insect stumbling across the sand.

** ** **

Seti negotiated the switchback path heading down into the town from the northwest. Djedi had taken the southern patrol, but only after a spell of argument.

Vandals would come from the river, Djedi had said. It was closer, and the danger was there.

"The desert is to the west," Seti said. "Think of it, Djedi: I could hide an army in the desert half a day's march from here. This village would never see it, never suspect it until it was too late."

"But the attackers came from the river both times," Djedi objected.

Seti folded his arms and frowned into the distance. "No one saw where they came from," he said. "They were first seen entering the village from the south. If I were leading an attack from the desert, I would go in that way. It would corral the villagers, would require no effort. Climbing a wall, I mean. Although that particular wall is nearly laughable."

"You sound as though you have led such attacks."

"I have," Seti said. "Not against peaceful villagers, but against a walled encampment. There are similarities."

Djedi frowned into space and then lowered his eyes. "I know nothing of these things," he said.

"You are learning," Seti said. "May I say that you are learning very quickly?"

Djedi looked up, a shy smile warming his face. "I am?" he said.

"Yes. You are doing very well. None of us knows everything. We have to learn."

** ** **

[155]

Dusk was dimming the bright rocks of the heights from gold to rose to soft purple. The moon had been growing over the past week. It lay just at the edge of the horizon like a great silver shield, waiting to climb the night sky.

A week had passed since he had spoken to Djedi of attacking encampments. The young man was an apt pupil with a good heart. Seti had been considering the possibility of tapping him for his own army. The thought that he would fret if he left his village occurred to him. Perhaps. But that would not rule out the possibility of changing his mind later.

He had spent the past several days patrolling with Djedi, watching him, and drawing some conclusions in his mind. He was returning that night from a private tour of the village's outskirts, noting the town's vulnerabilities, always looking to the west.

He could almost taste the danger, almost see it approaching. Almost. Not yet, and things could be done under Djedi's leadership to halt the peril.

He began the descent to the town, passing through the town's cemetery, approaching the well. Townsfolk paused to gossip, share news and food, laugh at the children.

He rested the shaft of his pike against his shoulder and passed the nearest tomb. No one had seen him yet. He could observe. He turned straight into the wide, black gaze of a child standing expectantly at the town's gate.

His breath caught in his throat as the child's face brightened, the eyes wide and sparkling. He held out his arms, his face glowing with welcome, came running on unsteady feet -

Seti remembered that child, and the man he had grown into, now locked away inside a black tomb, guarded by a carved stone statue staring wide-eyed into the dark.

In that moment the past broke through into the present, sweeping away all the years, bringing him back to the young man he had been, returning to his home and wife, seeing his first son hurrying toward him, chubby hands outstretched, beaming in greeting.

His heart seemed to stop. Had the years vanished? Was he going around again, repeating the years but with the full knowledge of all that had passed, the chance of righting all the little oversights, catching all the missed moments?

The boy ran past him as though he were a wisp of smoke. A young fellow, returning from his work at the tomb, dropped his tools and went to his knees as Seti had many and many a time, his arms wide open to catch the boy and hold him, laughing.

Seti smiled even as his heart seemed to crack within him. That child was gone. All children like him, who had called Seti 'Father' had vanished, though the men and women they had grown into still walked the earth. The moment of glad recognition, the wrigglingly delighted embrace of a child greeting him, was gone, never to return.

He raised his head, stepped backward, turned, and climbed the circling path, seeking a place where he could be silent and come to terms with this new loss.

He found the place, high on the hill overlooking the town and the tombs. Thebes was just visible as a faint glow to the northeast. He settled wearily, one knee drawn up, his eyes gazing unseeingly as all the questions he had wanted to ask his son came crowding around him:

Why were you smiling as you died? Did you smile at your escape?

That thought brought the breath rattling to a halt in his throat. Escape? From what? From a reality too burdensome to bear?

And then he knew: Kingship. But what choice had he? Nakhtamun was his son, Horus in the nest, as they all said, ready to take Kingship from his, Seti's, hands when the time came. There had been no need for haste or despair. He had planned it so carefully, giving Nakhtamun time to learn gradually, by himself, with good men around him-Nebamun the son of Kings, almost a father to him, unflinching and yet humorous. Nebamun had had his hand over Nakhtamun: why had he wanted to escape?

Didn't you know I would have died for you, gladly?

He repeated the words aloud, feeling their truth. "I would have died for you, gladly, Nakhtamun." The words fell into silence. It was too late.

He wept then, the tears he thought he had left behind with his youth.

It passed, leaving him spent against the still-warm stones of the heights. He closed his stinging eyes and drifted in the silence and faint glow of the night.

Oh, Nakhti, he said in his heart.

Words came to him, he knew not from where. *Can't I smile at a splendid day and a happy future after a time of unsureness?*

He brushed at his eyes with the back of his hand. "You had no future!" he said aloud. "And all I can see now is you with blood on your breast-smiling-smiling-as the arrows come one after another—"

The wind in the passes formed into words. *But you won't let yourself see me otherwise...*

"You have left me no other way."

The sigh of the wind was the only response.

He closed his eyes and let himself drift.

This must stop, he thought. *I am breaking my heart over what is gone. It is time to turn toward what is to come.* He sat forward and gazed down over the town. The streets were slightly outlined in lights.

He closed his eyes and felt the wind cooling his cheeks. *One less bereavement to fear,* he thought.

He heard footsteps presently along the upper path. A weary man, by their cadence. He knew who it was. He relaxed and waited.

Kenamun's head appeared over the rise. He started as he saw Seti, but he collected himself and came forward with a wry smile.

"Master Foreman," Seti said with a half-bow.

"Master Sa-Ramses."

"Why are you about at this hour?"

"I like to sleep in my own bed."

"It must be comfortable indeed to risk the edge of the desert at this time of night."

"What danger would find me?"

Seti only smiled.

Kenamun waited, and finally shrugged. "I have not encountered it, myself," he said.

"No one of this generation has, until recently," Seti returned. "But the danger is there and it will not go away."

Kenamun lowered himself to a rock. "And may I ask why you are here in that case, Master Sa-Ramses?"

"I can give good account of myself," Seti said. He sighed and sat back. "I could, if pressed. But to speak the plain truth, I could not stay where I was. And there was nowhere else to go."

Kenamun frowned at him. "Shadows?"

[158]

"A little boy. Gone, never to return. I had two such. One is dead. Both are lost to me now." His voice wavered.

Kenamun raised his eyes to the swath of stars called 'the crocodile's path'. "You never lose them entirely," he said.

Seti looked over at him. "You survived..."

"You will, as well." Kenamun had not looked away from the stars. "I promise."

XL

Seti was speaking quietly with Kenamun several days later, as the workers were gathering their tools to head to the Tomb. The morning coolness had not faded, and the hills held the lingering glow of sunrise. Djedi approached them, acknowledged Seti's salute with a touch of self-consciousness and then turned to Kenamun.

"My apologies for interrupting," he said, "but I had some ideas for the drill. Did he tell you, Master Kenamun?"

"Drill?"

"Yes." Seti nodded to Djedi. "It was his idea."

Djedi beamed. "I thought it would be a good idea to pretend that we are being attacked. People would have to think about where to go and what to do."

Kenamun's expression grew thoughtful. "Your idea, Djedi? It's a good one."

Djedi ducked his head, caught a look from Seti, and squared his shoulders. "I thought it would take the strangeness away. If-if people could think 'I am supposed to run up the hill to the tombs', instead of thinking 'What will I do?' That is what I thought."

"It's a good idea," Kenamun said again. He raised an eyebrow at Seti. "Will you be organizing or herding?"

"Herding, I think," Seti replied. "At least, that is where Djedi says he will place me."

Kenamun nodded. "With the troop assisting-rather like herding geese, I would imagine, Djedi. Tell me more."

Djedi straightened. "We would set a signal for the beginning of the drill. The men in the troop would be assigned their posts, and we would see how things went. I think we would have to rehearse?" He looked at Seti, who smiled and nodded.

"Several times, I would think," Kenamun said.

Seti coughed, opened his kit and began sorting through the brushes. "I thought so."

Djedi paused. "Yes, and we could also look into some of those areas of weakness we identified."

Seti examined his brush and then transferred his gaze to Djedi.

"Areas of weakness?" Kenamun repeated. "What do you mean?"

"The people could be in one of three areas at any time," Djedi said. He dropped to the ground, arranged himself comfortably, and drew one knee up. "Make that four: we have the tomb that is being constructed at the moment. His Majesty's. There's that encampment near the tomb where some of us spend the nights when we're on our ten-day stretch. And then the town itself."

Seti frowned and set the brush in its slot in the palette. "What is the fourth?" he asked.

"The areas between," Djedi said. "At any time there are people going between one or another of the locations. Women, specifically."

"And you think they're vulnerable simultaneously?" Kenamun asked.

"They could be," Djedi said. He frowned at the smooth earth before them and drew a quick sketch. "It wouldn't be hard to isolate the groups. Here's the tomb-here. The encampment is here, and the village is away from both."

Seti eyed the sketch. "That is right," he said. "An attacker with fifteen men could isolate each location, and those between those spots would be out in the open and at their mercy."

"Exactly! We need to examine each area and see which is the most dangerous. Once we know that, we can take steps to better protect ourselves."

"Sound strategy." Seti looked up to find Djedi eyeing him in a speculative manner that set his teeth on edge. Kenamun had caught the expression and was watching with the hint of a smile.

Djedi effaced the dirt sketch with a swipe of his palm and straightened. "I need to go to the Tomb," he said. "My way will take me past the outpost. I can look over those sites and see what I would recommend for strengthening them or-or making them less easy to surprise."

Seti expression shifted to a frown. "I...see. And I am to go to the women of the village, then?"

Djedi raised limpid eyes. "Why, yes. They all gather at the great well in the morning, laughing and chattering... You won't have to go far in this heat."

The cool breeze had strengthened. Seti turned his face to it and cocked an eyebrow at Djedi. "'This heat'? It is afternoon now."

[161]

"The day will get hotter." Djedi met Seti's straight gaze and added, "It can be oppressive for those not used to it. I took that into account when assigning you this task."

Kenamun coughed.

Seti spared him a look. "Is that so?"

"I don't want to subject you to too much too soon," Djedi said. He shifted under Seti's thoughtful stare.

Seti grounded his pike. "I see," he said again.

Djedi looked at Kenamun, who was rubbing his chin with the hint of a smile. "It will be easy to handle, and you won't tire yourself..." He trailed off as Seti's frown deepened to a scowl.

"Listen, Djedi," Seti said. "You are a commander of men. If you want to give an order, do so at once. Don't try to talk your way around it. If you have an unpleasant or difficult task for a subordinate, tell him so. Don't try to back him into it or explain yourself or feign excessive care for his health. It is transparent and will only make your subordinates laugh at you at best and judge you a shirking coward at worst."

Djedi lowered his eyes. Kenamun's smile widened.

"Well?"

Djedi squared his shoulders. "I will speak with the men at the tomb and the outpost," he said. "You will go to the senior women of the village and speak with them."

Seti bowed. "As you command, Sir." He stood silently as Djedi hesitated and then started to move away. "Djedi," he said.

The man turned.

"I still like you." He smiled as Djedi's wary expression split into a relieved grin. *And may the gods have mercy upon me,* he thought.

Kenamun lifted an eyebrow. "Some might say, 'They are only women'," he mused.

"Such men are fools."

"Possibly. You will meet my sister, Henetre, who is chief among the women of this town."

"You frighten me."

"Why? She appreciates a well-set-up man. You are exactly to her taste."

Seti eyed him. "You terrify me."

"Not at all. Be straightforward with her and she will return the favor."

"I suspect I am far below her weight."

"Do you, now? You may be right at that."

"I see." Seti shouldered his kit and straightened. "If I fall on my pike in embarrassment, will the village provide for my entombment?"

"Most certainly," said Kenamun. "And there is a magnificent one we can use near at hand. I can't imagine that His Majesty would begrudge it..."

XLI

Nefer set her jug beside the others and smiled at Henetre. "What a lovely day, Grandmother!" she said. "Such a wonderful breeze, even after noon!"

Henetre returned the smile. "Enjoy it while you can, Nefer," she said. "The Khamsin is coming..."

The women around them nodded. A cool breeze in the afternoon was an unlooked-for blessing. Best to remember that worse weather would be coming.

"Father Peri thinks it won't be so harsh this year," Nefer said.

Henetre cocked an eye at her. "And do you think he can discover the truth when it isn't under his own nose?"

"I think he can perhaps guess the weather," Nefer said.

"Who can?" asked Nebet, the new wife of the town's chief painter.

"Father Peri," Nefer said.

"He does have some native intelligence," Nebet said. "Surprising for a priest." She chuckled and began to add a description of Father Peri's shortcomings, and then stopped. "Speaking of a man..." She said.

Nefer followed her gaze. A man was approaching from the northwest stepping out of the sun's brilliance. She shaded her eyes and watched as he moved easily down the slight incline from the village. A scribal kit was looped over his shoulder and he carried a dagger at his belt. She recognized him after a moment: the man who had knelt to speak with the children at the well, and had seemed to be grieving.

He stopped beyond the well and stood waiting.

"A man!" Henetre snorted. "Just what we need to foul things up!" She straightened and stared at him as he gazed back at her. She raised her voice slightly. "Well? Why doesn't he come here instead of dawdling there?"

"Maybe he doesn't want to disturb us," Nebet suggested.

"A considerate man!" said the Town Scribe's daughter. "Will wonders never cease?"

"Does such an animal exist?" Henetre asked the sky. She eyed the man, who was still waiting quietly. "Standing like a stock!"

The group of women drew closer together, eyeing him.

Nefer began to smile. "He is the new man who is working with Djedi," she said.

"Sa-Ramses? That's *him*?" Nebet asked, a hand to her heart. "Why haven't I seen him before?"

"Kenamun tells me that he is rather quiet," Henetre said.

"I must say, he doesn't look like I expected him to," Nebet said, eyeing him. "*Very* nice, indeed!"

Heads raised. The man lowered his head.

"He heard you," Merithor said.

Tetisheri, Nefer's niece, tipped a grin. "How good to see a tall, well set up man! How old do you suppose he is?"

"Who cares?" Nebet asked. "That graying hair is fetching! Especially with those dark eyes! I'd love to run my fingers through it!"

The man blinked.

Henetre eyed the man. "What a pity his tunic is so long," she said. "He seems to have nice, long legs..."

The man shook his head.

"A good spread of shoulders, too." Nebet said, eyeing them. "Do you think he has a chest to match them?"

Tetisheri pretended to fan herself. "Ladies! You're making me dizzy!"

"He is a warrior," Nefer said. She smiled at the others' expressions. "I was married to one. There is a look..." She watched him turn away. "Stop it. You're embarrassing him," she said.

"A little embarrassment won't hurt him, if he is like other men," Henetre said. She contemplated his back. "*Definitely* a good pair of shoulders! He isn't a stonemason; must be an archer. He isn't wearing a kilt: such a pity! We can't get a better view of his backside!"

The man spun back on his heel, stared for a moment, then sat down on the low wall, shaking his head, and began to laugh.

"Good morning!" Henetre said. "Did you wish to speak with us?"

"I am not sure now," Sa-Ramses said. He rose and went to the entrance to the well enclosure. "Captain Djedi told me to get some information from you about your actions during the day. We're looking at ways to make this town safer for everyone." He paused and added, "We need to know what you do, where you go from day to day. It will help us to know how we can best protect you.

Henetre looked up at him. "What we do?" she repeated. "No, I suppose it isn't generally known by the men-much they care!"

Sa-Ramses took a step back and sat on the wall, bringing their eyes level.

Henetre's expression eased to a smile. "Thank you. I was getting a crick in my neck." She suppressed the smile. "We will show you around, sir. Nefer will be happy to escort you."

Nefer, who had been watching as he spoke, blinked as she heard her name. She came forward, one of the little girls beside her.

The child saw Sa-Ramses, pulled her hand away and went running to him. Sa-Ramses scooped her up on his lap and was rewarded with an ecstatic embrace.

"She knows you?" Henetre said.

"We're old friends. She has taken to bringing me water when I return from patrol."

"Along with the rest of that crowd," Nefer said. "What do you want to see, Master Sa-Ramses?"

"Djedi's concern is the town's vulnerable areas-the tomb, the servants' housing, the outpost and the village."

The women were all listening now. "The village?" Henetre repeated. "But-there's a wall..."

"The wall is useless for defense," Sa-Ramses said. "A determined group could scale it easily." He smiled at the startled expressions. "Djedi wants to identify any weak spots. My orders are to discover where you go and what you do." He added, "If that is convenient."

Henetre was frowning. "He feels that we—"

"No. He is not expecting an attack."

Nebet's face was suddenly white. "Are *you*?" she asked.

Sa-Ramses spoke gently. "No. They would not be so foolish."

The women looked at each other. "You seem very sure," Henetre said.

"I *am* very sure." Sa-Ramses allowed the words to sink in for a moment. He rose, kissed the child and set her down. "If I have met with your approval in all regards, perhaps that escort can show me where you go." He smiled at Nefer and turned to the rest of the group. "That is, *if* I have met with your approval?"

XLII

The north-east path connects Deir el Medineh to the Valley by way of a high-sided slash through the rocks before it reaches the Valley of the Kings. Nefer and Seti had paused to gaze down along the path before descending to it. They had spent time following the women's movements from well to servant's village, circling the village, visiting the workers' outpost and now moving through the landscape, as one might take an easy stroll.

"We sometimes come this way after visiting the outpost," Nefer said. "We often deliver food to the job site midday, whether it's His Majesty's tomb or another. We come in pairs when we do to help carrying things, though we will take a donkey with us to their work sites, if we brought one along."

She caught the flash of a grim smile. "What?" she said. "If worse comes to worst, we can ride it away from danger."

Seti frowned along the path. "A barefoot man with a sprained ankle can run faster than a donkey. And if I were driving my chariot, I could make circles around a donkey at its top speed." He broke off. "If I had a chariot," he amended.

She lifted her eyebrows. The amendment had been somehow forced.

"Do you usually take the cliff-top paths?" Seti asked.

She considered. "Not always, for all that you will have a beautiful view of the river. Somehow this way seems protected."

Seti frowned at the pathway and toed a rock aside. "Is this ever flooded?"

"It has been known to happen; not often, though. One of the tombs was excavated from the valley floor. It was filled with water and was abandoned. That was in my grandfather's time."

"That explains a few things I had wondered about," Seti said. "The cliff-side tombs..."

"They are more secure," Nefer said. "This route *is* rough, I know. But it's a pleasant alternative to the cliff-top path, especially on warm days, since the high cliffs keep this valley shaded.

Seti gazed back along the path. "You are certainly hidden from the deserts to the west. Do traders come from there, ever?"

[167]

"Once or twice, that I have heard," Nefer said. "They came when I was a little girl, but then I left to marry and was gone for some time. I understand trade has increased under His Majesty's rule."

Seti was frowning up the cliffs to either side. "Which way do you usually travel between the halfway spot and the work sites?"

"Our usual path?" She paused and then nodded. "I will show you on the way back. Sometimes it can be hot, but it's faster. We should be fine today."

He was gazing down along the steep valley; he turned to look back over his shoulder. "The footing is poor here," he said. "Not conducive to speed, certainly. That could be a benefit."

"I have known plenty of boys who have turned their ankles trying to run here," she said.

"I wonder if any donkeys came to grief," he murmured with a lifted eyebrow.

"I cannot say, sir," she replied, but with a smile.

He took the whitewashed board from his kit, spat on his cake of ink, and cocked an eye at her expression. "Don't ever lick anything a scribe has written," he said, working the saliva into the pigment. "Unless he is someone you happen to kiss regularly."

"Thank you," she said. "I won't. What are you writing?"

"Observations. I daresay I will remember them when I speak with Djedi, but in case I forget anything... Lead on if you will."

** ** **

They moved through the valley, Seti walking quietly while Nefer told him of the daily activities of the women of the town. Some of them held religious ranks and performed duties at the temples near the village. Others administered properties. Many of them were literate, as Nefer was. The children generally stayed around the town, under the eye of the older citizens, though they sometimes did run away to the river -as any child would.

"Do they help with the cattle?" Seti asked.

"They do chores, work with the herders, go to the schools taught by the local priests-and play truant when they can get away with it," she said.

"What of the very old?"

"They're cared for by the village," Nefer said.

[168]

Seti looked back over his shoulder toward the outpost. "It seems a good place," he said.

"It can be, sometimes," she said. "Or it can be very limiting. My husband found it so."

He lifted his eyebrows.

"Families live here for generations," she said. "The sons step into the fathers' places. The daughters marry the sons of others... Some of these families have held their positions-Outline Scribes, Sculptors-for two hundred years. There is little change, and as the town grows, we run out of room."

"I understand it was something of a miracle that I was given a house."

Nefer shook her head. "You would have been quartered with someone there and made very welcome. My grandmother, or Grand-Uncle Kenamun would have seen to it."

He looked down with the touch of a smile. "I have been made welcome anyhow," he said. "More than I expected."

"You came at a good time," she said. "Here we are-this path ends and just beyond there the workmen's track into the Valley begins. You can see that it's more passable. I always love coming here-I feel protected by the Great Ones..."

She took two quick steps forward, smiling. "We are in the valley now," she said. "You can see the tombs-there, to either side—"

A crash and clatter behind her. She turned, startled.

Sa-Ramses' writing kit had fallen to the ground, the box breaking open and scattering cakes of pigment through the small stones of the path. He stood ashen-faced, one hand clenched at his breast as his eyes swept upward along the vertical pillars of rock that formed the sides of the valley. He took a faltering step backward.

Nefer heard him say something-a name, perhaps? She hurried back toward him. Had he injured himself while she was moving on ahead? Had his heart failed? Or-more prosaically, she thought-had he perhaps turned his ankle on a rock?

His gaze was frozen, withdrawn, his breath coming raggedly through parted lips.

"Master Sa-Ramses?" she said.

He started at the sound of her voice and turned, dragging in a shaking breath, his eyes shuttered, his hand clenched before him. "Mistress Nefer," he said. His voice shook.

"What—" she stopped and amended herself. "Are you hurt in any way?"

"Stabbed to the heart..." The words were so low, she could not tell whether she had heard them correctly. "I hadn't known—" He collapsed to his knees, his eyes wet, and lowered his head, his shoulders braced. He doubled against the ground after a moment and covered his face.

She bent over him. "Is there any way I can help you?" she asked, her outstretched hand inches from his shoulder. She stopped. He was usually so composed... To overwhelm him with offers of assistance would hurt his pride. She moved away toward some larger rocks and sat down, her hands folded before her.

He was gazing up along the cliff again, tears spilling down his cheeks. As she watched he turned and stared down the channel of the Valley. He looked along the pathway that led from this back spot to the royal necropolis' formal entry from the great mortuary temples. His mouth tightened; he shook his head and slumped where he knelt for the space of a breath, the back of one hand to his eyes.

And then he pushed to his feet and straightened, turning toward her, his expression nearly composed once more. His foot struck the writing box. He looked down at it, knelt and began to gather the brushes, the pigments, his movements slow with exhaustion.

She came forward to help him.

They reassembled the box together in silence. He closed it, set it in the satchel at his shoulder, and sat back on his heels, his eyes lowered. "I am ashamed..."

"There is no reason to be," she said.

"I never meant to-to trouble you."

"You did not. I am glad you aren't hurt."

"No," he said. "Not hurt. Not me. If only it had been me..."

She looked at him.

He dried his eyes with his sleeve and tried to smile. "Old memories," he said. "Some not so old..."

She located a cake of dried red pigment and offered it to him. "A death?"

"My son." The words were barely spoken. "My second child. I never knew until it was too late. Now he's locked away in the dark, in a jumble of grave-goods, and I never even had the chance to tell him all that—" He closed his eyes, opened them, and rose, the back of his hand to his eyes again.

"I was taken unawares just now. I will be fine." His voice shook. "I am sorry I subjected you to this."

Her expression eased. "You needn't apologize," she said. "I have felt grief, myself... I come this way, sometimes. So quiet and beautiful... It's peaceful, though many are buried here. And it is a good place, I can feel it."

She remembered his words: *locked away.* "Tombs contain what we, the living, put in them," she said. "Stored by us. Those who are buried have no need of those things. They have moved beyond this world into the Land of the West." She looked at him. "Do you know the old saying: *So just and fair, where fear is not?"*

Seti's eyes filled again, but his expression was no longer frozen. He swore silently as he struggled to master himself and looked up at her after a moment with almost his usual calm.

The day was beginning to fade. Looking over her shoulder down the line of the valley to the town, she could catch the smell of cooking fires in the distance. Evening would soon be blooming out of the approaching sunset. But it was still light, and he was still suffering.

She turned back to him. "It is growing late," she said. "Are you ready to return to the village, Master Sa-Ramses? Or would you care to walk with me a little longer and enjoy the afternoon? A longer path borders the cliffs. There are some beautiful views of the river and of Thebes beyond it. It is a good way to go and... And collect oneself, as I have discovered."

He looked down at his hands, loosely clasped on his knees. "Collect," he repeated almost silently. "Yes. If we may."

"I will show you my favorite views," she said as he pushed himself to his feet. "It *is* beautiful. And I have found it to be healing."

He nodded and offered his arm. "We will do that," he said.

She set her hand in the bend of his elbow and then smiled up at him. "You will enjoy the path."

A smile warmed his tired face. "Thank you," he said. "With all my heart."

[171]

XLIII

Seti leaned back against the wall of his house and let the lingering warmth sink into his shoulders. The day's storm of emotion had left his eyes stinging and dry; he closed them with a sigh and surrendered to his exhaustion.

Nefer had walked with him through the deepening dusk along the paths overlooking the Nile. Twice when they were within sight of the village, she had told him of another path that was worth exploring. He had gone with her each time. He smiled wryly. Exploring had had nothing to do with it. He had been badly shaken, and she had had the exquisite charity to understand and allow him to regain his composure.

They had finally returned just at sunset, when the streets were dark and the villagers in their homes preparing the evening meal. She had told him to wait by the road, away from the crowds, and went to the well to fill his water skin, then accompanied him to the step of his house. She had left with a smile and a quiet word. He had watched her and then gone into his house.

He drank some of the water; he had not realized that he was thirsty, but now it took all his self-control to avoid draining the skin at once. A pottery jug of wine was on a shelf in the kitchen cellar. He had poured himself a cup and then took a fresh loaf of bread from the pile of seven that had been left by the village baker. The bread and the wine were beside him. He would eat and drink presently. For now it was good to sit in the fading warmth and drift.

Laughing voices in the street below him jolted him awake. Running feet on the steps leading to his terrace... He opened his eyes to see two children watching him with wide smiles.

"Taking a nap?" said the boy-what was his name? The son of one of the stonemasons? His sister was smiling and offering a bowl with a spoon of fired clay.

"Even grownups get tired," Seti said, opening his eyes a little wider and taking the bowl from the boy as his sister approached and looked solemnly up at him.

The question of a nap was abandoned. "Mother wants you to have this for supper," said the boy. "It's her best stewed beans. They're good."

The girl suddenly leaned forward to kiss his cheek and smile at him. The children were gone before he could thank them.

The kindness shook him, a little. He listened to the sound of their footsteps clattering down the steps and their laughter in the street, then raised the bowl.

He could catch the scent of onion and cumin-and maybe some shreds of roast duck? He hadn't thought he would be hungry after the day's turmoil, but it seemed that he was wrong. He lifted the spoon, tasted... And the next moment he was looking into a nearly empty bowl, pleasantly warmed by the meal, the kindness that had provided it, and the smiles of the children.

It wasn't the worst day of his life, he thought. That had happened some time ago. But the raw emotion and the suddenness of the shock had exhausted him. He was content to sit against the warm wall of the house, eat the rest of his supper-provided through the kindness of people who only knew him as a visitor and yet shared what they had, and reflect on all that had happened that day.

He broke the loaf of bread and sopped it in the juice from the beans. He could smell yeast, and the baker had been a little extravagant and coated the loaf with sesame seeds. Lavish feasting, indeed! Had he done that for everyone? How could Seti find out? Or was it perhaps better to simply accept the possibility that he had been treated generously?

The cup of wine was on the floor beside him. He raised it and sipped, letting the wine slide gently down his throat.

He turned his mind to that day, to the moment when, looking up along the steep sides of the canyon, he had realized that he was looking at his son's tomb, reliving his frantic pain at finding the tomb closed and sealed.

He had needed to bring the bow and the ring, to be at his son's side-no matter that he had died long before-and present his gifts and say his farewells.

He had been with many people as they died. He had wept at their passing, he had gone on to fight-but this had been so different, this need to bring his son a gift, to say what he had wanted to say. And the memory of his son's statue sitting wide-eyed in the blackness, as though his son himself was there, locked away, lost....

Those who are buried have no need of those things. They have moved beyond this world into the Land of the West.

He could almost hear Nefer's quiet voice. *So just and fair, where fear is not...* His mind understood: why was his heart so slow to accept? He raised the wine to his lips again and sipped, savoring the taste that somehow blended with the stillness after the day's storm. It was so good to be silent, still, to stop fighting the exhaustion and wait for healing.

"Sa-Ramses? Are you there?"

But perhaps not yet, he thought with a sigh, setting the cup down. "No," he said quietly. "I've gone to walk along the hillside track."

He heard footsteps on the stairs, a tap on the wall.

"Come on ahead, Djedi," he said, and tried to pull himself more upright.

Djedi stepped onto the terrace. He was carrying a rush basket that was giving off wonderful smells. "I knew you were joking. I brought some broiled fish and some beer!" He stopped as he took in the bowl of beans and the bread. "Oh! You've eaten? What did you have? Just that bowl of beans! That isn't much. Have some of this fish!"

Seti eyed the fish and the jug of beer. "That's barely enough to feed you," he said. "Unless you've eaten already. And I am drinking wine just now. I doubt beer will agree with me."

"Pooh!" said Djedi. "There's plenty for both of us! At least take this one!" He dropped one of the largest fish into Seti's nearly empty bowl and sat down. "Though you're right about the beer. I'll drink it." He did so, lifting the jug itself to his lips and taking a hearty swig.

Seti hid a smile and sipped his wine.

"Did you learn much from the women?" Djedi asked. His voice was very casual.

"I certainly found it educational," Seti said.

Djedi raised the jug again. "That's good! What did you learn?"

Seti smiled up at the emerging stars. "I learned that I am still quite handsome, despite my age," he said. "The term they used was 'fetching'. One of them had her hand to her heart. I learned that I would please them better if I wore shorter kilts and went about bare-chested."

"They said *that*? To *you*?"

Seti closed his eyes. "I said it was educational," he yawned. "I also learned that my graying hair is not at all disgusting to women-indeed, one of them wanted to run her fingers through it. *After* she had a chance to admire my chest."

"What!"

Seti yawned again and opened his eyes. "Oh, yes. I am surprised they didn't tell me to strip then and there. They thought it was a pity I wasn't displaying my backside in a way that would leave less to their imaginations. They said this to my back. I turned and they decided against pursuing that subject."

Djedi was staring.

Seti stretched his legs out before himself and tipped the last of the wine in his cup down his throat. "I am obviously not a stonemason," he continued after setting the cup down. "They didn't say how they had come to this conclusion. Not muscle-bound enough? Perhaps because I had my tunic on and they couldn't see my chest? Or my rump?" He eyed Djedi's lap. "*Do* stonemasons have muscular backsides? Or painters? Stand up and let me look."

"I'd have run away!" Djedi said.

"Yes: that is why you and Kenamun sent me in your place." Seti lifted the fish in his fingers and bit into it. He raised his eyebrows and took another bite. "This is good!" he said when he had finished chewing.

Djedi was staring in front of him with the look of a man facing an unimaginable horror. "That sounds terrible!"

"I survived," Seti said through another yawn. "Well. I promised that you would come to them in the morning wearing only your shenti so they can look you over, backside and all." He lifted the bowl and the fish over his head as Djedi spit out his mouthful of beer and began to choke. He set the bowl to the side and thumped Djedi on the back. "I told them you'd bathe thoroughly and oil yourself," he said between blows. "Do you know how to flex your chest muscles?"

"You *didn't*!" Djedi wheezed.

"That *was* what you wanted, wasn't it?" Seti asked. "I gave them my word. You aren't going to force me to back out of it, are you? That will shame me and I will have to resign and leave."

"I might as well go naked!"

"I don't imagine that group would mind," Seti said, pulling off a piece of fish from the backbone and licking his fingers. "They're all experienced wives and mothers. They certainly seem to know what pleases them."

[175]

"I won't go!"

"Coward!"

Djedi jumped to his feet and stared at him, his face reddening. His eyes widened and he crashed back down to his stool. "You were playing me like a fish on a line!" he said.

"I was?"

"Admit it! Damn! I fell for it, too! What an ass I am!"

Seti pulled off another piece of fish. "They'd be more interested in the ass that you have," he said.

"You aren't fooling me!"

"No? Show up in your shenti tomorrow and see what they say."

Djedi shook his head. "Have some more fish."

Seti took it from him with a smile. "Thank you," he said.

"You *were* joking, right?"

"Was I?" Seti pulled off more fish, chewed, and leaned back against the wall, his eyes closed. Things were blurring around him; he opened his eyes again. He'd sleep shortly.

Djedi was eyeing him with a touch of worry. "Are you all right?" he asked. "You're pale. You seem exhausted."

"I am," Seti said. "It will pass. Listen to me: we need weapons for this group."

"But we have mauls and staffs," Djedi had said. "And the stonemasons are strong..."

"Strength is good," Seti said. "And yet I know a man in his late sixties-strong, hale and hearty for all that-who could stand behind a wall and take down every stonemason in this village at thirty paces as they all approached him at a run."

"Sixties!" Djedi exclaimed.

Seti managed a smile. "He is a Master Archer," he said. "The finest I've ever known. What good are mauls and staffs against such a man if you are in the open and he has a quiver of arrows at his back and a good bow in his hands?"

"I...see," Djedi said. "I guess we do need better weapons... Bows?"

"There's no time to teach archery. No one said that the attackers had bowmen with them. I am sure you would have if that were the case. So we need weapons. Spears, pikes, knives..."

"Where will we get them?" Djedi had asked.

Seti lifted his eyebrows. "We will tell Count Intef."

"The *Vizier*?" Djedi gasped.

"I believe that's his name," Seti yawned. "We can tell him that we need them. He should give them from the royal armory. He holds public audience tomorrow. You will ask him then."

Djedi had been prepared to argue, but one look at Seti's white face changed his mind. "We will do it," he said. "You will come with me, won't you? I'll call for you in the morning." He stood, suddenly brisk. "Maybe you'd best get some sleep," he said. "You've been doing all the work-yes, you have! Shame to me for that!"

"No shame to you at all," Seti said, slowly getting to his feet. "You're learning. Quickly. No, I don't need to be escorted anywhere."

But Djedi would not hear of it, and he accompanied Seti inside and waited until he was abed before leaving.

Seti fell asleep to dream of the ocean, foaming and green around him, and the tinge of his son's smile against it.

XLIV

The royal palace complex at Thebes had begun its existence as the home of the Theban Princes who had risen up against the Hyksos centuries before and founded the XVIIIth dynasty. The original modest building had grown during the course of the next two and a half centuries, sprawling across thirty acres along the edge of the fertile land on the west bank of the Nile, south and west of Deir el Medineh. The affairs of Southern Egypt were administered from there, with the Southern Vizier holding his audiences when Pharaoh was not in residence. While all people were allowed to attend the audiences and present their petitions for review, the rooms were crowded with high-ranking nobles, officials and priests.

Djedi moistened his lips and wondered if he should turn and leave. He had arrived early, as Sa-Ramses had directed him, had made his way to the audience hall after asking an impassive guard where it was, and had hesitated inside the door, looking around with enormous eyes. There were so many people there, all dressed impressively, all bathed and anointed. He thought he probably shouldn't be there. He knew nothing of audiences and noblemen.

Soft voices murmured in the rooms, though he heard arrogant tones once or twice and caught the speakers eyeing him and then sneering. Even the guards looked intimidating! He could paint sufficiently, and Sa-Ramses said he was shaping to be a good fighter, but he was as out of place here among great lords and priests as a duck in the desert.

What had Sa-Ramses been thinking? Djedi ran his tongue over his lips again and reflected that he had better stop that action before he ended up with sore lips as red as a prostitute's.

** ** **

They had met that morning. Sa-Ramses had written a letter to give to the Vizier and said briskly that the sooner they got started the sooner they would be back with their haul. He had explained how the audience was conducted, told Djedi what to expect and how to behave. Djedi had listened, nodding where appropriate-he knew nothing of audiences or Theban politics. Sa-Ramses had experience, and he had been content to agree to his plan. It should have been easy: show up at the hall for the Vizier's weekly audience with Sa-Ramses beside him, stand quietly as Sa-Ramses presented his credentials, and answer any questions the Vizier might direct to him after Sa-Ramses had finished talking...

But Sa-Ramses had escorted him to the main entrance of the palace, handed him the sealed letter, and then said, "I must be off now. I've errands to run in Thebes, and they may take all day. We will meet by the docks, just outside the temple of Amenhotep the Magnificent, by the northernmost of the seated colossi. If I am late, wait for me."

"But you're—"

"You will be fine," Sa-Ramses said.

"But—" to his embarrassment Djedi was stuttering.

Sa-Ramses had started to walk away. He had turned, eyed Djedi, and then took two quick steps back, to set a reassuring hand on his shoulder.

"Listen to me, son," he said. "You are as good as any man there, and better than most. You are intelligent, courageous and honest. Don't let anyone make you feel like a fool: you aren't one. If I thought so, I'd go in with you. Do you understand me, son?"

Djedi felt himself blushing. "Y-yes, sir," he said.

"Go, then," Sa-Ramses said. "Do Deir el Medineh proud." And he had turned and walked away.

✶✶   ✶✶   ✶✶

The audience hall was covered with the most marvelous frescoes, floor and ceiling. Looking up, he could see a tapestry of celestial cows and stars; his feet were on a painting of darting fish in a stream. The colors were beautifully laid on, and if he-

A cough at his elbow. "His Excellency will see you now."

The voice, beside him, made him start slightly. He saw one of the officials before him, waiting. The man's gaze was somehow scornful.

Djedi could hear Sa-Ramses' words again: *You're as good as any man there, and better than most.* He squared his shoulders, lifted his chin, took the letter from his belt and followed the man up the center aisle, over the frescoes, to the foot of the dais.

He went to one knee as he was announced, stated his name, and then looked up at the Vizier.

The man was older, stocky with age, but with a broad, intelligent face. Lines beside his mouth and around his eyes showed that he smiled a great deal. "Very well then,

[179]

Commander Djedi of Deir el Medineh," Count Intef said. "What is your petition?"

Djedi offered the letter." We need Your Excellency's assistance," he said.

** ** **

Intef frowned at the young man before him and then at the packet of papyrus. It looked somehow familiar... He opened the message. The characters danced before his eyes. The message itself was brief, without preamble:

> *This letter will serve as your authorization to release fifty spears of excellent quality with sharp bronze blades, the same number of pikes with bronze blades, and that number of long knives with sheaths from the armory at Thebes. You are to detach them immediately and present them to the bearer of this message, whose credentials I have determined to be impeccable. The weapons will most likely require an oxcart with oxen to transport them; if that is the case, one should be provided. And you are to refrain from asking any questions until I come personally to speak with you.*
>
> *You are also to keep yourself well and healthy, old friend, and know that I am, myself, well in my heart and healthy in my body.*

Intef lowered the letter and looked at the man before him. "W-who—" his voice shook. He sat back, and said more clearly, "Who wrote this letter?"

"My second-in-command wrote it this morning," the young man said. He eyed Intef's blank expression and added, "He's an army scribe."

"An army *scribe*?" Intef exclaimed. "But that's—" he stopped and looked at the letter. ...*you are to refrain from asking any questions until I come personally to speak with you*. He closed his eyes, opened them, and saw that the young man, Commander Djedi, was watching him. He schooled his voice to calm humor. "I will have these assembled and brought to you directly," he said. He raised his voice to

[180]

address the throng. "This audience is ended. We will resume tomorrow.

** ** **

Sa-Ramses was waiting at the rendezvous point when Djedi arrived. "How did His Excellency receive you?" he asked, frowning distastefully at the pair of laden donkeys provided by the Vizier.

"He was very kind," Djedi said. "He read the letter and said that he would have the weapons assembled for me. He went with me to inspect them personally. We had wine and date pastries while we waited. I liked him..." He added awkwardly, "I don't know whether you had anything to eat, so I asked if I might bring some for you."

Sa-Ramses lifted his eyebrows as Djedi presented a wooden box filled with date treats. "Then it went well," he said, sorting through the pastries and selecting one. "I told you it would." He bit into the pastry, looked at it with raised eyebrows, popped the rest into his mouth and reached for another. "You just have to remember who and what you are," he said as he chewed.

"Where were you?" Djedi asked.

"I was down at the docks," Sa-Ramses said. "They always need scribes there. I was busy. I learned of some juicy gossip from Bubastis, sent six love notes, penned a letter from a student to his parents trying to reassure them that the young drunk was *not* a drunk, helped to write a letter to be taken north into Mitanni, and completed an accounting of supplies received from a sender. Some items requested and paid for in grain were missing. In exchange for this I was given...let me see... A length of cloth, some nice, ripe perseas, a composite bow that's as good as any I've seen that master archer use, a pouch of bowstrings and two quivers of well-fletched arrows. It was a profitable—"

He stopped in mid-sentence and looked beyond Djedi with a suddenly cold stare.

Djedi had been listening with a grin. He stopped and looked behind him. There was nothing out of the ordinary; throngs of people coming and going... He turned back to find Sa-Ramses smiling at him but with the hint of a glitter in his eyes. "What is it?" he asked.

"You did very well," Sa-Ramses said. "I have one more thing I must do. Would it be too much to ask that you bestow

[181]

these with the rest?" And he offered the bow and arrows and moved purposefully into the crowd.

** ** **

"My instructions were explicit!" Seti lowered his voice when he saw some of the throng looking at him.

Count Intef was gripping him by the shoulders and scanning him with wide, relieved eyes. "You didn't say I couldn't come to you," he said. "I asked no questions-I ask none now! I only wanted to see with my own eyes that you are well and safe after disappearing so suddenly when you were in such a state."

Seti hid a smile as he relented and embraced Intef. "And did you look to see if you were being followed?" he asked.

Intef pushed away. "Do you think I am a fool? Of course I did! I may have become old and stout, but I haven't lost my wits!"

"No, but you have lost your ability to read. I said I wanted a pair of oxen! And you send donkeys? Have you gone blind?"

"You said to send oxen if I thought the requisition warranted them. These two donkeys are sturdy and strong, and they can easily carry the supplies."

"I don't suppose you sent a pair that don't bray!"

"I haven't heard them, but they are robust enough to do that well."

"Don't try me too far, Intef!"

"Don't try to bluff me, Se—That is, sir. You are fighting a smile."

He looked up at Seti. "Are you, " he began, and then he amended himself. "No questions. Please: will you send to me if you need help?" he asked. "If we were to lose you—"

Seti nodded. "I will," he said. "I promise. And I will keep in communication with you." He stood silently as Intef reached for his hand, gripped it, hard, and then released it.

"Keep yourself safe," Intef said.

XLV

Two days had passed since the audience with the Vizier. The men had been given their weapons, and Sa-Ramses had set up a time every morning where the men were taught how to use them. Who would have known that the butt of a spear or a pike was as important a weapon as its blade? Or that the pommel of a dagger could be used in close fighting? The results were very satisfying.

The journey to Thebes had been profitable, but it had also brought some disturbing revelations. He had seen Count Intef, dressed like a commoner, slipping into the crowd. And he had seen the man's reaction to Sa-Ramses' letter, as well as Sa-Ramses' reaction to Intef's appearance. Things were fitting together, but what should he do?

He did not know. He sat down, his back against a rock, and puzzled things through. What should he say? What should he do? The train of thought, followed over several nerve-wracking days, was making him dizzy. He closed his eyes with a sigh. The breeze on the path sifted through his hair. He was so tired. If only...

** ** **

"'If only— What?" The voice was light with suppressed laughter.

Djedi opened his eyes to an upside-down view of Sa-Ramses looking down at him. He tried to struggle to a sitting position, slipped sideways and ended up flat on his back on the path.

Sa-Ramses laughed and unlimbered his bow. "Stay where you are," he said. "You've been going at a run since I came, and there's no need. Things are doing well under your command."

Djedi took a deep breath and rolled to his hands and knees.

Sa-Ramses hid a smile. "Have it your way," he said. "But you've earned a breather." He sat down beside Djedi and set his bow on the ground.

Djedi blinked the sleep from his eyes. "I think we need to talk about the command again."

"Command?" Sa-Ramses repeated. "Of what?"

"The troop!" Djedi said.

Sa-Ramses' expression was odd for a moment, but it eased into amusement. "Have you been out in the sun without a headcloth by any chance?" he asked. "Or are those fools going on about your 'experience' again? You are the troop commander, not me. I am merely your lieutenant."

"They have a point. You do have more experience in fighting than me."

"I have more experience in everything than you," Sa-Ramses said, "Being, as I judge, more than twice your age." He considered. "Well, perhaps not painting. In that I am a complete novice. And I am not likely to learn it."

"I just have a feeling that we are running out of time. There's so much that—that we need to do, and so little time. And your word carries weight. As it did at the audience."

Sa-Ramses lifted his eyebrows. "I wasn't there, Djedi. I was taking dictation down at the docks. Something, incidentally, that I plan to do again tomorrow if you don't object."

"But the town needs a good commander as quickly as possible!"

Sa-Ramses shook his head. "I thought we had put this foolish notion to rest. What brought it back into your head? You remind me of a time one of my horses clamped his tail down on a wasp and went careening of, dragging his harness-mate with him while I cursed and fought to bring him under control. I finally abandoned the chariot, which was wrecked in short order. All the nag had to do was lift his tail."

Djedi stared. "Are you saying that I am behaving like a horse with a bug up its arse?" he demanded.

Sa-Ramses, caught up short, blinked. "Ptah save us! It sounds as though I am! I apologize! I certainly meant no disrespect..." The next moment he was lying back against the ground, convulsed with laughter.

Djedi grinned.

Sa-Ramses sat up after a moment and wiped his eyes. "Oh, my! The picture that conveys... I haven't laughed so hard in..." His voice hesitated. "In a long time," he finished. "It's been so long..." He looked up at Djedi's expression. "No! Don't say anything! You will just set me off again! Please b-believe me- I meant no offense!"

Djedi smiled. "Was he hurt? The horse?"

"*I* wanted to hurt him," Sa-Ramses said. "My staff was laughing too hard to be of any use. Stupid animals!"

"Your staff? Or the horses?"

"Both!"

"Now, if you had a staff–"

Sa-Ramses spoke over him. "This troop was your idea, Djedi. You formed it, you command it–and may I say that you are doing very well? Will *I* command it? No!"

"No?"

"No! The fact that I was in the army doesn't immediately make me a candidate for every military position that comes up." He eyed Djedi's expression. "You're making me proud, lad," he said more gently. "You have become a commander of men. Just continue as you are. I promise, if I think something needs to be set right I won't hesitate to tell you privately."

He smiled at Djedi's expression. "You've made me as proud as though you were my own son." He paused and added, "You'd like each other."

Djedi hesitated.

"What is it?" Sa-Ramses asked.

Djedi looked down for a moment. He raised his eyes again and looked straight at Sa-Ramses. "I have a request to make," he said. "I ask it as a favor."

Sa-Ramses' brows drew together fractionally. "What is it?"

"If I ask you a question, just one time, will you... Will you promise to answer me truthfully?"

The frown deepened for a moment and then eased. "Yes. I will. What do you want to ask?"

Djedi hesitated, all the questions he might ask whirling in his mind: *Who are you? Why have you come here? Why do you bother with us?* He looked up at Sa-Ramses, straightened. "Are you a General?" he asked.

Sa-Ramses frown eased to a sudden smile. Yes. I am. But not at this moment. For now I am simply making myself useful serving under a fine young man that I would be proud to call friend and even son. Does that satisfy you, Djedi?"

Djedi felt an answering smile growing. "Yes," he said. "Thank you. I will ask no more questions.

[185]

XLVI

Yet another festival, Seti thought. *A small one, this time.* He wondered if the non-festival days might not be fewer than the celebrations. In this case, one or another of the Kings was being honored. They honored dead Kings, which saved him the odd experience of having to participate in his own festival. *Something to be grateful for,* he thought.

Djedi rose and raised his hands for silence. They had agreed that he would prepare the town for their first drill, but the evening breeze, whistling past Seti, who was seated on the wall, blurred his voice. Seti set his cup on the ground and leaned forward to listen.

...no more taken by surprise... ...Meet them on our own terms... Proud of you all...

"Proud." Seti said the word under his breath. Djedi was a son to make any mother and father proud. A son...

His eyes stung and the feast was oddly blurred. He remembered Nakhtamun beside him as they watched the armies of Muwatallish of Hatti. He remembered him limbering his bow with a smile.

In that moment Seti had realized that he could not control his son's fate. It was then that he realized that Nakhtamun was a man.

He pushed to his feet, holding his cup.

Djedi was answering questions, his eyes bright. The focus of everyone's eyes, most of them approving. He was gesturing, explaining with no reference to Seti.

As it should be, Seti thought.

But he had forgotten that taut, concentrated gaze...

Small farewells, he thought. *Unexpected.*

He slipped from the wall and went to the shadowed side to gaze out over the valley. After a moment he found himself fighting tears. *I am not sad,* he thought, blotting his eyes with the hem of his sash. *Why this?*

"Master Sa-Ramses?"

Seti swore and dabbed at his eyes again.

Footsteps, a pause as a throat was cleared, and then the steps approached.

Seti linked his arms about his knees and sat back.

Kenamun approached from the edge of the wall. He was holding two filled cups in his hands.

"Sa-Ramses?"

[186]

"Here," Seti said.

Kenamun came around the wall and offered a cup. He sat and took one back. "It's cooled," he said.

Seti nodded.

"How are you?"

Seti smiled and sipped his beer. He looked up to see Kenamun watching him. "I am well, Master Foreman," he said. "Sit down. It is a beautiful evening."

Kenamun sat, took his cup back from Seti, and sipped. "You can see the river from here," he said. Always in sight, shining in the sun, shimmering in the moonlight."

"Something to hold to in changing times," Seti said.

Kenamun nodded and balanced his cup between his fingertips. "Farewells crop up," he said. "Don't they? No warning."

Seti cleared his throat. "No," he sighed. "No warning. He's a fine lad, Djedi. Reminds me of one I lost."

XLVII

Djedi had announced the first drill for the next day. Everyone at his place, the women and children going on as before, the men in the troop ready at a moment's notice to go to their stations and perform their tasks.

Seti had drawn Khatef, the junior of the Outline Scribes, as a companion. To Seti, that day the man had the quivering intensity of a rat.

The leader should be anyone other than Djedi," Khatef said. "He is not fit to command."

"Let me remind you, Master Khatef, that you are under Djedi's command at this moment."

"He should be removed and another put in his place."

Seti frowned. "Are you saying, sir, that you wish to forcibly remove him?"

"Not forcibly remove him; but with his history of wild actions the town fathers should tell him to resign before he can do any real harm."

Seti's frown deepened. He looked back along the path and then turned to the man.

"Be honest, Master Sa-Ramses," said Khatef. "You have experience. It is obvious that you are a fighter. You should be commanding this group."

Seti frowned. "While I am flattered by your confidence, he said, "let me remind you that you had nothing before Djedi offered to form this group. Djedi persuaded you to volunteer. If he hadn't, you would all be helpless if your nightmare came pouring along the streets. Commander Djedi recognized the danger and did something about it."

Khatef's expression shifted. "He is too young. And he is disrespectful to his betters."

Seti's smile had vanished. "No one is born old. He is a good way to being the commander you need."

"I tell you he was wild as a boy. No one could control him after his parents died. Master Kenamun had to take him in hand."

Seti folded his arms and leaned a shoulder against the wall. "He isn't a boy now."

Khatef shook his head. "He's a troublemaker," he said. "You should command, not him."

"Whether or not I might be able to command, the commander is Djedi. And he is commanding you at this moment. Do you realize that what you're suggesting is mutiny?"

Shouts from down the street. Seti frowned, listening.

"Once a troublemaker, always a troublemaker," Khatef repeated. "We need someone with more steadiness."

Seti eyed him with increasing distaste. "You sanctimonious sack of wind!" he said. "You aren't fit to serve beneath him! And be glad you're serving under him and not me: if I were your commander in fact I would have you up for mutiny at this moment!"

Khatef drew himself up. "Now see here!"

"Get to your post. We're having a drill."

Khatef's jaw dropped. "You dare speak to *me* like that!"

"I do." Seti brought two fingers to his mouth.

"I have never been so insulted in my life!"

Seti lifted his eyebrow. "You have passed your life among amazingly tolerant people!"

"You *dare*-!"

Three piercing whistles split the air a moment later. "That was the signal for the drill," Seti said, lowering his hand. "Get to your post."

Khatef stared. "Now wait!"

Three more whistles.

"You're away from your post," said Seti.

"You disgraceful, mannerless *beggar*!" Khatef choked.

The commotion around them dimmed for a moment. Eyes widened. Henetre folded her arms.

Did he really say that?

Who's he talking to?

Sa-Ramses?

He's an ass!

"You damned, officious *rat!*" Seti said through his teeth. He raised his fingers once again and sounded the signal. "Your charges are being butchered," he said. "You'd better go do something about it and stop beating your gums if—" He stopped as Djedi, who had been staring, moved forward and set a hand on his arm.

"If you have something to say, Khatef," he said, "Then you'd better say it to me!"

Khatef stared at Djedi, his teeth set.

"No?" Djedi said. "Then get to your post!"

**   **   **

"I've never seen Khatef so furious," Neferhotep said later that afternoon. "He could barely speak."

"Well, that's a blessing," Kenamun said. He was eyeing the points of his chisels. He set them down and wiped his hands. "I was getting a little tired of his litany of perfections."

"Be serious!"

"I am serious. Tell Khatef not to be such a fool."

Neferhotep shook his head. "I don't know. He's a bad one to cross... And Outline Scribes are hard to find."

Kenamun's expression might have been a grin if his lips had not been closed. "I don't recall Benetamun singing his praises," he said, running a thumb along the edge of his adz. "And if he's as difficult as you say, I'd say let him go. We can apply to Opet for a promising candidate."

"Be serious!" Neferhotep repeated.

"I am," Kenamun said. "Khatef has his *shenti* in a twist because Sa-Ramses gave him a piece of his mind, if I am sifting through the jumble of complaints accurately."

"He's a bad one to cross."

Kenamun set the adz down. "I've heard that before, Nephew, and not just this evening. I haven't seen anyone suffering for telling him to fling himself into the Nile. I'd be less likely to cross Sa-Ramses. I've been hearing a lot from various people here who heard the whole thing. Your mother cornered me and said she couldn't believe Khatef had the balls to say what he did, as though the world waits on his every word." His smile widened a little. "She called Khatef a little shit and said that Sa-Ramses was too much of a gentleman to answer him as he could have."

Neferhotep stared. "'Balls!'" he repeated. "I don't believe my *mother* would use that word!"

Kenamun folded his hands across his stomach and tipped a smile. "Would you care to lay a small wager?"

"No!"

"Bring her here."

Neferhotep stared. "Amun help us! She did!"

"She *was* rather annoyed," Kenamun said.

"She's right about Khatef, certainly." Neferhotep frowned before him. "But the man says he has His Majesty's ear."

Kenamun did grin. "Did he, now?" he said. "His Majesty? Last I heard it was Count Intef, with the High Priest of Amun as a backup. He wasn't clear why His Holiness should be one of his admirers. I should ask him. His Holiness, I mean. I suspect I would be the recipient of a blank stare." He dismissed that line of speculation with a chuckle. "But why doesn't he complain to Pharaoh, if they're such fast friends?"

Neferhotep stared at him. "You're smiling!"

"That's right." said Kenamun.

Neferhotep frowned as Kenamun's smile widened.

"I don't understand."

Kenamun considered. "Let me put it delicately," he said. "If I had to choose between putting Khatef in a temper and angering Sa-Ramses, I'd choose to annoy Khatef."

"You can't be serious!"

"You keep saying that, Neferhotep, and I keep telling you that I am. For the last time, I am as serious as death."

"He's a man of wealth! He's a fine craftsman!"

"That's open to debate," Kenamun said. "Benetamun had a few things to say."

"Have you seen what Sa-Ramses wears?" Neferhotep demanded. "Not rags, certainly, but everything is worn."

"Khatef again. Sa-Ramses' clothing is spotless. He came here with his belongings in a satchel, but he's always presentable. He hasn't spent any time here dawdling and saving his clothes. Have you seen his weapons? They glitter." He added, "And have you had a chance to see what he wears at his neck?"

"That pendant? It's usually under his tunic. I saw it once."

"It is a *gold* pendant, Neferhotep. Shaped like a lion's head. It is called 'the gold of honor'. It is awarded to a warrior after a battle. For heroism. And it is generally given by the King, personally. This one has some age to it. And, speaking as someone who deals with sharp tools, you might want to take a look at Sa-Ramses' weapons. Not just their condition, but their quality. Something to think about."

"I don't understand."

"You don't have to. Take my word for it: Khatef is a nobody."

"Maybe you're right," Neferhotep sighed. "I liked Sa-Ramses the moment I met him, and that's the truth. But Khatef's valuable, too. At any rate, Khatef's saying he will get Sa-Ramses dismissed."

Kenamun lay back, laced his hands behind his head, and indulged in a luxuriant fit of laughter.

"It isn't funny!" Neferhotep exclaimed.

"Oh, it is!" Kenamun said. He returned Neferhotep's stare. "I will tell you some time," he said. "For the rest, it is under my control. You will see."

XLVIII

Seti closed the door behind him and set his spear down. The drill had gone fairly well. Better, in fact, than he had expected, though he had had to raise his voice once or twice to get the townsfolk moving. Khatef, for one. Djedi had had some understandable shyness with the people of his own town. *He will get over it quickly*, Seti thought. It was hard to remember that the lad was barely twenty. Only two years older than Ramesses.

He thought of Ramesses in the late afternoon. He would be with his children by the pond at his estate, perhaps. Or, more likely, with Bint Iset and Nebamun at the Temple of Ptah. Iset was fifteen years older than Ramesses; more like a mother than a sister.

He smiled at the thought and then paused to reflect that he was not so shaken now. When had that happened?

A fist upon his door interrupted his thoughts. He went to the door and opened it.

Henetre and two of the other ladies were ranged before him. The others had their arms full of clothing.

"Aha!" said Henetre, pushing past him into the room. "I *thought* you'd be in, Master Sa-Ramses!" She looked around. "You haven't eaten yet? Excellent! You will dine with my family! Kenamun will be there and Father Piay from the temple! *And* the other Masters from the village."

Seti had turned to face her. "I have a supper set out for me," he began.

"Pooh! Probably cold fruit and some tough squab!" Henetre said with more accuracy than she could have guessed. "*I* know how those servitors are! You will dine with us. Change your clothing and come to my house. Others will be there, as well..."

She frowned at the door. "...which reminds me. Nebet! Tetisheri!"

He stood aside as the others came in.

Henetre put her hands on her hips and looked him up and down. "You're taller than most here, but unless you're trying to wear an old man's long tunic-which you do rather too often for your age-that doesn't matter." She handed four garments to Seti. "We have some clothing for you. The townsfolk offered their best for you, you know. Kaya sent several good tunics, but he's such a squirt I told him you'd split them at the seams.

[193]

As it is, they're all a little short but you've got a good pair of legs. The shoulders, now, might be a problem, but these sleeves are generously cut. Put them on!"

He looked at them and then at her. "Excuse me," he said.

"We're all married women!" Henetre said. "It isn't as though we haven't seen our husbands dressing."

"But, ladies, you are not married to *me*," he said, and left the room, reflecting that while it was a retreat rather than a rout, it wasn't in as good order as he would like.

He took the top tunic-a plain one bordered with blue stripes-and pulled it over his head. A sash was in the pile; he cinched it about his waist and hoped this determined group was not going to inquire after the state of his shentis.

They were waiting, seated on his stools, as he came back.

"Well, then!" Henetre said. "That looks fine! Turn around!"

He obeyed, suppressing a smile until he saw Tetisheri's round eyes begin to dance. He covered his grin with a cough.

"That is perfect!" Nebet said. "You *will* take them won't you Master Sa-Ramses?"

"This is too generous," Seti said. "I do have clothing."

Henetre snorted and fixed him with her bright eyes. "Somewhere up north with the rest of your family, no doubt! Aha! I am right! Take these." She eyed him. "Does your *wife* know you're here kitted out like a beggar?"

He lowered his eyes. "My wife died last year," he said.

Henetre's expression softened. "I see. I am sorry, but it spares us the shame of her knowing how badly you were treated this afternoon."

"I am sorry too," Nebet said.

Henetre cleared her throat and added "Keep them. These are yours as long as you need them."

✼✼ ✼✼ ✼✼

He descended the steps to the street the next morning, shouldered his kit, and frowned down the street. The townsfolk were moving along the main street, the workmen moving out toward the circling path, children walking beside their mothers, the older ones carrying jars for water, the younger ones holding toys.

Some of the older children, out of tot-hood, were shuffling off toward the small temple that lay south and west of the town. Father Peri held class two mornings a week, teaching the basic skills of reading and writing. He sometimes asked

[194]

the town scribe to help teach, but since Wahankh had been called away from Deir el Medineh indefinitely, he had been handling the classes by himself. He had shyly approached Seti the day before, asking if he might be willing to teach the children two days that week.

Seti had folded his arms and considered.

Father Peri had mistaken his thoughtful frown. "I meant no offense, Master Sa-Ramses," he had said. "I know you are a busy man, with...with the concerns that have everyone worried. But I have seen your hand-it is even and well-formed. Even if the children could see how you write... But I will understand, certainly."

Seti, who had been Scribe of the Armies for a time, had smiled suddenly. "Teach the children?" he had said. "I would enjoy that."

Since matters had settled slightly, he thought that he could make an appearance that morning. He enjoyed teaching, and that day-

Khatef interrupted his thoughts by falling in beside him.

"Good morning, Master Sa-Ramses," he said.

Seti's mouth tightened. "Good morning, Master Khatef," he returned. They were approaching the well.

Khatef took a deep breath, stepped before Seti and stopped. The townsfolk around him stared.

Seti propped his foot on a nearby step and folded his arms.

"I wish to speak with you, Master Sa-Ramses," Khatef began.

"You are speaking."

"Yes... What I wish to say is this: I was wrong to speak as I did last night, both about you and about Commander Djedi."

Djedi, approaching from the street, stopped.

"I spoke without thought, and I spoke of things I...I thought years before, which might not be true now. In fact, as you said, they are not. I also overstated my own worth. And I insulted you, Master Sa-Ramses."

Seti straightened and frowned at the man.

Khatef lowered his head and stared at his hands. "You are a visitor, Master Sa-Ramses, and you have taken our welfare into your hands. You have kindly assisted Djedi in his efforts to establish a guard for this town, and even helped to train us. That alone called for my respect. You are a guest and my words were inexcusable. To call you...a beggar shows that I

am a mannerless fool at best. I am ashamed. I beg that you-
and Commander Djedi-forgive me."

Djedi beamed. "Of course we do!"

Seti smiled. "We need not think of any of this, or speak of
it again, Master Khatef."

XLIX

As the troop gathered by Djedi became more confident of their abilities, Djedi and Seti decided it was time to establish a rotation of tasks. Over the course of a sevenday they had taken turns patrolling the heights, escorting the women to their tasks, and policing the valley paths that lead to the town. On one of the first mornings, Djedi decided they needed a guard in the tomb; some of the others argued they were best suited. It would be a soft assignment where they could relax and chat with their friends. But Djedi, while agreeing with them, assigned the task to Seti.

With the troop looking on, Seti nodded, snapped his fist to his shoulder, and started toward the tomb. He paused at the entrance, drew a deep breath, and walked in, returning the greetings called to him as he went.

The light flickered on stark white walls, catching shadows on the hewn surface of the rock. Quiet voices, the tap of copper against stone... Seti looked up at the ceiling, his mind supplying the shape of the cliffs above him. And for a moment he could feel the weight of stone pressing down upon him, ton upon ton, ready to collapse and crush the fragile shell that was his body.

He drew an unsteady breath and lowered his eyes to a carving of himself accepting a necklace from Hathor. He could see the elegant shapes carved into the stone, the wide eyes, details of dress ... when had he worn a wig like that? All white, all blank... *But I am dead here...* he thought in confusion.

He forced himself to take a deep breath and relax his shoulders.

** ** **

Kenamun made his brisk way past the carvings at the tomb's opening. The hallways lined with gods and goddesses, many of them crisply cut by his own chisels. They were well done, and the colors being laid on made them stand out satisfactorily against the smooth walls. He admitted to himself that he preferred the carvings without the paint. It was easier to see the spare elegance of the forms, the play of shadows across the surface. But in the eternities to come it would not matter, he thought, so long as what he did was done well.

He slid the strap of his satchel from his shoulder and set it on the ground. His tools were getting heavier, he thought with a humorous grimace. Odd how that happens...

Heads raised at the quiet clink of noise.

"Good morning, Master Kenamun!"

Kenamun looked up. One of his younger apprentices, a stonemason's son who had a yen to be a sculptor. Kenamun nodded to him. The boy was shaping up well.

"Is all in place today?" he asked.

The boy ducked his head. "It is going well, Master Kenamun. I-I am carving the King's Name, as you told me to. I *think* it looks well."

"I'll be back to look it over once I make my circuit," Kenamun said. He straightened, frowned down into the tomb. The smaller pillared room had been swept clear of stone chips. The apprentices grumbled about taking the unending baskets outside, but Kenamun had simply lifted an eyebrow. Now the room was clear and ready to be inspected.

He stepped under the portal and stopped; his breath caught in his throat as he gazed at his carving of the King accepting a necklace from Hathor. The carving was as it should be, still pristine and white. The King stood beneath the two and gazed up at them, a quirk to his brows...

Kenamun closed his eyes for a moment and shook his head. *Two Kings?*

He opened his eyes again. And then he understood. He hurried over to Seti and seized him by the arm. "Have you run *mad?*" he demanded through his teeth.

Seti had been frowning at the carvings. He transferred the frown to Kenamun.

"What are you *doing?*" Kenamun said again.

"I am gazing at carvings" Seti said. His voice held the hint of a quiver.

"Have you run *mad?*"

"You are repeating yourself." Seti's voice had dropped.

"Don't quibble! *Here* of all places! What are you thinking?"

Seti folded his arms. "My commanding officer ordered me here. He thought we might wish to place a guard inside the tomb."

"Couldn't you refuse?"

"And be cited for insubordination? No, I cannot."

Kenamun looked at him.

"Don't stare at me. Rules must be obeyed. I of all people should not promote disobedience."

Kenamun frowned thoughtfully and finally nodded. "I outrank Djedi," he said. "You will leave now. I will speak with Djedi."

Seti's stance was subtly eased. "You could tell him that close places make me dizzy."

Kenamun looked more closely. "You're pale," he said. Come outside with me." He raised his voice. "It was good of you to come here, Master Sa-Ramses. I have a message for Commander Djedi which I ask that you carry, yourself."

L

After the disastrous day in the tomb, Seti was given tasks that kept him on the reaches or in the town. He took several turns walking with the women of the town, usually carrying either his bow or his spear. This had raised some eyebrows, but he had merely said that he had a feeling and he wanted to make certain that any necessary warning was given immediately.

This day he was shepherding a group of about ten women. They were joined as they were leaving by the wife of one of the workers. She was bored sitting at home and waiting for her baby and thought the stroll would do her good.

Seti, eyeing her, caught Henetre's eye and shook his head. "She's too far along," he said when Henetre was beside him. "She'll slow us."

"She might go into labor, come to that," Henetre agreed. "The baby hasn't dropped, but it won't be long." She went to the girl, Sheritra, spoke to her with a smile, and then watched, resigned, as Sheritra burst into tears.

Seti closed his eyes and drew a breath as the sobbing continued.

"I can't reason with her," Henetre said, beside him. "She'll obey if I give an order…"

"…but it would be unkind," Seti finished. He set his bow on the ground and folded his hands on the top. "We will turn around halfway," he said at last. "We are bringing nothing that is urgently needed, and this can be an exercise. It may do her good, and it will be good practice."

"The rest of us can go on when she turns back," Henetre suggested.

Seti looked down at her. "I… am not certain that is a good idea," he said slowly.

"A feeling?"

"They come upon me, sometimes. We are safe for now. We'd best get moving." He straightened, set the bow over his shoulder, and motioned to the group. "Put Sheritra in the center," he said, and was silent as they set off.

The day was turning pleasantly cool, and the ladies were enjoying the walk, which Seti kept at a slower pace. He began to frown as they approached the halfway mark. He stiffened and turned toward the desert as they neared the path that split toward the temporary housing.

[200]

"What is it?" Tetisheri asked.

Seti raised his hand. His expression changed to a scowl, and he drew his forefinger sharply across his throat when the murmur continued.

"What was that?" Nebet gasped.

"Silence," Nefer said.

Seti cocked his head and listened for a moment. "I hear something," he said almost soundlessly. "I am going to take a look. Sit down and keep silent at all cost."

He moved quickly up the slope on his hands and knees, keeping low to the ground. He paused near the edge. They saw him stiffen and go backwards. Once on the path he went briskly to Henetre. "Gather everyone," he said. "Get together in a tight group. Sheritra should be in the center again."

"But why?"

His eyes narrowed slightly. "Because I judge it best." He looked over his shoulder. "You will be returning to Deir el Medineh as quickly as you can."

"But there's no one—" Henetre began. She stopped as he limbered his bow and took out an arrow.

"Do as you're told," Seti said. "Now. I want you to head directly to the village." He broke off to frown westward. He shook his head and then turned to them, "Right. You have your instructions. Get going."

"What!"

He raised his hand again. "Quiet!" He untied his sash and pulled his shirt over his head. "Someone give me her kerchief," he said as he shortened his kilt and re-tied the sash.

Nebet had been watching him with her eyebrows raised. She began to grin. "Nice..." she said.

He frowned at her. "This is not the time for foolishness," he said quietly.

Merithor offered her kerchief and watched as he knotted it loosely about his neck, turned the knot behind him, and pushed it up over his head, bringing the crease behind his ears and settling the folds.

"What are you doing?" Henetre asked.

"I am making myself look like a soldier," Seti replied. "Where's that bow-thank you! Give me the quiver, too."

He set the quiver between his shoulder blades, settled the strap diagonally across his chest, ignoring the wide stares and the one woman who was pretending to fan herself. "We have

[201]

some would-be visitors," he said. "I am going to take a look. I will warn them off. The rest of you start back to the village."

"But we can't leave you here if there's danger!" Henetre said.

Seti straightened and met Henetre's gaze squarely. "You are a leader," he said. "I do not say there is danger here and now-or not great danger-but answer me honestly: if one action could lead to twenty deaths and the other to only one-which would you take?"

One woman raised her hand to her mouth.

Henetre's smile faded. She met his gaze and nodded.

Seti lifted his bow. "Gather them into a group. Put Sheritra in the middle with the taller women to the outside. Walk in a tight formation and support her. I don't want them to see her."

Henetre frowned and then nodded.

"I see you understand me," he said. "Don't let her be frightened. There is probably no need, and these nightmare thoughts will do her no good so close to her time. Now go. I will rejoin you when I can."

"Someone should stay with you," Henetre said.

He frowned for a moment. "Perhaps," he said. "I don't think they will come to me, and I don't plan to go to them. Pick someone who can run, in case I have to send word to you."

She nodded. "Tetisheri will stay."

"Fine. Now listen: I will be calling out, shouting things, maybe. That has nothing to do with you. Keep moving. If you hear other voices shouting besides mine, step up the pace. Do you understand me?"

Henetre smiled. "Yes, sir," she said.

He turned and began to climb the steep slope to the edge of the cliff. He paused just below the ridge to gather his weapons, take a deep breath, and cautiously raise his head.

A group of eight men stood some yards away. They appeared to be scouts rather than soldiers... Armed? He watched for some time. Knives, most likely. He saw spears, as well, clumsy-shafted with points lashed on with twists of sinew. Crude but deadly enough. No archers in sight, either, but they were approaching the track. He pushed to his feet and gained the level ground.

"Who goes there?" he demanded.

The group stopped and turned toward him, hands on weapons. Their hair was plaited with feathers, their leather cloaks covering little else. Libyans, as he had expected. He drew an arrow from the quiver and nocked it.

One of the men stepped forward. "Who are you?"

Seti raised the bow. "I asked you first."

The man was staring narrowly at him. The stare lowered to the gold pendant; he frowned. "We are herdsmen," he said at last.

"Where are your herds, then?" Seti had spoken in their language. It startled them. When they did not reply he said, "Lost? All of them? Unfortunate for you!"

The men in the group traded looks.

Seti showed his teeth in a cold smile. "Shall I ask my commanding officer to send the garrison to help you look for them?"

One man lifted his spear. Another man tried to peer beyond his shoulder.

"You have a garrison here?"

Seti's smile deepened.

More quiet conversation. "You are lying," the leader said.

Seti drew the bow. "Then see *this* truth!" he said through his teeth and let fly.

The leader jumped back with a curse.

Seti nocked another arrow. "Come closer!"

They backed away.

Seti cocked his head, as if listening. "I have run into intruders!" he shouted over his shoulder. "Tell them I need them here now." He turned back to the group. "Get back to your herds," he said, loosing the arrow at their feet and smiling as they retreated. He nocked another one. "If we see you here again, the garrison will look for your cattle!"

**   **   **

"We can wait a moment or two," Nefer said, smiling at Sheritra. "Catch your breath. We have moved swiftly." She saw Nebet's expression brighten and looked over her shoulder.

Seti was approaching at a run, Tetisheri beside him. "Get moving!" he said with a nod to the girl, who continued on. "We have to get back to the village." The headcloth was bunched in his hand. He folded it with a flick of his fingers and gave it back to the owner. "I've sent her on to alert the town," he said. "She is a brave little one."

Henetre nodded. "She's a good runner."

"Excellent." Seti twitched his shirt back from Merithor and pulled it over his head, lifting an eyebrow as Nebet said 'Pity!'

under her breath. He looked around, saw Sheritra, and hurried to her side. "How are you?" he asked with a nod to Nefer.

Her eyes were wide and shadowed in her pinched face. "Will they kill me and the baby?"

He dropped to one knee and took her hand between his. "Why would anyone want to do that?"

"B-but they hurt the others!"

"These aren't the same people," he said. "And they would have to hurt me first if they were. What talk is this? We are going home, and you will go to your own bed with a nice, warm posset to help you sleep, and your husband will rub your feet for you."

Her lip quivered, but she nodded. "I am sorry I'm slowing things down."

"You won't be for long," he said. "I will get you home. Put your arms around my neck."

She obeyed, stiffening as he gathered her. "But—"

"I am going to carry you," he said. "You weigh nothing, even with the baby, and we can go quickly."

Her eyes filled. "This is too much trouble," she said.

He smiled into her eyes. "Hah! If I don't do this my wife will come from the Land of the Blest and give me a scolding!" He settled her and then rose to his feet with a grunt. "Lie back and close your eyes. You will be home before you know it."

Sheritra looked up at him, then at the other women. At a nod from Henetre she subsided against his shoulder and closed her eyes.

Nebet stood before him, her head to one side. "When can *I* take a turn?" she asked.

Seti directed a look at her. "When one of those marauders hurts you and you are injured and unable to walk! Get moving!"

[204]

LI

Tetisheri had run as fast as the wind; Seti's group met Djedi and a contingent of the townsmen pelting along the track.

"Were you attacked?" Djedi demanded.

Seti settled Sheritra against his shoulder. "We encountered intruders approaching the main path. I sent them on their way, but I judged it best to hurry back here." He saw Tetisheri over Djedi's shoulder. "Well done!" he said. He looked down at Sheritra. "Wake up, child."

She opened dazed eyes and looked up at him. "Are we home?"

"Yes, Little Mother. Safe and well, and you needed the sleep." He nodded to a man who had come running up with Djedi. ...And here is your husband, waiting for you.""

Her arms were still around his neck. She tightened her hold for a moment. "Thank you," she said. "I was so frightened."

"There's no need, now," he said.

He set her carefully on the ground, holding her until her husband had his arms around her before pushing to his feet. He staggered for a moment. "She had a bad fright," he said.

Henetre gripped his arm and steadied him. "You need to call Mother Seshet to her," she said. "The baby has dropped."

Sheritra looked away from her husband to hold her hands out to him. "How can I thank you, Master Sa-Ramses?"

He took her hands between his. "Bring us a healthy, lively baby as beautiful as you," he said with a smile to her husband before turning back down the street.

Nefer was waiting for him, her eyes shadowed. She bowed as he approached her and then straightened. "Shall I call Seshet?" she asked. "She's carrying very low now."

"Henetre already told her husband to," he replied.

Nefer nodded. "I think another two days will see a new baby."

"Maybe not that long," he said. He frowned up the street. "She should do well..."

"You are returning to your home, aren't you?" she said.

"No. I will be patrolling the hilltop path this evening," he said.

"You stood off a group of intruders and then carried a heavy load for long time," she said. "No, sir, do not tell me that Sheritra weighed nothing. She's a healthy girl and carrying a full-term baby."

"She didn't feel that heavy."

"That was the excitement of the moment," she said. "It is gone now. There are others in the troop who can patrol."

"They lack my experience," he said. "They will delay me. For this one time I will go alone."

"Then I will accompany you," she said.

He frowned.

"It is daylight still," she said. "And I can run at need."

"I doubt there will be any need this afternoon," he said.

"I am coming with you nevertheless," she said. She lifted her chin at his expression. "No, Master Sa-Ramses. Absent an order from one of the foremen-who are at the tomb, or were the last I heard-or Henetre, who will most certainly *not* give such an order," she smiled at his expression, "I will accompany you."

He frowned and then nodded. "Stymied," he said. "Well done."

"You aren't angry, are you?"

He laughed and shook his head. "Not I," he said. "Come with me and keep your eyes open."

They walked along the track circling the back of the town, she keeping her eyes on the surrounding landscape, he frowning at the gaps in the hills.

"They were scouts, weren't they?" she said.

He paused and lifted his eyebrows at her.

"My husband was a soldier," she said. "A group intent on fighting would not be diverted by one man, no matter how persuasively he might speak, or how impressively he might bluff."

"Bluff!"

"I could hear it in your voice," she said. "Others might not have."

"You surprise me."

"I observe things," she said. "I can...sometimes feel emotion."

"Emotion..." He stopped and faced her. "I have wanted to apologize to you," he said.

"Apologize, sir?"

"For...for that day in the Valley of tombs. I was taken unaware-a memory, returning suddenly... I never meant to

[206]

embarrass or trouble you." He paused for a moment, his color slightly heightened. "Your tolerance was beyond kind."

Her heart turned over within her. "There is nothing to regret or apologize for that, sir," she said. "We have all known such grief... Or, perhaps, some of us..." She paused. "And to lose a child..."

He looked down at his hands gripping the pike. "He was a grown man."

"That is a greater tragedy," she said. "You had longer to love him."

He stopped and looked up at the darkening sky. "I...never thought of it that way," he said.

"I suspect you didn't have much time to think," she said. She saw that he had raised his head and was frowning along the track.

Two men were approaching: Djedi and Isesi. Seti grounded his bow and waited for them to come up to him.

Djedi bowed to Nefer and then turned to Seti. "Isesi and I will take over from you and patrol the path," he said. "You should go home, have a meal and get some rest."

Seti frowned. "I can make the patrol," he said. "I am familiar with the people we encountered, and I know what to do."

"You have done enough," Djedi said. "You've earned some rest."

The frown deepened. "It is no trouble for me to continue, he said. "I know what I saw..." He paused as Djedi raised his eyebrows.

"You escorted the women a fair distance," Djedi said. "You stood off a group of armed men. And then you went back to your charges and carried a pregnant woman the better part of a mile at a brisk pace. And I was told that you were keeping a lookout as you went. Am I right?"

"Who told you?"

"It doesn't matter," Djedi said. "Is it true?"

"Henetre!"

"Is it true?" Djedi repeated.

Seti lowered his eyes." "It is," he said. "But—"

"Then you have done enough," Djedi said. "You are relieved. Go back to your home and get some rest."

"But—"

Djedi folded his arms before him and frowned down at them. "You have shown me what it means to be strong. I am learning. I think." He looked up. "And you have also taught me what is important for a commander. We must protect those who depend on us." His gaze grew very direct. "And that includes those under our command. You have done enough today. It is time to rest." He took a breath and added, "What would you do if you were talking to me and the situation was the same but our positions reversed?"

Seti's frown was back. It deepened to a scowl and then lightened, "I would order you back to your home. And if you continued to argue I would threaten to report you for insubordination."

"Well, then," Djedi said. "We can talk about what happened tomorrow." He lifted his eyebrows, "*After* I deal with your insubordination!" He slapped Seti on the arm with a grin.

Nefer hid a smile. "Master Sa-Ramses can escort me back to the village," she said.

"That would be good, Mistress Nefer," Djedi said. He was actually grinning as they turned away.

"Well done, Djedi!" Seti said under his breath.

"I beg your pardon?"

Seti shook his head. "Never mind. That young man is the best I have ever taught."

LII

"That was a fair-sized group," Seti said. "They did not have the look of anything particularly organized, like an army but they were all young and strong. I thought they might be a scouting party."

Djedi nodded and sat back against the wall of the tomb. They were up in the hill cemetery overlooking the village. The courtyard to the small tomb gave a good view of the surrounds to the town. The sun was rising, and with it the bustle of the town. "How were they armed?"

Seti folded his arms and settled himself more comfortably on his knees. "Adequately. Spears, that I saw. Not particularly well made, but effective enough if the lashing does not come loose. Knives. I didn't see any long blades or bows."

Djedi nodded again, his brows knit. "They don't sound very organized," he said.

"They were not."

"And you drove them away alone?"

Seti frowned down the hillside. "Let us say that I made them think that attacking me might not be a good idea. They left of their own accord."

Djedi pushed out his lower lip, his brows knit. "You were along that path the women take," he said. "You must have seen them at one of the gaps opening to the desert?"

When Seti nodded he said, "They would have some trouble getting past a defender there-high sides and a narrow track and... And no way to go around you without killing you."

Seti smiled. "Exactly," he said.

"How did you manage to convince them?"

Seti drew one knee up. "It didn't take much effort. .I had to. And I picked my ground. They thought I was a soldier with a troop to back me." He paused and then said, "You have my account, which I can write up for you. What are your commands?"

"It must not happen again," Djedi said.

Seti nodded.

"We have the group..." Djedi paused. "We have the group," he repeated. "If we train them, have them practice..."

"Are they good enough to fight off an attack?"

"If they are trained, they will be," Djedi said.

Seti was frowning. "Do we have time to train them?"

"What do you mean?"

Seti raised his eyes to Djedi's. "If that group decides to swing around and attack the town tomorrow, could we fight them off?"

Djedi chewed his lip as he considered. He finally shook his head. "I believe we have time. You warned them off and they left, thinking we have a troop of soldiers here. They would likely be cautious."

"They only saw and heard one man."

"But they left, nevertheless." Djedi sat forward. "We have weapons, we can train them—"

Seti frowned. "You seem very sure of that."

"I am sure that we can do it! And they're used to handling mauls and axes."

"And brushes?" Seti suggested.

Djedi stared. "Be serious!"

"I am."

They traded stares before Seti looked down. He frowned at his hands, raised his eyes again and said, "You could approach Pharaoh through the Vizier and request a squadron of men to be quartered here."

"We don't need one!"

"Don't you?"

"It-it would be a lot of trouble and expense."

"The Crown pays the cost of its soldiers, Djedi-unless you approach the Governor, but that is not his rightful concern, since you are royal workers. Pharaoh would support your defenders."

"Where would we house them?"

"That would be His Majesty's concern."

"I tell you, we don't need a troop!"

Seti shifted to a cross-legged position. "Are you saying that, Djedi, because you truly believe it? Or is it simply because you want to?"

"We can speak more on this tomorrow."

Seti looked up at him. "'Tomorrow and tomorrow and tomorrow'," he said. "You say that too often. Let me tell you, Djedi, you need to hoard your tomorrows, use them wisely, for tomorrows will run out and you will be left with only yesterdays, wondering where tomorrow went and desperately wishing to have them back, just long enough to say a word, make a gesture, bind a wound, give one last kiss..."

Djedi's expression shifted to a frown. "I...see," he said.

Seti folded his arms. "You will," he said. "And we need to decide this now. I ask you again, are you saying we need no help defending ourselves, Djedi, because you truly believe it? Or is it simply because you want to?"

Djedi stared. "I don't..." He looked down.

"Let me ask you this way: Tell me why you want to train the townsfolk rather than request a troop from His Majesty."

"We need to learn to take care of ourselves!"

"What is wrong with having in the town people who are hired specifically to fight for the town?"

"We will be dependent on them !"

"Egypt is dependent on its armies to do the things that armies are mustered to do-fight foes and defend citizens."

"Yes, but if the armies are somewhere else, Egyptians need to fight, don't they? Did Kamose and Ahmose have an army to drive the Hyksos out?"

"As a matter of fact, they did."

"No! Two brothers who fought together—"

"—at the head of their army."

"—and drove the Hyksos from the land—"

"—leading their armies after their father was killed and left to dry in the sun," Seti finished.

Djedi drew himself up. "We don't need that troop. We had one once."

"What?"

"During the bad times right after Thutmose I died... They became renegade and turned on the town."

Seti thought for a moment, scowling. "Yes," he said slowly. "They were put down by the Royal Army. We need reinforcements."

Djedi was frowning. "I-I—" He broke off, gnawing his lip.

Seti sat back. "What is it?" he asked.

Djedi drew a careful breath. "I...am the commander here," he said.

"Yes."

"It is my judgment that we don't need to apply for troops at this moment."

Seti lifted his eyebrows.

"...and so we will not."

"Can we speak of this further? We are confronting a dangerous situation; else you would not have decided to form the guard. We do not have the luxury of time. Your talk of Kamose and Amose, while interesting, is beside the point and-if you will take my word for it-inaccurate. I have told you that there is danger. Why are you hesitating?"

Djedi sat silently for a space, his brows furrowed. "I know we could have the army," he said. "But-but we would be depending on the Army for our protection..."

"And is that a bad thing?"

Djedi looked up. "It could be," he said. "They would not be interested in the town's welfare. No, listen to me! It would only be an assignment to them, and they would not fit in. But even if we did agree to have a troop quartered here, His Majesty is a great warrior. Everyone who knows about such things says so. What would happen if he decided to gather his armies and go after the Hittites or-or march south into Kush?"

"Do you think His Majesty would leave any of his subjects, dependent on his might, helpless?"

Djedi hesitated. "Not His Majesty. But there are plenty of people who want to curry favor with the leader-whoever he might be-and go to excess. His Majesty would never leave us to fend for ourselves, but others might." He paused.

Seti folded his arms and leaned back against the stone behind him.

"So you see, I thought we needed to learn how to defend ourselves. We needed form our own force-I could see it in my mind, how we would be, depending on no one, if the need came."

"So you would not object to an army detachment when the time was right?"

"When the time was right-no. But it isn't right now."

"I encountered those scouts, Djedi," Seti said. "Something is coming. Something with power. And it will be coming soon." He watched the expressions cross Djedi's face. "You must believe me: I have been a soldier for a long time. I can feel these things. We must get some protection now."

"No," Djedi said, though the words came slowly. "We have some time."

"Do we?"

Djedi straightened. "I say that we do."

Seti nodded. "Very well," he said.

"'Very well'?"

"Yes." Seti smiled slightly. "Do you want me to get to my feet, salute you, fist to heart, and march away?"

"I'd..." Djedi moistened his lips. "I'd like to know that you don't hate me."

"Hate you? For giving an order? Don't be a fool!"

"But you want a garrison!"

"Yes. You don't. You are the commander. I will obey." Seti added, "I reserve the right to say 'I told you so' when you fall flat on your face. If, that is, we're both still alive to talk of it."

Djedi looked down. "I am sorry," he said. "I just think we will be able to fight them ourselves. You were able to rout them by yourself."

"I was lucky. And I picked my ground."

Djedi shook his head. "No. We will not trouble His Majesty."

"Can we approach the town fathers, at least, with the question?"

Djedi folded his arms and frowned down at his feet. His expression lightened and he looked up. "We can," he said.

"Well, then—"

"When Benetamun returns from Edfu."

"What?"

"He left for Edfu yesterday. We need all the Master craftsmen present to make a decision."

**   **   **

And that, Seti thought, *is unanswerable.* He was up the side of The Peak, his back against the sun-warmed stone. He drew his knees up and cursed his anonymity, not for the first time.

They needed reinforcements. If not right away, then sooner than Djedi thought. And they would get them. But how?

He let his gaze swing toward the Nile, glittering in the afternoon sun like a valley filled with stars. A ship was making its way south, heading toward the Aswan quarries, maybe? The granite quarried there was in high demand at Opet.

He blinked away the thought of the Nubian lowlands and gazed into the distance. He could see himself standing up before everyone and announcing that he was His Majesty. They would all laugh at him. He could see it in his mind's eye. They would clap him in prison for his own protection. Kenamun, who knew the right of things, would speak up and be imprisoned, as well.

They would watch the slaughter of the town from their prison cell, and Seti would shout "I told you so!"

The mental image made him laugh.

[213]

Well. It was an interesting dream, but the reality was troubling. He had the duty, as King, to do what was best for his subjects. He would go to Intef as soon as possible. It was time.

And he would be gentle with Djedi.

LIII

Seti turned to motion to his escort, who joined him at an outcropping of rock. "Down there," he said. "What do you see?"

The group turned and frowned into the valley below them.

Wide terraces holding wrecked columns glinted in the sun.

"It is Deir el Bahari," one man said.

"And what do you see there? Anything unusual?"

They traded looks, turned, and frowned down at the sloping, graciously proportioned temple built by Hatshepsut.

Seti set the butt of his spear on the ground and waited as they talked among themselves and argued over what was to be seen. He eyed the temple expanse. The irregularity, to him, was like a fist to the eye. How could anyone miss it? But they overlooked it. Was it a common sight? Well, then, they would learn to see the common with new eyes.

He held his peace. They would never learn if he did it for them.

He let his gaze swing toward the Nile. A boat heading south before the prevailing wind. A small craft: it did not seem to be one to brave the rapids south of Swenet. A family group on an outing?

"Master Sa-Ramses?"

The respectful voice broke into his reverie. He blinked away the vision of the Nubian lowlands and turned to the patrol behind him.

"Did you find anything?" he asked.

"There were donkeys there," Khatef said. "We could see tracks. We think one is tied in the portico of the temple, but we can't tell without going down there."

"And what would you do?"

"Send a report by runner to Captain Djedi. Give our conclusions but make no plans."

Seti's face warmed in a smile. "Excellent! You do yourself proud, Master Khatef! Few would notice those tracks, and yet they could mean so many things. Intruders like Bedouin, a merchant on his way to the city, with wares from the north. Or attackers. "Which do you think?"

They looked at each other, hesitating. One man finally stood forward, Kheti, a stonemason.

"I think it's a couple traders," he said. "Raiders wouldn't be riding donkeys, would they? Anyone can outrun a donkey!"

Seti laughed. "Well done, Kheti. You all can go back to your homes now. Tell Captain Djedi that I am pleased with you all and wanted him to know."

Smiles, bows. They left.

** ** **

Seti's smile faded. They were learning very quickly. In fact, the village had some really intelligent people there. And some truly oblivious idiots.

He frowned slightly. It was growing late, but he did not feel like going back to the village just yet. He could do a circuit, and maybe cut through the Valley, taking a look around.

He frowned at a nearby rock, smoothed by weather and time to what appeared to be a comfortable seat, and sat down cross-legged to do some more thinking.

Deir el Medineh was a village that was out of the ordinary. It was situated in an area that would not normally be settled, far from water and arable land. It was populated by a specific group of people dedicated to a specific occupation-And could he imagine anything more soul-killingly dull and repetitive than carving tombs? Their abilities were rare and priceless. They were singular citizens and perhaps...

He stopped. No, there was no 'perhaps' about it. Royal intervention was required.

He slid from the rock, dusted his kilt, took his pike with him and started along the donkey path back to the village, frowning over what should be his next step.

He stopped and looked up at the sky above The Peak. It was so clear it seemed to ring, and the presence of the Nile, felt more often than seen, was reassuring.

Time to be up and be doing, he thought.

He followed the track up toward the heights. The village's cemetery was spreading up the slope now, the result of generations of workers living and dying there. It was a forest of small pyramid-shaped chapels. He paused to frown over the question of whether anyone in that town had any conception of a 'forest'. Probably not. He gazed up at the pyramidions, his mind full of the image of tall trees whispering in a breeze, swaying to the motion of the wind...

A dark shape, moving quickly, caught his attention. A smaller animal-a cat, most likely. He looked more closely. Upright ears, slender, graceful-a jackal. It saw him and melted away among the rocks, leaving him to do some thinking.

A jackal this close to a settlement? They moved in pairs, mating for life, he knew. But there was plenty of hunting and scavenging for them closer to the desert. Why were they here?

He shouldered his pike, looked around. Attacks by jackals were not unknown-if they had something to gain-such as food during a time of scarcity. Were there others?

He moved among the rocks, looking for tracks, not easy with the footing. He gave it up. One jackal at least, but if he was away from his usual haunts and this close to a settlement, he was either sick-which he had not appeared to be-or else trying to avoid a hazard in his own territory. They tended to live near lions, he knew...

And that is the sum of my knowledge, he thought with a wry smile. It was enough. He would speak with Kenamun and Djedi and suggest that they warn the villagers. And, maybe, have the patrols keep an eye out for the creatures.

What could be driving them this way?

He dismissed the question until he could give it more thought. He had other things to consider, some of them delightful enough to make him smile. Sheritra had approached him through her husband, asking whether he would object to her naming her new son after him. How could he possibly object? She wanted him to come to their home once she was out of her confinement, to hold the baby and bless him.

His smile dimmed a little as he thought of other years and other babies, and chances long past to... To what? Cuddle them? Kiss them? The past was past, the present coming to him moment by moment, as he had learned. Each moment brought its own joy, and if he were to think of the times he had missed, why should he not think of the times he had enjoyed?

[217]

LIV

He was smiling as he descended the path through the village necropolis when he saw another jackal. It stood to reason that they would haunt that area, since the townsfolk left offerings at the tombs. The growing darkness brought them out, but if the cemetery was a haunt of jackals at any time, it would be a good idea to place it off limits at night or require that the townsfolk visit in groups.

He frowned again at the question of what might be driving them toward Deir el Medineh. It bore some scrutiny.

Movement out of the corner of his eye. Another jackal. He shifted his grip on his pike and looked around. He saw one of the townsfolk quietly kneeling beside an offering slab in the courtyard of one of the tombs. Nefer.

She was quiet, self-contained. Not in an access of grief, apparently, but pensive and heedless.

He looked along the path as he weighed his choices, and then decided that there was no choice, after all. He gathered a fistful of stones, settled himself on one of the walls, looking away from her, and disposed himself to wait and watch along the path.

Time passed. He caught motion from the tomb; she had stood and was starting to turn toward the doorway when she saw him. Her eyes flickered for a moment, the starlight catching a shine on her cheeks. "Master Sa-Ramses," she said. Her voice quivered.

He bowed. "Mistress Nefer."

She was silent for a pause. "Are you waiting for me, sir?"

He caught a touch of annoyance and nodded toward the path. "I was keeping some jackals from calling on you."

"I heard stones," she said.

"I threw one or two..."

She looked back at the tomb. "My Husband. He died...some time ago. And my child. I found myself remembering... In the silence."

"Yes," Seti said.

Her eyes raised to his.

"Sometimes the past takes us unaware." He looked out over the Nile for a moment, then turned back to her. "It is restful to be quiet," he said. "Away from the noise of life. Of other voices and thoughts. It gives us a chance to...to heal."

She looked down and away, her fingertips brushing at her eyes.

He watched her, hesitating, then set his pike aside. "There is no need to return immediately, Mistress Nefer," he said. "The sunset is still beautiful. We can walk along the river path."

She looked down. "You are giving me the chance to collect myself," she said.

"If you wish." He retrieved his pike and waited for her. "You did as much for me, once."

** ** **

They took the ridge path, looking at the night sky, reflected in the river. A light breeze was rippling the water, sending the lights shimmering. There was no need to speak. The constellations rose higher in the sky, the Path of the Crocodile bright against the rich night fabric.

She spoke finally. "*Were* there jackals outside, then?"

"There were," he said.

"They would not have attacked me."

"You seem very certain of that. Could you have fought them off if they had?"

"I would have tried."

"And so I stayed," he said. "Besides..."

"Besides..?"

He looked down at her with the touch of a smile. "You stayed with me that whole afternoon."

She lowered her eyes. "How could I not? I know that way of feeling, of living. It is hard..." Her voice broke again. "Our children... Even now I remember and regret the things I never said, until it was too late."

He stopped and waited as she turned toward him. "Children?"

"A child. Dead far away. I came back here. The tomb was ready. But there is nothing here and everything to regret."

He chose his words carefully, thinking of the years when he judged petitioners and gave counsel in the audience hall in Memphis, in the years that he had been Vizier.

"Our children sometimes leave us too soon," he said, looking down and away from the sparkle of tears in her eyes. "You can give them birth, or cause them to quicken in a womb... You give them the best childhood you can, try to be the father that you should be. But, ultimately, they will leave you. A month, a year... Through marriage, through distance-you do lose them, or part of them you loved. All that you can do is hold to what you did have and remember the care you gave them. And the love. And also remember, for we sometimes do forget, that what we gave was the best we could at that moment. And it was sufficient, no matter how we may dream of what we might have done, if only we had known."

She was gazing up at him with an arrested expression, her eyes bright in the sunset. She nodded, once. "Let us enjoy the stars," she said. "Walk with me. I don't want to return yet."

** ** **

They moved through the deepening night, sometimes silent, sometimes speaking quietly. He saw tears, but her composure returned, and she smiled at him as the time passed.

The moon was beginning to lighten the eastern horizon. They watched it come curving slowly into the sky.

"It is late," she said. "This place is no longer as safe as it was... Let us go back."

They did not speak as they went along the path. He offered his hand to help her over some rough spots in the track; she did not release him. They moved together in silence, looking down over the lights of the town toward the distant shimmer of the Nile.

The wall of the village rose before them. They paused.

"Sheritra wants to name the baby for you," Nefer said.

Seti smiled. "I was honored," he said. "But he's their firstborn. Surely her father, or his—"

"They want to name him for you. They asked me about it and I suggested that they approach you."

He lifted an eyebrow.

"I told them it was a good idea. You were so kind to her."

"She was exhausted and frightened and near her time," he said. "What else could I have done other than what I did?" He looked down the street. "It is quiet now."

"They're asleep," Nefer said. "We tarried a long time."

He smiled and shook his head. "Time changes from moment to moment, as I have discovered. Life stretches before you into eternity-and you find that the years have passed, leaving you wondering where they went." He looked at the dark windows. "But they aren't likely to look at us and wonder what we have been up to."

"I don't care what they think," she said.

"You should. You can't live a lie-and you don't want a lie to color your reputation."

[220]

She stopped and faced him. "Do you care?"

"Of course I do."

They were at her doorway. There were so many things to say, and no words with which to say them. She turned, facing him full. Her hands rose to his shoulders, settled there. "Stay with me tonight," she said.

His frown appeared for a moment. "I did not expect to be invited in simply because I escorted you home," he said.

She lifted her chin and looked at him. "The invitation was not issued because I wished to pay you for keeping nonexistent jackals at bay," she said. "And I cannot imagine that a man of your quality would expect such a payment, no matter what service was rendered."

His expression was an odd mixture of regret and assent. "I can promise nothing, Nefer."

"I am not asking for promises, Sa-Ramses," she said. "I only want your company through this night."

"I don't understand."

"There is nothing to understand. I love you."

"Nefer..." He looked down and away from her. "You are a beautiful woman. Kind, gallant... One to cherish. But I can't make any promises, ever."

"I need no promise from you," she returned. "No keepsake to treasure. Only your company this night. I know it can't be for long. What drew you here is losing its strength, and I think you will soon be gone. I, too, am moving toward changes. But during this time that we have been together, during the days I have watched you and walked with you, and this night, when you ... when you spoke so gently to me-your wisdom—" She faltered. "I love you."

He raised his eyes to hers. "No promise," he said. "Why would you chance it?"

She moved toward him with a smile, her hands curving behind his neck. She drew no closer. "There is no risk with you, Sa-Ramses. I have nothing to fear from you. I love you, that is all. How could I not?"

He gazed down at her, at the curve of her mouth, the warm eyes that were so like Tuia's, gone now for a year. Shadows, but mourned and missed. And this woman, so kind, so valiant... And, he realized, dear to him now.

He took her in his arms, smiled at her, and kissed her.

[221]

LV

Seti stepped out onto the terrace and closed the door quietly behind him. No one was astir. The sky was still dark but growing pale toward the east; he could see the moon hovering just above the western horizon, beginning to catch a reflection of the emerging sun. Daybreak would be coming shortly, and with it the clamor and bustle of the town. He looked over the rooftops. But not yet. No one had seen him. He lifted an eyebrow. It was the result of the lack of a guard force. That would change. Meanwhile, he could return to his own house and prepare for the day and not worry about any hint of gossip.

He descended the steps that led to the street from the side of the house and moved soundlessly up the main road, turning off at his house.

He stepped inside. Someone had been there that evening: a flake of limestone, covered with writing, lay on one of the low stools. Limestone flakes were plentiful and free; they were often used in place of expensive papyrus. Who had written it?

He lifted it, turned it over, and eyed the signature with a grin. A note from Djedi. The village scribe must have hated teaching him. His script looked like nothing so much as cuneiform scratches. From what Seti could decipher, Djedi liked the idea of a mock attack and had already selected the attackers. He was in haste to go to Thebes for the evening and couldn't speak with Seti that night. Friends, apparently; a birthday...

He went to his sleeping chamber, undressed, and went to his bed, to lie there with his arms folded behind his head, looking up at the ceiling and thinking over his plans for the day. But he smiled to himself and thought of Nefer again.

Tuia had said years ago, on the eve of one of their many partings, that a night spent in the arms of someone who truly loved you and understood who you were could change your life. He smiled again, closed his eyes and dozed...

It was brighter when he awoke again. He indulged in a luxuriant stretch and then lay back for a moment, thinking of the coming day and all that he hoped to accomplish. He could not escape the feeling that many lives were depending on his actions. So it had been since he became King three years before, but this time the lives that depended on his actions were those of people he knew personally and had come to love.

He decided that he had lain abed long enough. He had things to do, and quickly. He arose, tied a new shenti, donned a kilt and straightened his bed. A tap sounded at the door as he reached for his tunic. He draped the garment over his arm and went to the door.

Djedi, who looked offensively wide-awake and cheerful after what must have been a night of drinking, was standing on the doorstep with Kenamun beside him.

"I didn't want to trouble you, Sa-Ramses," said Djedi, "But I was up and about, and I saw Master Kenamun. We were talking about drilling the villagers..."

Seti stood aside and motioned them into the house, pulling his tunic over his head as he did so.

Kenamun hesitated at the door. "Did we wake you?"

"I have been up for some time," Seti said. "I was just dressing..." He pushed his hands through his hair. "I will groom myself better before I go out. Have you had breakfast? There's gruel here-the servants left it for me last night."

"I saw," Djedi said. "I stopped by. You weren't in... Did you take a turn along the paths last night?"

"I did. I've been seeing jackals hovering around the edges of this village. It did not make me happy."

"Jackals?"

"Yes. They don't usually come this close to human habitations. I don't like it: it puzzles me. I saw several among the tombs."

"The offerings," Kenamun said.

"I think so," Seti agreed. "We can talk this afternoon."

"This afternoon?"

"Yes. After I return from the docks." He raised his eyebrows at Djedi. "I have some business there, and once it is done I will be offering my services writing letters. For now-if Commander Djedi agrees-I would suggest that we tell the townsfolk not to venture out alone and tell them why."

Djedi frowned, but the expression eased. "Jackals? They might attack children... I will say something, or..." He broke off and looked over at Kenamun. "If the Senior Foreman could pass the word... I think his word would weigh more than mine."

Kenamun's expression grew thoughtful, but he nodded. "I will do it," he said. "But don't sell yourself short, lad. They'd listen to you now."

** ** **

The battlements of the royal palace of Thebes shivered in the mid-morning light. Dawn had faded; the brassy brilliance of midday was building to its afternoon crescendo. The lines of the palace shattered into ripples as a papyrus skiff crossed it. Seti watched it move across the reflection, smiling at the family gathered on the small deck, the father poling the boat, his wife behind him with a baby on her lap while an older child stood beside his father and watched the landscape pass. The boy saw Seti and waved, then pointed.

The family smiled and called greetings. Seti returned the smile and bowed where he sat. How many times had he journeyed so with his young family before fame and high position had placed him in palaces...

Seti was sitting by the docks, sorting through his kit. He had given a message to a courier heading to the Vizier's palace and was now waiting for a response.

He heard voices in the street; a mother shepherding her gaggle of children down toward the well. A donkey brayed somewhere close. He spared a wry thought for the reaction of any number of highly bred horses he had driven in the past thirty years to that specific noise.

Why on earth should it upset them so? And yet it did.

He smiled to himself, remembering a time when he was quite a young man driving his chariot in review before Pharaoh Ay. It had been a splendid day, much like this one, with the sun glinting from arms and armor, the blare of trumpets, the exclamations of an admiring public. But then the intrusion of a braying donkey had made everything go disastrously wrong. It had been as bad as a text he had copied as a schoolboy learning his letters:

> *Come, let me tell thee of the miserable calling of the Officer of Chariotry, my son. He is given rank because of his grandfather, the father of his mother. He has five slaves, with two helpers among them. His Majesty comes; he hurries to get his horses from their stalls in His Majesty's presence. When he has secured a fine pair of horses he gloats. He goes to his home town and*

[224]

*trampleth it underfoot, but he does not yet know
how badly it will be for him.*

*He squanders the wealth he received from his
mother's father, using it to buy a chariot. Its pole
costs three months' wages and the chariot costs
thrice that amount. He is overturned in a thicket;
his feet are cut by his sandals and his shirt is torn
by thorns. When the commander comes to muster
the troops, he is mocked. He is thrown upon the
ground and beaten with a hundred stripes! Be a
scribe, my son, follow this great calling, pleasant
and abundant with possessions. How joyous you
are every day!*

He remembered his horses stampeding straight at Pharaoh
as he sawed at the reins and cursed, picturing his team
careening into His Majesty, sending the Lord of the Two
Lands flying heels over head. He had thought in the brief
moment that he had that it might be a good idea to simply
abandon the chariot and trust the horses not to send any other
humans flying, but then he thought that he might experience
something rather more unpleasant than a lecture from his
commanding officer if he did that. So, he had remained with
his team, wrestled them aside at the last possible second. He
would never forget the horror and shock on Ay's austere face
under the double crown. He ended up on the ground in the
wreckage of his chariot, dodging his horses' kicking hooves.

No one had had the nerve to beat him, especially after Ay
had gathered his wits and commended Seti for keeping a
mishap from becoming a disaster, but he had had to tolerate
pointed fingers, laughter, and snide remarks for several weeks.

Being a scribe was no sinecure, either. Right at that
moment Seti could think of several times when he served as an
army scribe, thought longingly of his home and family and
wished that he had been able to ride in a chariot. And his mild
dislike of donkeys had risen to intense distaste after that
mishap.

"I need a letter for my wife, Master Scribe."

The voice, deep and soft, was above him. He looked up,
squinting a little in the sun. A stocky man with a broad,
intelligent face, was looking down at him with his eyebrows
raised. He met the man's gaze and began to smile. "By all

means, Master," he said. "Something to send the lady? A love letter, maybe?"

"That would be...interesting," the man said. "It may make her view me with less annoyance."

"Sit down Master," Seti said. "I have the perfect letter for you..." He drew a folded document from his scrip. "See if the phrases please you..."

The man took the sheet from him and scanned it. A sudden, intense frown was firmly suppressed, and he sat back and read it again. His mouth twitched. After a moment he lowered the document and looked up. "Do you think this will work?" he asked.

"It always has worked for me," Seti said. "But then I've been fortunate most of my life."

The other lifted an eyebrow. "I will take it," he said. "It may well persuade her. Thank you." He paused. "Master Scribe," he said. "I have enjoyed talking with you, and I have some questions about this letter. Would you care to discuss it with me over a bite and a sup?"

"As disheveled as I am?" Seti asked with a grin.

"You look like a prince."

LVI

"'Cram yourself into something that isn't a robe of state, leave your wig behind and get over to the docks'," Intef said. "What a way to summon an old friend!"

"We've been friends too long for you to take offense," Seti said.

"That is debatable." Intef eyed the rough cup of beer and then raised it to sip. "Perhaps I am naive, Seti, but I can't fight the conviction-odd, I know!-that you must have had some reason for summoning me so abruptly aside from the urge to indulge your strange sense of humor by abusing me!"

Seti topped his cup from the jar of beer before him. "You already know, Intef-you have the message."

"Ah yes," said Intef. "The message..." He drew it from the scrip at his belt and frowned thoughtfully at it. "Are you quite serious?" he asked.

Seti frowned and set his cup down. "How long have you known me? I'm as serious as death! I am surprised that you are questioning me."

Intef nodded. "I was...simply curious, but as you command..." He sat back and looked straight at Seti with an expression of bland inquiry. "Should I wash my feet before you start kissing them?"

"*What*? Give me that letter!" Seti snatched it from Intef's hand, opened it and read, scowled at the blank cover and then put it down with a shout of laughter. "Damnation!"

"I gather there was another message?"

"There is," Seti said. "It's in my scrip."

"Along with a parcel of love-lorn notes!" Intef grinned. "My wife would lay me low with a blow of her staff and then laugh me to scorn! What on earth could have made you compose such a piece of twaddle?"

Seti folded the message and handed it back. "I will have you know, my lad, that it is a standard letter. A classic, in fact, taught in schools. How did you come to miss it? Were you asleep? This particular letter is very much in demand among my young, male customers."

Intef poured more beer, sipped and then spluttered his mouthful over the floor as Seti added, "Actually, some of the older, more substantial men have bought it as well."

"For their concubines, no doubt!"

[227]

Seti considered. "Based on their names, I suspect the women in question were-shall I say-housed separately in an establishment that welcomed all comers."

"You're a warrior!" Intef snorted. "When did you start talking like a mealy-mouthed scribe?"

"I *am* a mealy-mouthed scribe, Intef. Been one for decades."

"That's right. 'Scribe of the Armies'. How could I forget your meekness while leading a charge of chariotry?"

"The one not precipitated by donkeys? I was busy cursing during the other."

"I remember the language," Intef said. "In fact, it's one of my most treasured memories." He shook his head and looked at the letter. "Seal it," he said. "I will give it to my wife and see what she says."

"You might be surprised at her reaction, based on what my repeat customers have told me," Seti said. He frowned into his scrip and took out another message. "*This* is what I wished to give you. It's urgent, and I think you will find everything in order."

Intef took the document and opened it after giving the superscription and seal a quick look. He read it and then looked up with a frown. "A garrison?"

"It's warranted," Seti said. "I saw some of the nomads that have been troubling them. There's strength behind them, I think. I had thought they were perhaps several weeks away from here-but I can sense organization..."

"A scouting mission, then?"

"That is the sense I had," Seti said. "The townsfolk originally spoke of raiders coming through-abusing an old man-taking items of little value. I think these people are different."

"But the town is close to Thebes," Intef objected. "Wouldn't you think that would deter them?"

"It would depend on the numbers that are backing them up," Seti said. "A large group, looking for land. The village is not in a very fertile area: would the Theban officers think it worth coming to blows?" He poured more beer into his cup and frowned down at his reflection. "And, too, they may have heard from the others that no one hindered any attacks."

"That's a good point," Intef said. "But still-let us discuss this for the sake of argument-It is only a small town. Would marauders or wandering nomads want to control it?"

[228]

Seti nodded. "There is that objection," he admitted. "But consider this: it may be a small town but having a group camping on what is essential Thebes' doorstep is not good. They must be stopped. And that does not take into account the nature of the town itself. Those people, as a group, are irreplaceable."

Intef nodded, his eyes fixed on Seti's face. "And you have grown to love them," he said.

"How could I not?"

"How, indeed?" Intef said. "Why Seti! I believe you are blushing!"

"Don't try me too far," Seti said. "Or I'll remember that I am your King.'

"You've never forgotten," Intef said. "That is why you are a good King. I will have the garrison set up, as you have ordered. Shall I send the order at once?"

"Get it underway, if you would," Seti said after a moment's concentrated thought. "I am actually going over my commander's head. Don't laugh, Intef. I am serving under a fine young man, but he has to wait until the town fathers decide what to do. One of them is away in Edfu and they have to hold off until his return. I gently suggested going to the Town Fathers and saying that this is an emergency, but the boy doesn't know what I do, and I am not willing to give myself away. And even if they were all there, the town fathers, from what I can see, take forever to argue over the number of chisels they need to carve my tomb, I suspect that the decision won't be made before the Nile has turned."

"What of Kenamun? He's a foreman."

"Yes," Seti said. "The Senior Foreman. He also knows who I am. He recognized me and spoke to me privately. I don't want to put him in an awkward situation."

"What can be awkward about being a friend of Pharaoh?"

"If your neighbors and friends are angry with you for not telling them..."

"There is that." Intef reached for the jar of beer. "I can send troops over tomorrow, but it will be rushed."

Seti frowned and sat back, absently chasing sesame seeds with a fingertip. "That might be a good thing," he said after he licked the seeds off. "As soon as it can be arranged at any rate. Space is limited there-best to set up an encampment."

"That may take some time," Intef said.

"Can they be quartered at one of the mortuary temples?"

"I will see what can be done. Do you think we have any time to spare?"

Seti broke off a piece of crust, set a small onion on it, bit into it and chewed. "I'd like to say we have plenty of time," he said. "But I don't know..."

"That group impressed you."

"In a way. They could have rushed me. In fact, I am not sure why they didn't-except that I carried a bow. As I said, they appeared to be scouts."

"Well, they must have received an impression of determination."

"Or else they had a large force in reserve. Large enough, they may have thought, to take the town and dispatch me and my force at their leisure. And the terrain was good for me, too."

"That makes all the difference," Intef said. "And if that swayed them, then I think they're more experienced than we had hoped."

"Exactly," Seti said. "They are probably reporting to their people now. They will be back." He paused, frowning. "And I am uneasy..."

Intef folded his hands and watched him.

"Things don't feel right. I am seeing jackals close to the town..."

"Something in the desert is driving them toward you..." Intef mused. "Something large enough and dangerous enough to make them nervous."

"That's what I am afraid of." He looked for more seeds and then shrugged. "And that is why I am uneasy." He hooked the gold pendant from beneath his tunic, slipped it over his head, took the ring from the cord and handed it to Intef. "If I need the forces at once I will send to you. This ring is the token I will use. It does not matter who carries it: the request will be coming straight from me."

Intef turned the ring in his hands and then looked up at Seti. "Tuia's ring," he said, handing it back. "I'm sorry, old friend. She was... a beautiful woman."

Seti smiled. "It is always with me." He slid the ring back on the cord and set it around his neck again.

Intef frowned at the Gold of Honor. "You still wear it," he mused.

"It means a great deal to me. I remember that fight..."

"As do I." Intef lifted the document. "Shoulder to shoulder against overwhelming odds there on the border. Will you ever forget Achtoy rallying our forces-and then falling with a spear thrust to the eye? He was a darling of the gods, that he lived after that."

"I thought we were dead men," Seti said. "But we won." He lowered his head. "We won, and I've never forgotten. Well. You have the order."

Intef folded the note. "I will get things underway," he said. "This young fellow, Djedi, must have impressed you if you're making him an officer."

"He is impressive," Seti said. "Very young, with no army background. But he's the one who determined to set up a corps of guards. You will like him-plucky and generous."

"I think I will," Intef said. "So. What do you plan to do now?"

"Take dictation at the docks," Seti said. "It's what I told them I'd be doing today. After that, we will see. I have that feeling... I will be in touch. If anything changes, be ready to act quickly."

"I will be ready," Intef said, pouring the last of the beer.

LVII

Seti paused to look back toward the river. He had accomplished that day all that he had hoped for-but he had the nagging feeling that it was not nearly enough, and before much more time had passed he would wish that he had, in fact, done more. But what else could he do other than what he had done?

He turned back toward the approaches to the village, raising his eyes to the Peak. It seemed to glow in the reddening light of sunset. He gazed at the Peak and thought *What more could I have done?* The lowering sun was silent behind him, the Peak monumental and calm in its glowing sunset. He relaxed. He had done what he could, and the rest-

Angry voices— Crashing, clangor, the thud of racing feet—

He stopped, aghast. Raiders? They weren't ready! *He* wasn't ready!

He raced along the donkey path toward the town, his mind whirling with nightmare images of destruction and bloodshed. He rounded the bend in the track leading to the ascent to the village and saw a crowd of workmen circling a lone man, who was trying to back away from them.

The workmen were armed with mallets and mauls, sticks and, here and there, the glint of a knife. Although a knife was sheathed at the man's belt he had not drawn it. He was instead doing a fair job of holding them off with a plain staff. As Seti watched it came across one man's shoulders and send him stumbling. He was shouting something, but the uproar made it impossible to understand him.

The crowd surged forward as Seti watched, the man disappearing suddenly from his sight. He saw raised fists, heard shouts—

He ran forward, his hand at his knife, arriving just as Djedi strode over, pulled one of the workmen off and sent him spinning.

"What are you *doing*?" Djedi demanded, hauling another to the side.

"He's an intruder!" someone shouted.

"He came from the west!"

Djedi frowned at the group. "Idiots!" he snapped. "Is *this* why you went after him? The *west*? Amun's breath and bones!

The last I knew, the sun doesn't set in the southeast! Stand aside and let me look at him. Did you kill him?"

Seti moved forward to look over Djedi's shoulder as the crowd moved back, showing their target.

The man was down on the ground, curled into a tight ball, his arms shielding his head. Seti could see blood.

"*Kill* him!"

"Stand back, all of you, or fight *me*!" Djedi snapped. "Twenty against one! And he armed only with a staff! Were you sired by dotards, that you should fight like this? Were you trained to arms by old women? Or half-wits?"

"*You* trained us!" The words had come from the edge of the crowd.

"Who said that?" Djedi demanded.

Seti began to grin.

"He knew how to use that staff!" someone shouted.

"He has a knife!" another pointed out more quietly.

Djedi dropped the question of half-wits. "Who fights with a knife by keeping it sheathed at his belt?" he retorted. "Shame on you all! Move aside and let me see him!"

They parted. The man had pushed himself to his knees and was dusting his clothing off and straightening his tunic. He looked up and saw Seti. His eyes widened and he started to flatten himself against the ground. He caught himself, straightened and forced a grin.

Seti had dropped his dagger. "What the devil are *you* doing here?" he demanded as the other hurried after the weapon.

Djedi's eyes had narrowed at that exchange, but he moved aside to give him a good view.

"Well met, Uncle Sa-Ramses!" Ptahemhat, Commander of the Corps of Guards at the Temple of Ptah at Memphis, said through a split lip and a grin, offering the retrieved knife. "I have a message for you from my father, who asked me to carry it to you since I was coming this way. He sends his kindest regards, as does my wife." And he held out a folded, sealed parcel of papyrus.

Seti took it with an exclamation of annoyance Frowned at it, and handed it back.

Djedi was looking from Ptahemhat to Seti. "Do you know this man?" he demanded. "The scouts said he was acting furtive."

"Furtive!" Ptahemhat repeated. "I was walking along, twirling my staff and whistling."

[233]

Seti raised his eyebrows.

Djedi frowned over Ptahemhat's shoulder toward his accusers. "They didn't tell me *that*," he said. "They just came pelting over to say that they'd cornered an intruder. *Do* you know him?"

"Yes, to my cost!" Seti replied. "He's a grown man now, but a more obstreperous, pert nephew can't be imagined."

He flashed a look at Ptahemhat and then schooled his voice to kindness. "The men are to be commended for their vigilance," he said. "But perhaps next time they should take the suspicious person prisoner and bring him to you for questioning."

He turned to Ptahemhat. "Commander Djedi, I have the honor to present my nephew, Ptahemhat. Ptahu, Commander Djedi is the officer in charge of the guards of this town." And he smiled at Ptahemhat's stunned expression, hastily altered to a smile.

** ** **

"A cat commanding a lion!" Ptahemhat exclaimed some time later. He was seated in Seti's reception room with a cup of cooled beer in his hand. His hurts had been tended and he had eaten a quick meal. "It is ludicrous! Why are you putting up with it?"

"Not so loud!" Seti said. "These houses are jumbled together and there is little privacy. Why? Maybe the lion is exhausted and wishes he were a cat. Or maybe the cat is really a lion cub and just needs some training from a lion. Djedi is a good man, as you will find out. He needs experience, but I like him. I would have him in my army without hesitation. He has earned my complete respect, and he deserves yours, as well. What made you come here?"

"His Holiness sent me," Ptahemhat said. He took the message out and handed it to Seti.

Seti broke the seal, cut the twine tying it, and spread it, frowning at the even, elegant writing. He raised his head after a moment, swearing.

Ptahemhat lifted his eyebrows.

Seti smiled grimly and read aloud:

My Dearest Sa-Ramses,

I am sending this message by the hand of your nephew, Ptahemhat, whom I know you

[234]

have missed during your time away from your family. I have sent him to bear you company and assist you in your endeavors in far-away Thebes, the great Queen of cities, second only to Memphis for beauty.

As you know, it was the good pleasure of the Lord of the Two Lands to give me full scope to exercise my judgment and discretion in all matters pertaining to the welfare of this land and its people, from greatest to least, with obedience to my commands required from highest to lowest. With such a fiat from His Majesty himself, I am confident that all the steps that I am taking for the welfare of Egypt are proper and will prosper.

You, my dear Sa-Ramses, may, perhaps, disagree with my actions. You have told me, in an earlier exchange regarding my situation, that you have settled on a bout of singlesticks as the means of resolving any conflicts.

Your knowledge of procedures is faulty. As the one being challenged, I have the right to select the weapon of resolution. I choose to settle my score on the archery court at the Temple of Ptah when you return. It will, perhaps, serve to make matters more equal, I tottering on the verge of my dotage, as you have so kindly pointed out in our most recent discussions.

Be kind to Ptahemhat, my good nephew. He should be of immense use to you, and I have directed that he remains with you to serve as your bodyguard until I recall him.

I embrace you and look forward to seeing your face once more. My only regret, and it is a truly profound one, is that I cannot see it as you read this message.

Your loving uncle,
Nebamun

Seti threw the message down. "That *bastard*!" he said through his teeth.

[235]

Ptahemhat hid a smile.

"Did he have you read this?" Seti demanded.

"He was sealing it when I arrived," Ptahemhat replied. "He told me what it said."

Seti eyed the amusement in Ptahemhat's expression and swore again. "So I am to be saddled with *you*!"

"It would seem so." Ptahemhat said. "His Holiness thought it shouldn't be too difficult for you. He says, in fact, that I have grown up to be a fine and sensible man after being such a pain in the ass as a youngster."

"Did he actually say that?" Seti demanded.

"Words to that effect. At any rate, you are right: you're saddled with me."

Seti eyed him. "Get out!" he said. "I command it!"

"I am under orders," Ptahemhat said. "Lord Nebamun told me that they were given with all the weight of His Majesty's power, which had been handed over to him by you, and have not been withdrawn according to your directions. I can't disobey them." His grin softened to a smile. "I don't like it any better than you, Sire."

Seti swore again. "Oh, all right," he said. "It would be suspicious if I ordered you out. And you'd best call me Sa-Ramses."

"I was wondering about that," Ptahemhat said. His smile grew crooked and then straightened. "Well," he said, "I have delivered the message as I was charged. And I am here to stay."

Seti looked at him.

Ptahemhat offered a packet wrapped in cloth. "His Holiness sent these with me. I am ordered to hand them over to you after you have stopped cursing and trying to throttle me and, by association, His Holiness."

Seti frowned at the package and then sat down and opened it. Jumbled within the layers of cloth were three cylindrical gold necklaces, two rings, and a falcon pendant of gold set with lapis, turquoise and carnelian. He stared at them and then looked up at Ptahemhat. "And what am I supposed to do with them?" he demanded.

"I imagine His Holiness thought you might wish to wear them," Ptahemhat replied.

"Wear them? I am an itinerant scribe! Where would I have found them?"

"You are also a King."

[236]

Seti frowned. "And another thing: What are we to do with them?"

"Hide them," Ptahemhat replied with a promptness that made Seti's mouth tighten.

"Servants come to clean the houses in this village," Seti said.

Ptahemhat shrugged. "Are they thieves?"

"No. But they might think that I am one!"

"I rather doubt it, Sire. They will probably think I brought them."

"Stop calling me 'Sire'! People might hear you!"

"They will probably think I am your son."

"Worse and worse!"

Ptahemhat suppressed a smile. He paused and then said more quietly, "I am ordered to congratulate you on the birth of your newest grandchild, a healthy boy. Lady Iyneferti has named him Khaemwaset."

LVIII

The next morning Seti took Ptahemhat along the path leading to the encampment. He stopped and stood silently, slowly scanning the ridge. "It was here," he said. "A group of the women were going along the main path toward the temporary housing. They'd been planning to go into the Valley. Looking at my tomb, I gather." he grimaced. "At any rate, something felt odd, so I went to look. I found a group of men a distance away. Shouting distance, and they didn't have to shout for me to hear them.

"We spoke at some length, then I sent them packing and accompanied the ladies back to the village. That was nearly a sevenday ago." He fell silent, frowning, then moved up the steep slope.

Ptahemhat followed him, pausing as he settled on his stomach near the top of the slope. He hesitated and then went down on his hands and knees beside him. "Do you see anything?" he asked.

"I am not sure..." Seti said, almost under his breath. He propped himself on his elbows and frowned westward toward Libya, the land of the Tjehenu. "I saw jackals..." he said.

"Here?"

"In the village. Coming from the desert, coming among the villagers. Something driving them in, I thought. I went to Intef yesterday."

"Sire?"

Seti directed a look at him and then pushed to his feet. "I told you not to call me 'sire'," he said. He frowned westward and then squared his shoulders. "Come on," he said, moving quickly down to the path. "There's shade there-we will sit for a moment."

Ptahemhat selected a comfortable spot, indicated it to Seti, and found another for himself. As he watched, Seti opened his kit, took out the palette and a brush, and then settled himself cross-legged with his kilt stretched tight across his thighs.

"Sire?" He amended himself when Seti shot him a look. He sat back and watched as Seti spat on the black cake and worked the saliva into the pigment with the brush.

"I have a dispatch for you to take to Intef," Seti said as he wrote. "The Vizier of Upper Egypt," he added. "Take this with you, " he paused to pull the pendant over his head, remove the ring and hand it over. "And I will have a message for you to

[238]

take in a trice. You have been to Intef's palace before, I know, when you accompanied His Holiness in past years."

Ptahemhat slid the ring on his little finger and then sat quietly and watched as Seti wrote. "I am telling Intef to send the troops that we discussed at once. Tell him that I asked you to say that I want them immediately. Without delay. A squadron of chariotry and two of archers."

He scowled at the document, blew across it, and then folded it and handed it over. "Take it to Intef now. He's expecting word, and the ring is your pass to admit you to his presence. There is no time to waste."

"Do you see anything, S-sir?"

Seti's frown was slightly puzzled, "I *feel* something. And I am not inclined to argue with the feeling. Get going." He stood. "Ptahu—"

Ptahemhat turned back.

"Go with the gods and return safely."

**   **   **

Deir el Medineh was humming into its usual activity as Seti reached the southern gateway and paused to question some children. Djedi was at the village apothecary...

He found Djedi leaning against the jamb, his arms folded, smiling. His smile widened as he saw Seti.

"We must speak, Commander," Seti said. "Quickly."

The smile faded. "What's wrong?"

"We will be under attack shortly. I would stake anything I have on it."

Djedi's eyes flickered, but he nodded. "We'll go aside." He saw the apothecary's expression. "Stay here, Master Suti," he said. "I may have some instructions for you and the others in a moment." He turned to Seti once they were out of earshot. "What is it?"

"Attackers are coming. I went to the heights, to look westward, and saw dust rising in the distance. A cloud of it, caused by the movement of a body of people. I believe it is the main force from that group of scouts. They are coming in numbers, and they are coming quickly."

Djedi looked over his shoulder. "How soon?"

"We have some time. *Some* time. But we must not overestimate it."

"Understood."

"You were not there to approve the action, so I took it upon myself to send my nephew to Count Intef asking for

[239]

reinforcements to be sent here at once." He took in Djedi's frozen expression. "I apologize, Commander," he said. "I never meant to overstep–"

Djedi raised his hand. "Please," he said. "You have taught me everything I know, and you have your hand on my shoulder, like a father. I am your pupil. How could I possibly object if lives are at stake?" He paused and said more quietly, "And I would be honored if you would call me Djedi. It *is* my name."

Seti lowered his eyes. "Very well...Djedi."

Djedi folded his arms and frowned down at his feet, an echo of Seti's stance. "They're coming from the west? They mustn't get to the village. I know places where we can ambush them and hold them off. If-if your nephew is going for reinforcements, they may be coming with horses. We can buy time..."

"Exactly."

"Meanwhile..." Djedi turned back to the apothecary. "Pass the word, Master Suti. Tell everyone to go up the hillside to the tombs."

"A drill?" Suti asked.

"No. This is real. My force will be going forward to hold them off. Tell them to act as though it is a drill."

"Djedi!"

Khatef was approaching at a dead run. He skidded to a halt before them. *"They're coming!"*

"Make your report," Djedi said.

"We were doing a sweep patrol, " Khatef stopped and collected himself. "We had circled the hills and were planning to make an approach to the village when we saw a plume of dust rising to the west."

"Where was this?" Seti demanded.

"Near Hatshepsut's temple," the man said. "Near where we had that practice with a donkey."

"What are they doing?" Djedi asked.

"We couldn't see clearly. They were at a distance. But certainly heading this way!"

"A small group?"

Khatef frowned for a moment. "More," he said. "A large group."

"It's a good thing you ordered the evacuation," Seti said.

Djedi's brows drew together, but he smiled. "We will make it interesting for them."

[240]

Khatef had turned back from scanning his group of scouts. "My group is all here, Captain Djedi." "What are your orders?"

Djedi cast a quick glance at Seti, squared his shoulders. "Pass the word. We are evacuating the town. Everyone up the hillsides! Shelter in the tombs. We'll keep them all safe."

** ** **

Ptahemhat slowed to a walk and lowered his head, his hand pressed to his side. He had covered the distance from the path to the Vizier's Palace at a run, broken briefly to catch his breath and quell the stitch that threatened to clutch his side.

A river of humanity of all stations moved before him, channeling toward a high gateway west of him. He stepped into the current moved into the flow of people before him, channeling toward the Vizier's palace.

The slower pace let him catch his breath. Once in sight of the gate he moved briskly forward to one of the guards flanking the tall doors.

The man, a gold-adorned veteran, straightened and watched him approach.

Ptahemhat stopped before him. "I must speak with Count Intef at once!"

The guard lifted his brows. "Do you have a ring?"

Ptahemhat drew the ring from his finger and offered it across his palm.

The man inspected it, bowed. "Follow me."

** ** **

Henetre frowned around at the people clustered at the summit of the cemetery. The pyramid-shaped chapel roofs cast deep shadows that cut the near-noon heat. The breeze that had blessed them for the past weeks would eventually strengthen into the Khamsin, but for now it provided coolness and comfort.

A child whimpered near her. She caught its eye and smiled. "Don't cry. All will be well, and we will have a festival tomorrow to celebrate."

The plume of dust was closer now. "All will be fine," she said, and closed her eyes.

** ** **

"Is everyone safe?" Djedi called. "Good! Hold your places! We'll hit their..."

"Vanguard," Seti supplied quietly.

[241]

"Vanguard!" Djedi called. "It should shock them and give us time to fall back to Khatef's group."

"Tell them not to go forward," Seti said quietly from behind his sheltering rock. "If they run into the force they will be lost. The idea is to strike and then fall back, leaving them confused. We don't want them to get sight of us."

Djedi nodded.

The sounds were getting closer. Seti took an arrow from the pile at his feet, nocked it, and wished Nebamun were at his shoulder. But at least he could convince them that they were facing archers of a sort...

** ** **

Count Intef handed the ring back. "We have met before," he said.

"Yes, Excellency."

"Ptahemhat, son of Kaya, son of Kenamun." Intef pushed to his feet and strode down the main aisle of the room. "Come with me," he said at the door. "You have no doubt run a league, but you will be able to return in comfort, in a chariot."

Ptahemhat followed him into the enclosed courtyard. A word from Intef sent one guard running. Chariots and soldiers were pouring into the enclosure within a few heartbeats.

Ptahemhat stared at the gold-topped standards.

"The Division of Amun is ready to march," Intef said. "Now go and kill all those intruders!" He watched as Ptahemhat bowed to him and stepped into a chariot. The force turned and swept from the enclosure.

LIX

A volley of arrows poured into the attackers as they rounded the bend in the path, as swiftly as Seti could loose them. They had inflicted damage at the first ambush. Now they were at the more secure site Djedi had spoken of weeks before. Good footing, favorable terrain:

Seti dropped the question. Perhaps they would think that a squadron of archers was awaiting them.

"Here they come," said Djedi. "Get ready."

** ** **

One more time, Seti thought. The reinforcements from Thebes *had* to be coming. Here, at the approach to the village, they would be making their last stand, and if the army came— if it came—they would win.

Bright sun and dust coming down in streamers above the fight. Khatef went crashing to his knees, but a swing of his spear set his attackers stumbling, to be killed by his comrades.

Djedi was in the thick of the fighting, shouting encouragement, cursing at the attackers, giving orders. And as he watched, Seti saw the marauders trade looks and turn toward him.

"Eight to one!" Seti said through his teeth. "He's plucky, but he can't hold them off."

Khatef nodded. "Let's go," he said, and then raised his voice. "Hold fast!" he shouted. "We're coming!"

Djedi smiled and dodged a stroke. "Don't take too long!" he said, thrusting with his spear.

Seti sent an attacker reeling backward with a blow from the butt of his pike. A spear between his feet sent him slamming into the ground. The fall dazed him for a moment and he dropped his weapon. The point of a spear was at his throat; he looked along the shaft toward his captor, a pale-eyed bearded man who had the look of chieftain.

The man laughed as he withdrew the spear for the death stroke. He crashed to the ground as Seti hooked his foot about the man's ankle and pulled it back sharply.

Ye gods! Seti thought rolling to the side to dodge another spear thrust, *how many ARE there?* He kicked at the man's legs and was halfway to his feet when he saw the glint of a spear point coming down out of the sun straight toward his heart. There was no room to dodge it.

[243]

Djedi yelled his name.

The sound halted all movement. The fighters raised their heads.

The spear was descending slowly through the streamers of sunlit dust, inexorable, unavoidable. There was no room to move. Seti fixed his gaze on the face of his attacker with a scornful smile.

A shadow fell across him. "Draw your last breath, you bastard!" Djedi said through his teeth. He had found Seti's pike and was swinging it desperately. He knocked the spear aside, giving Seti a chance to recoil backward.

The spear raised again...

"*Djedi!*" Seti shouted, scrambling to his feet as the spear drove into Djedi's side. "*No!*"

**   **   ****

The General drew his horses to a halt. "I can hear shouting!" He turned to Ptahemhat, beside him. "Were they attacking the village?"

Ptahemhat frowned over his shoulder at the river of soldiers behind him. Spears shifted in the sun, the stamp of hooves. He turned to the General. "Not when I was sent to Count Intef. They were coming fast and furious."

"They're near the town itself by the sound." The General scowled along the path. "We need to go on the double. What is the best approach, Commander?"

"This way, My Lord. It leads straight to the main approach. The village is walled: a low wall, but there nonetheless."

The General nodded. "We will bottle them, then." He gathered the reins. "Who am I to report to?"

"You will know him when you see him, General."

**   **   ****

Seti fell to his knees beside Djedi as the tide of the fight swept past him. "Get the physician over here!" he shouted, gathering him. "Now!" He looked down at Djedi. "Does it hurt badly, lad??"

"It's not so bad..." Djedi said as Master Abeni dropped to his knees beside him. "But I am thirsty..."

Someone brought a skin of water. Seti poured some in his hands and held it to Djedi's lips. Abeni frowned at him and bent over the spear.

"Can we pull it out?" Djedi asked, his eyes closed. "It hurts..."

[244]

Abeni sat back on his heels. He lifted his eyes to Seti and shook his head.

Seti closed his eyes for a moment and then opened them. "Djedi," he said. "My son..."

Djedi opened his eyes.

"It is a death wound," Seti said. "There is no way to heal you. When the spear is withdrawn it will take your life with it."

Djedi tried to smile. "I think my tomorrows are running out." he said.

"We still have now," Seti said.

**   **   **

"I see them!" said General Mentemhat. "Forward!"

The force streamed toward the attackers.

**   **   **

Djedi closed his eyes and turned his cheek against Seti's shoulder. "Well, I tried..."

"You succeeded," Seti said. "The attackers are on the run, thanks to your work. Count Intef received an order from His Majesty two days ago, establishing a garrison at Deir el Medineh. By this order you, Djedi son of Kharu, son of Nebnefer, are Commander of Two Hundred, and governing the garrison. You were to work with Captain Kasaya of the Medjay."

Seti pulled the pendant over his head. "You were also awarded the Gold of Honor. Pharaoh ordered it two days ago. I will give you mine, until it comes."

"A garrison..." Djedi said. He was smiling. "You were right."

"Yes," Seti said gently. "All through your work."

Djedi closed his eyes. His breathing was shallower.

Seti shifted him more comfortably. "How are you, son?" he asked.

"I am tired," Djedi said. "I am still thirsty." He lifted his head to sip from the cup that Abeni held to his lips, then lay back with a sigh. "You weren't hurt?" he asked.

"No," Seti said. "You saved my life."

Djedi's hand tightened in Seti's.

"And through your actions, you probably saved this village and, through them, Thebes itself, from danger." He carefully set the gold of honor over Djedi's head and centered it. "Can you see it, son?" he asked.

[245]

Djedi was drifting into incoherence. He opened his eyes, focused on the gold. "Thank you," he said. "Just like yours..."

"You earned it," Seti said.

Djedi smiled sleepily. "Father...?"

Seti gathered him closer, thinking of another death even as a cool, aware corner of his mind paused to listen to the rattle and thrum of wheels, the quickened stamp of approaching feet. "I am here, child." He thought of Nakhtamun, held by another as he died. "I will be your father. I won't leave you until you leave me."

Djedi tightened his hold on Seti's hand. "You never would..." He smiled sleepily, raised his hand to Seti's face to brush at the tears that were running down his cheeks. "Don't worry about me," he said. "I will be all right." And then, consciousness gone, he lay as limp as a sleeping child.

**   **   **

Ptahemhat loomed out of the sun. "The force from Count Intef is here," he said.

Seti raised his head and saw the soldiers ranged behind Ptahemhat-archers, chariots, all that he had ordered. Their commander-the man looked familiar to him-was on one knee before him.

Men-Maat-Re Seti Merneptah shifted Djedi in his arms and resumed the rule of Egypt with a silent sigh. "You made good time," he said. "Well done." He nodded to the commander. "They were part of a larger force, General. There are more out there."

The man rose and brought his fist to his shoulder.

"Find them all," said Seti. "Cut them off from their camp and drive them into the river. Take no prisoners. You have your division with you? Excellent. Their encampment will be found and destroyed. Better to take too many men than not enough."

"...by your command," the man said.

His name came to Seti. "Thank you, Mentemhat," he said. "Go with the gods."

The soldiers straightened at a shouted command. Seti looked down at Djedi as they moved away. He gathered him closer. *Oh, Djedi.*

"It is time, Abeni," he said. "Draw out the spear. It won't hurt him. He's unconscious now."

"*Wait!*" The words were urgent, as peremptory as the hand that appeared, gripping the shaft of the spear above his.

[246]

Seti looked up.

One of the soldiers had dropped to his knees before him. An older man, wearing the Gold of Honor, with a kit at his shoulder. He bent over Djedi. "Wait," he said again. "Let me examine him!"

Seti's eyes widened.

The man smiled up at him. "Please: let me look at him first."

LX

Kenamun tapped at Seti's door and then entered the room. "I have breakfast for you." He offered a bowl of gruel.

Seti had been gazing before him, his eyes fixed on the middle distance. He took the bowl from Kenamun and frowned at it.

"Try to eat a little," Kenamun said.

Seti nodded and lifted the spoon to his lips. After his initial hesitation he found that he was shaking with hunger. He dug in.

Kenamun sat silently while he ate. He smiled when Seti put the bowl aside and offered a cup. "Drink this," he said. "It's warmed wine and water, with a touch of honey."

Seti took the cup with a wry smile, sipped, and then looked at it with raised eyebrows. "This is good..."

"It was a difficult day yesterday," Kenamun said. "Your actions saved the village. You might as well hear it from me. If you had not happened along as you did, and taken the steps that you did, we would all have been killed."

"There are many things that lead to a result," Seti said. "Djedi was the one who set things in motion. I went where I was meant to go..."

"Perhaps," Kenamun said, pouring more wine and adding water. "It is best to be grateful and continue as we are." His smile warmed. "I bring a message from Kamose: General Mentemhat's surgeon."

Seti set his cup down.

"It is good news. The spear did not go in as deeply as he had feared. It did some damage. Those were his words. But he says that the way Djedi was moving deflected the force of the blow. It nicked his lung, from what he could see, and injured one of the vessels, but leaving the point in the wound gave them time to slow and then stop the bleeding. Nothing vital was badly damaged. The worst was the pain and the loss of blood. He says that with the blessing of the gods, and his best efforts, which he promises, the young man should recover with a scar that the ladies will love."

Seti blinked at a mental image of Djedi dropping his kilt to display a scar. "Did he say that?" he demanded.

"No," said Kenamun. "I thought you needed the chuckle. You don't seem so wan now. Drink some more."

Seti obeyed and then set the cup down. "Does everyone know about me?"

Kenamun sat back and steepled his fingers together. "People here know you aren't exactly what you seem to be. I knew-but then I had recognized you, as I told you that night." He met Seti's gaze squarely. "I told no one."

"And no one said a thing to me."

Kenamun smiled. "They love you," he said. "This is an intuitive group: you were known to be...to be mourning someone you lost. A child, they thought since you love them. They closed ranks to protect you. I think they believe that you're a high-ranking General."

Seti took another sip of wine. "I suppose I owe you an explanation."

"You owe me nothing."

"You know it all, already," Seti said. "You saw me at my son's tomb. I had been taken unawares by his death. I learned it late and unexpectedly. Soldiers are killed. I know it. I just forgot, I guess. And death hurts."

He looked up at Kenamun. "I didn't even know that my son was far to the north in Palestine. I received the sort of tidings that fathers and mothers fear to receive. And I was not ready."

Kenamun stretched out his hand. "I know," he said. "How can you prepare for such a thing, no matter who you are?"

Seti shook his head. "It's time to be up and doing," he said. "The garrison will be put in place before I leave. The troops were to arrive within the next two days. I thought they could be quartered here until suitable housing was constructed. I suspect the word will be spreading that Deir el Medineh is not such an easy mark. That was Djedi's work."

He frowned. "I have met many heroes in my life. He is in the front rank, I think." He eyed the nearly empty bowl of gruel and lifted it again. "I suspect he knew, too."

Kenamun smiled. "You did not try to disguise yourself; you know. You merely appeared here and asked if there was a place for you. There was. There always will be." He added another heaping spoonful to the gruel in the bowl. "Have some more."

Seti looked down at his spoon and then raised it to his lips.

"He may well recover," Kenamun mused. "Physicians never give good news without equivocating. Much can happen, but I suspect Djedi will be up and about and up for

[249]

any mischief that suits him." He eyed Seti's growing smile. "I long had the feeling that he would leave this village and make his way along other paths, for all that he actually was a gifted painter. Have you any plans for him?"

"I want him in my army," Seti said. "I will speak with him if the gods are kind. He must stay here for a time: I named him commander of the garrison, to be under the eye of General Mentemhat. He commands the Division of Amun, and he knows a good man. But in a year, perhaps two... He has a place with me if he wants it."

"Will you be leaving now?"

Seti closed his eyes.

"Not yet," he said. "Not until the garrison is in place."

LXI

Seti sat back and frowned at the document he had completed. "Intef is expecting this. He has the troops ready; it only remains to house them."

"I would have thought we'd have more time," Ptahemhat said.

"I did not. But we had less time even than I thought," Seti said. He folded the message, sealed it, and handed it to Ptahemhat. "Here."

"We were very fortunate," Ptahemhat said, taking the message from him.

Seti's mouth tipped into a wry smile. "I've been a soldier too long to believe in good fortune. You earn your successes. Now take this to Intef immediately."

"If he has any questions," Ptahemhat began.

"He won't." Seti eyed the sheet as he slid his brushes back into the palette. "There's a message for Djedi, as well. Go safely," he added.

Ptahemhat straightened. "Yes, Sire."

"Not so loud."

Ptahemhat hesitated. "So Intef will quarter troops here?"

Seti's expression grew grim. "He's about to receive a royal order," he said. "He'd better."

Ptahemhat stared.

Seti looked at him with a lift to his eyebrows. "Well?"

Ptahemhat looked down. "The girls will be falling all over themselves when the soldiers arrive."

"They usually do," Seti said.

"They do?"

"You were never in a garrison, Ptahu, were you?" Seti said. "I'd recommend it to any man who thinks he's ugly."

"That could cause some problems," Ptahemhat said.

Seti put his scribal kit aside and stretched his legs out before him. "It could also have a good effect," he remarked, closing his eyes.

Ptahemhat hesitated.

"This village is showing signs of inbreeding," Seti said. "Outcrossing tends to strengthen bloodlines. It will be a good thing for all." He looked Ptahemhat over, then lifted an eyebrow. "You're a well-set-up fellow," he said. "You would be doing them a kindness-keeping them from producing straw-haired, vacuous offspring in the years to come."

[251]

"Sire!"

Seti reached for the sheet of papyrus. "Don't be so prudish, Ptahu. Sebnit would understand, and your youngest was asking for a sister when I saw her last."

"Sire!"

"Sit down," he said, reaching for a brush. "I've something to add..."

Ptahemhat settled back on his heels, his hands folded before him.

Seti lifted an eyebrow and wrote, beneath his signature,

> *I charge you to select comely men of good disposition. Courage, honesty and humor-they will be well able to support association with this collection of singular characters. The billet should serve to everyone's benefit, now and in future.*

Ptahemhat stared.

Seti sat back and laughed as Ptahemhat collected himself, took the message, bowed and left. The laughter faded into a chuckle as he took up brush and papyrus again. Outcrossing-

The brush fell from his fingers and landed on his lap in a splash of black ink. "Nefer," he said. And sat back, thinking furiously, his brush between his fingers.

He reached for another sheet of papyrus and began to write.

** ** **

"'Well-favored men of good character'," Intef repeated pensively. He eyed Ptahemhat with a lifted eyebrow. "Did he say he was going to post you with this garrison?"

"Excellency!"

LXII

Seti paused, his eyes traveling up the steep wall of rock. This was the place, weeks before, where he stood and gazed, appalled, at the marks of his son's tomb. He could catch an echo of that moment of stunned agony, but it was as faded as old ink on discolored papyrus.

He faced the cliffs hearing in his mind a quiet voice from that terrible day:

What is here is what we put here. ...Those whose bodies are buried here have no need of those things. They are not sleeping in those tombs. They have moved beyond this world into the Land of the West.

He settled cross-legged, sat back against the rock and looked up at the face of the cliff, remembering the darkness of the tomb, the jumble leaping into existence by the light of a flaring torch. In his mind he saw his son's statue, seated upright, the pensive, slightly sad expression, all in darkness...

He closed his eyes for a moment, willing himself to face the image and consider it.

What was in there? Furniture, food, equipment, a statue, a coffin...a...body, no longer used.

No longer used.

Then why were they there?

Because we need to put them there, he thought to himself. *Because we need to be able to say, 'I did this for him because I loved him so much. I wanted him to have the best that I could bring, even though I know... Though I know that the Blest are happy in the land of the Blest'.*

Gazing up the cliff face with the eyes of his heart he could almost see the interior of the tomb blaze into light, and through the rock he could see his son-in the living, blessed flesh of the West-rising up through the boundaries of the tomb, more solid than the stone, brighter than the starlight... He saw him fade, as though he had stepped into another room.

Gone from that space, but not departed from being... Could it be? It was hard to grasp, hard to imagine, but he stared, dazzled, at the star-filled sky, working it through. Not departed from being, but nevertheless gone, never again to be met, smiled at, embraced, in this life. It was a farewell, and painful for all its reassuring nature. He closed his eyes, half-blinded by the stars and feeling, almost, as though they were running down his face like tears.

Warmth beside him, the scent of lotus. Nefer.

"Sa-Ramses?"

"Nefer," he said, his eyes still full of stars. "You came. I planned to speak with you tomorrow."

He could feel her hesitation. "I received your message this afternoon," she said. "And I saw you leave. I was concerned."

He looked at her, remembering. "About me?" he asked. "But why?"

"I told you," she said. "I love you..." She paused, her hand almost touching his face, but hesitating just short of the contact. "Has the path reached its end?" she asked.

He smiled at the cliffs. "It has," he said. He looked at her profile, silver in the starlight that flashed from her eyes as she turned toward him. A slight, indrawn breath... The gentle touch of her hand against his face.

"Oh, my dear," she said.

His hand rose to cover hers. "He is not here," he said. "Not locked away in the darkness. That thought had...troubled me, once." He looked down again. "But he isn't near me any longer."

She said carefully, "Is it another death, then?"

He considered. "No," he said at last. "In this life, apart from death, loved ones leave, never to be seen again. Or not in years..." He looked over at her. "I know you understand me."

"I do," she said.

"It is sad for those of us left behind," he said. "The black-eyed little boy who ran along the river and wanted to drive my horses is no more even though the man that boy grew into is still walking the earth."

"There are compensations for that," Nefer said.

"So I have seen," he said. "And yet, much though I love the man that little boy became, and the children that he brought, in his turn, to sit on my knees, I miss the little boy, and wish I could hold him on my lap and listen with my knowledge that the precious moments will soon be gone forever."

A wind rose, feathering cold and crisp along his cheekbones. He rose and held out his hand to her. "It is late," he said. "And there may well be things to fear along this path if we linger."

She took his hand and let him pull her to her feet. Facing him, she looked up at him. "Is your heart whole now?" she said.

He took her hand between his. "It will be. Soon. It is nearly time for me to leave..." He hesitated. "Nefer."

She looked up at him.

"You gave me love and comfort when I was lost. I accepted it and returned it wholeheartedly. We must part soon, I know. But if there is a child..."

She met his gaze.

"I will acknowledge it," he said. "And I will provide for it and for you and your family."

She frowned and looked away for a moment. "I have not asked for that."

He released her hand. "I must, Nefer," he said. "No man should do otherwise." His gaze sharpened as she hesitated. "I promise I can support my children."

Her eyes met his, and she nodded. "I will accept it," she said. "If there is a child I will teach it to honor its father."

"Will it know that it came about through love and kindness, not through a moment's passion?"

She met his gaze for a long moment and then nodded. "I will tell the child when it is time," she said. "I promise you."

He unknotted the cord of the necklace and drew it from inside his tunic. "This is the first Necklace of Honor that I won when I was younger. Please: take it and keep it as a token of my promise."

She stared at it, feeling its weight, the warmth of the gold. "The first?" she said. "Was there more?"

"There was," he said. "Horemheb was a fighting King, and I served under him. Listen to me: I am giving this to you. It will speak for me if I am somehow not able to. And if you or those you love are ever in need it can be broken apart and sold. Will you take it?"

She lifted the necklace in her hands. It was heavy, the three cylindrical strands draping over her fingers. She raised her eyes to his with the shadow of a frown. "Who are you?" she asked. She saw the shift in his expression. "No. What you tell me won't change the way I feel about you. But-who *are* you?"

He smiled ruefully. "I was named Seti for my grandfather," he said. "My father's name was Ramesses."

"Sa-Ramses..." she said, half to herself.

"I was a soldier for many years. And I am a scribe."

"And you are King now," she said.

He lowered his head. "I am sorry, Nefer," he said. "I couldn't…" He paused. "I never meant—"

She frowned at the necklace and then at him. "'Never meant' what?" she asked. "Never meant to behave like the man that you are and make me love you because of your kindness and courage? Never meant to be a friend to me-and a friend and protector to this town? There has never been any shame attached to you," she said. "Or to the love I have felt for you. Never."

He looked away.

"My dear! I do believe I've embarrassed you."

"I have known worse embarrassment than hearing a beautiful woman tell me that she loves me."

She began to smile. "Were there other women?"

"Before my wife? Perhaps one. I was very young when we wed. Only you, afterward. Will you take the necklace?"

She smiled up at him. "I will take it," she said. "And I tell you now that I will always love you, whatever the future brings, and think of you with contentment over the years." Her eyes were wide in the night. "I will miss you."

"I will miss you, as well, 'Beautiful one'," he said.

She raised her hand to stroke through his hair as the setting sun painted the old hills and valleys rose and gold below the stars. "But you are not leaving yet," she said as she drew his face down to hers.

"No," he said with an answering smile as he gathered her closer. "Not just yet."

LXIII

Nefer straightened and raised her head in the morning breeze. *Another cooler day*, she thought. *A blessing, not to have to worry about searing heat during a time of change.* Her husband's tomb lay before her; she had brought some delicacies from the morning's meal as offerings for him and their little daughter. She thought of her words to His Majes— *No*, she thought, *to Sa-Ramses.* She had told him what she had realized for herself: *what we put in a loved one's tomb is for ourselves. The Blest are happy in the Land of the Blest. It is for our own comfort that we remind ourselves how much we loved.*

How much we love. She smiled down on the sweets on the offering slab. *You have sweetness-and my love, always-where you are. And I will see you in good time. But time passes and I must pass on, as well.*

The blare of a trumpet split the morning silence. Sa-Ramses had assembled the corps of guards the day after the battle and commanded that a watchman be positioned on the heights. Her smile widened. That is how she had heard it described. In actual fact, from what her uncle had told her, he had nodded to the men, praised them for their courage of the day before, and then suggested mildly that until the garrison was established and working with them under Djedi's command, they should position a sentry on the heights and provide him with a trumpet to sound an alert.

This had generated a great deal of discussion among the men, Kenamun had said. A trumpet? Why so? Couldn't they just yell?

Her grandmother had lifted her eyebrows. "They are still giving the man back-talk!"

"So it would appear," Kenamun said.

"Knowing who he is!"

Kenamun's frown had grown pensive. "He hasn't actually said who he is, Henetre."

Henetre's brows had drawn together in a frown. "They have eyes. They are *supposed* to have brains! What more did they need to be shown in order to draw a conclusion for their feeble selves? Has the man been so long with us and they so unobservant? That General going to his knees before him! What more do they need to know?"

"His rank, perhaps," Kenamun had murmured.

"What of it? All they need to know is that the man-the gods bless his Ka!-outranks them!" Her tone had altered. "I am glad to hear the good news about Djedi. That young man is a hero! And Sa-Ramses, as well. I thought to bring him some roast goose and perhaps some good wine."

Kenamun had sat back. "He would like that," he had said. "He would like it even better if he were to eat it sitting down with his friends in your house this evening, Sister."

Nefer had enjoyed the supper, which had been free of the shadows of fear and regret. Now, savoring the breeze as she hurried to the hillside path, she admitted that he was right.

The trumpet rang out again. She could hear the sounds of the village gathering. As she made the descent to the main path, she could see movement in the distance-a glitter of sunlight on metal. Nebet was standing on her doorstep, watching.

"Could you see anything, Nefer?"

Nefer shook her head. "Sun on metal, approaching."

Nebet's eyes dilated. "Weapons?"

"Possibly. They would be ours however, after the rout two days ago."

Nebet considered and then smiled.

People were streaming along the main passage, channeling toward the gate and, beyond it, the temple. She saw Khatef, his pike on his shoulder, frowning.

"I hear horses," Nefer said.

Khatef looked at her. "Horses? They aren't attackers, then."

Nothing more was said until they arrived at the temple's small courtyard. A squad of Medjay archers had drawn up at attention. Three chariots were waiting, the morning breeze ruffling the feathers dancing above the horses' bridles. The gold-topped Standard of Amun glinted in the morning sun.

"The Division of Amun," Nefer said to herself. She looked up along the street.

"He's coming," Nebet said beside her. "He's coming in order to leave."

His Majesty strode down the street, followed by two guardsmen. He wore the Gold of Honor around his neck, wrist– and armlets, a circlet of gold about his headcloth. She could see the faint curve of a smile. *He is preoccupied,* she thought.

The townsfolk began to kneel.

His Majesty stopped. "You have feet," he said. "From now on, stand on them when you face me."

Sidelong glances. Henetre stood and smiled at him.

"Very good," Pharaoh said. "And now I must leave you. I thank you for your courage and your loyalty. You have gladdened my heart and given great service to this land. I leave you with regret."

A nod. He stepped into the center chariot, nodded to his driver. The squadron turned and left the courtyard at a smart trot, the Medjay following them at a lope.

Nefer looked down at her hands.

"Well, that is that," Henetre said. "I will miss him..."

**   **   **

Khatef frowned down across the valley toward the river the next afternoon. He could see the activity there, where the architects sent by His Majesty were blocking out the structure that would house the Deir el Medineh garrison. Added to a small temple to Amun, it would be built like a Syrian Migdol fortress, they had said. Reporting to the army, but subordinate to the village. It was a good thing, he thought. Djedi would approve. By all reports he was recovering well.

The warning trumpet blared in the afternoon stillness. Khatef swore and made his way to the gate. "All right," he sighed. "What is it?"

The guard, wide-eyed in the sun, said, "We have a... a visitor." He nodded to the man standing quietly beyond him. Tall, aging, with white-streaked hair-

Khatef began to kneel.

The man stopped him with a hand under his elbow. "My name is Sa-Ramses," he said with a smile as Khatef straightened. "I was here until some time ago. I... ask to return and greet my friends and give them my thanks."

Khatef realized that he had been gripping the man's shoulders, beaming.

Seti's eyes moved to the stream of townsfolk coming toward them, narrowed in a smile as he saw Kenamun and Nefer.

They were around him now, crying half-embarrassed greetings, questions.

"I could not sail for Memphis without taking the proper leave owed by one who has been made not only a guest but a friend and a brother. May I come in?"

[259]

LXIV

Memphis

Nebamun propped the tip of the bow against his instep, bent the shaft, and slipped the sinew string from its notch. He frowned and eyed the string. It was getting worn, time to use another. The last time a broken bowstring had raised a welt on his forearm was more than a decade ago. He didn't care to have it happen again at his age. He knotted the bowstring, pulling the knot tight so that no one else would want to use it. The breeze rose; he raised his head and closed his eyes, tasting the scent of the flatlands beyond the irrigated land, the flowers from the temple gardens. His lines had fallen into pleasant ways, all unexpectedly all those years ago...

He spared a thought for himself at twenty-five years of age, his life, as he thought it, all in ruins around his feet. If he had known then what he knew now, looking back, he might have smiled. Might have.

But the past, though interesting, was past and he had some concerns that needed to be addressed. Ptahemhat had left for Thebes some time ago. Surely he would have had occasion to write a report and send it by royal courier! Had something gone wrong? He wished, not for the first time, that The Two Lands were rather less long and thin. A nice, compact parcel of land, perhaps. Rather like Hatti...

His private apartments lay to the right. He swung the door open and entered. He was tired, no visitors this afternoon. He closed the door behind him, set his bow against the wall, and indulged in a luxuriant stretch.

"You make me feel old." The words came through the hint of a chuckle.

Nebamun turned at the sound of the voice, his heart pounding.

Seti was reclining at his relaxed ease in one of the low chairs, watching the breeze tossing the roses through the window. A warm smile was brightening his face.

The quiver clattered to the floor, sending arrows rolling underfoot. *"You!"*

Seti rose and retrieved the scattered arrows. "In the flesh, Father," he said sliding them back into the quiver and offering it to Nebamun.

The High Priest took a step backward. "You were *supposed* to go somewhere private-one of your estates, one of the temples. You were to rest and recover-I did not tell you to drop off the face of the earth and leave your nearest and dearest open to suspicion of murder!" He eyed Seti's expression. "You don't believe me?"

Seti put the quiver on a low table nearby. "Oh, come now. You are exaggerating. Your messages never—"

"Messages get intercepted!"

"You could have told me to come back. I gave you authority to do so."

Nebamun's rigidity eased. "I would never be so cruel," he said. "What were you doing?"

"I was fighting marauding Libyans."

"*What?* You weren't supposed to go into combat!"

Seti smiled down at him. "You could have ordered me to fling myself into the Nile," he suggested.

"Don't try me too far! You would have led a revolt." Nebamun began to smile. "And you would have assembled an overwhelming following and defeated me soundly."

"I would never fight against you, Nebamun."

"You wouldn't have to. You're back. And you are smiling. When did you arrive? I had no word from Ptahu."

"I forbade it. Things were happening quickly, and I knew that I would be leaving in short order. I wanted to come to you myself. It was time. And here I am."

"And are you heart-whole?" Nebamun asked.

"As much as anyone can be." He spoke more quietly. "How can I thank you enough for all you have done for me and mine through this time?"

"I need no thanks," Nebamun said. "You had me worried."

"You hid it well," Seti said drily. "And I might have known that you had the brains and the reach to hamstring me from Memphis when I was in Thebes..."

"Seti—"

He turned.

"Look at me." Nebamun frowned up at him and suddenly smiled even as he swore and brushed at his eyes. "Well, you're back. Have you spoken with Ramesses?"

"I came to you first. I'll find him now."

Nebamun nodded. He looked up a moment later as Seti's hands settled on his shoulders. "What is it?"

[261]

Seti pulled him into a quick embrace. "Thank you, Father," he said. He straightened. "Now where is that son of mine?"

** ** **

Ramesses settled his third son on his lap and smiled at his wife. The garden caught the afternoon breeze, now heavy with the scent of roses. Hori and Rai were at the pond again, playing with their boats and squabbling over scraps of papyrus for their sails.

Nefertari, his wife, smiled as Rai looked up, and blew him a kiss. "His mother misses him," she said.

"She will be out of her confinement soon," Ramesses replied, settling the baby against his shoulder. He smiled at the children, laughed at Hori's attempts to rig the boat.

Such a beautiful afternoon, he thought. *If it could last forever...*

Hori looked up at him, as though he had read his thoughts. The black eyes widened. Hori threw the boat aside, scrambled to his feet, and tore past across the garden to launch himself into his grandfather's arms.

As Ramesses turned to watch, Seti gathered the boy and held him long enough to bury his face against his hair. His eyes were bright as he drew away.

Hori snuggled closer for a moment. "Where were you?" he demanded. "You were gone forever!"

"I was traveling." Seti pushed to his feet with Hori in his arms as Ramesses and Nefertari hurried toward him. "It was a long journey." He kissed Hori and set him on the ground and smiled at Nefertari. "You have given me a fine grandson, Daughter."

Ramesses stopped before his father, scanning him, tallying the changes.

Seti's smile dimmed a little. "I had to go, Sesse," he said "Your brother..."

Ramesses took the step between them, gripped his father's hands. "I know. I know." He bent to lift Rai in his arms. "I am so glad to see you back here. I was worried."

Seti eyed him with a touch of irony. "Even after Nebamun sent a bodyguard?"

"He sent a bodyguard? He never told me!"

"Are you serious?"

"I am. ...Where were you?"

"I was serving as a scribe in the workmen's village near the necropolis at Thebes. I would have thought you knew."

[262]

"I didn't," Ramesses said, holding out his hand to Rai.

"What?"

Ramesses lifted his younger son in his arms. "I promised."

"Of course..." Seti said. "I had forgotten." He cleared his throat. "We have plans to make. I've a fine son to acknowledge formally as Crown Prince. And we both have a death to avenge."

Epilogue
Canaan Three Months Later

"This is the fortress, Sire," Senwadjet said.

Seti frowned at the sun-bleached stones, framed by mountains rising almost purple to either side.

Ramesses drew up beside them. "Is it abandoned now?"

Senwadjet bowed. "I made certain of it at the time, Highness," he said. "And I sent a corps of archers here two nights ago and cleared it again. People had been staying here once more. Nomads..."

"Armed?" Seti asked.

"Yes. Although in this area arms are necessary."

"Armed but not an army," Seti mused. "As before?"

"Exactly, Sire."

"I will look inside," Ramesses said.

Seti's brows drew together fractionally, but he nodded. "You are in command, Sesse," he said, and watched as Ramesses shook his reins and drove toward the fortress.

The wind had raised, bringing the scent of far-off forests, of grasslands in the sun. He closed his eyes and turned his face to it, then watched his son vanishing into the stronghold-

Seti raised his head, suddenly grim. "Nakhtamun..."

Senwadjet turned toward him. "Sire?"

Seti frowned at the gatehouse. "My son..." He urged his team forward.

**   **   **

The stones of the fortress rose about Ramesses, dark in the mid-morning sun. Looking back through the gatehouse, he could see a rectangle of sun-washed space before him; the hills smoothing to grassy flatlands beyond it. His gaze moved to the doorways that opened to this courtyard, indented in the walls, room enough to hide an archer...

This is where it happened, he thought. He looked back at his horses, tethered to a protruding timber and then raised his eyes along the stretch of the walls: windows opened on the upper story, looking over the inner courtyard. He could see how the ambush had been laid-the archers positioned, waiting for the King to come.

He heard the rattle of approaching hooves.

**   **   **

Seti loosened the pressure on his horses' bits; they bent to the ease and increased their speed, the collected trot quickening to a canter until they were almost in the shadow of the tower. He drew up, then, looking at the gatehouse, picturing it stuccoed and painted, peopled with soldiers and traders—

His mouth tightened.

"Sire!" Senwadjet, beside him.

The horses jibbed at the bits, steadied, circled and plunged through the dark doorway.

** ** **

Ramesses saw the horses approaching at a smart trot. Seti's hands loosened the reins as the gateway's shadow fell across him.

Ramesses watched as his father swept through, his eyes moving to the places that an archer would hide, well inside the opening. The horses halted shaking their heads.

"Father!"

Seti stepped down from the chariot, frowning at a darker patch of sand and rocks.

Nakhti...

He dropped to his knees on the spot, raised his eyes to the darkness around him. *Nakhti...*

In his mind he could see, as though distant and somehow detached from him, the many, many comrades he had fought beside, who had gone before him through the portal to the West. Those he had held, all he had mourned and missed. *Here*, he thought, *this very spot.*

But it was only a patch of gravel and dust in a tumbledown fortress, notable to Seti as the place where his son stepped away from this world and into another place. There was nothing about it to keep him there or hold it precious.

Seti looked around at the various vantage points, picturing each holding its archer, swept a glance over his shoulder and shook his head at Ramesses. "I have seen it now," he said. "It has been a long journey from there to here. The ambush was well-enough laid, but the death was a gift." His smile tipped into irony. "We all make mistakes. Sometimes we survive them."

He looped the trailing reins on the chariot rail and smiled at Ramesses. "It has been a long journey for you, as well, Sesse. And how are you?"

"I am all the better for seeing you smile again."

[265]

Senwadjet had come into the courtyard and was standing silently.

Seti acknowledged his bow and turned back to Ramesses. "You are the commander of this foray. You have seen this place..."

"Yes, Father."

"And your orders?"

Ramesses looked around at the sturdy stonework, at his father standing where Nakhtamun had probably been that day...

"Destroy it," he said. "Raze it to the ground. This is a strategic spot, but there are better ones. We can build another fortress."

Afterword

Welcome to *The Memphis Cycle*. Or, more accurately, the second book of *The Memphis Cycle*. Perhaps you have read the others; maybe you have yet to discover them. Let me tell you about them.

In her preface to the reissue of *Rocannon's World*, Ursula le Guin commented that those who create worlds think that they do so with perfect freedom and no bounds. To the contrary, she comments, once a fact is stated in a story, it becomes as immutable as an engraving in stone. A writer certainly has the freedom to create, but then he is limited by the boundaries of the world he has created. It is not for the faint of heart.

A Killing Among the Dead was the first book that I wrote in what would become *The Memphis Cycle*. It is not included in this compilation. The story, which is the last in the cycle, takes place at the very end of the New Kingdom, just before the dynasties of Ramesses ran out and Egypt disintegrated into a collection of principalities. The action takes place in the village of Deir El Medineh, the town that housed the craftsmen who, for generations, constructed the tombs in the Theban Necropolis. A young man named Ramses is a major character. He reminds the hero of some of the carvings found in the mortuary temples of the early Ramesside kings. When he comments on it, a friend says this:

> *"Oh, an old story," Duwah said, summoning a smile. "Pharaoh Seti was grieved by the death of his oldest son, Nakhtamun, who should have succeeded him. He came to the Valley of the Kings to mourn. He met a maiden of the town, and she...eased his grief, shall I say? She married a village man soon after, though she and the king had had a summer together, and within six months of that marriage she had borne a fine, strong son who bore a striking resemblance to the son Seti had lost. Ramses is a direct descendant of that baby."*

The hero took shelter in Nakhtamun's tomb, and the tale progressed. I paid little attention to this passage after I finished

[267]

A Killing Among the Dead. I was busy writing other things, including *Pharaoh's Son,* the second book written in *The Memphis Cycle* and the third in the series. But when I went back to write *The City of Refuge,* I found myself considering the tale again. Seti mentions his children in that story, including his second child and oldest son, Nakhtamun.

As *The Memphis Cycle* began to develop, though, and the characters to step forward with their personalities and histories, I found myself remembering Seti's summer of mourning. And so *Mourningtide* came into existence in a shape far different from the way I had first envisioned it. I knew more about my characters, both historically and fictionally, and I could place the facts into their proper settings.

Since this is 'Historical fiction', I am listing some of the areas where I followed my own judgment or imagination. Seti and Ramesses were historical characters, as were Seti's daughters and his son-in-law, who had the same name as his wife. Their tomb was excavated near old Memphis. In my story line Seti's queen, Tuia, died a year before the action begins; history has shown that she survived her husband by many years and held a position of honor and influence in her son's court.

In this age of electronic research, where a question is quickly answered (accurately, we hope and pray) by an impromptu search engine query, it is hard to remember that our knowledge of history, especially the events of centuries ago, is sketchy at best. As an illustration, you will read variously that Seti died in his sixties, in his forties, just barely forty-five, no older than forty. He reigned ten years. No, fifteen years. No, twelve! The means of establishing these lengths of reign depend, apparently to a great degree, on the presence of a king's name on jugs of wine or beer. Because of the imprecise nature of our actual knowledge, if the premise of a story can be defended like a doctoral thesis, it is valid.

A hazard of writing historical fiction that follows a timeline is the departure of a beloved character. People grow old and die, and so do characters. Lord Nebamun, who made his debut in *The City of Refuge,* has one more book in which to make an appearance before he takes his final bow. *Kadesh* tells of his last involvement with the family of Seti and Ramesses. I will miss him. But he plays an important part in Mourningtide. I hope you enjoy it.

[268]

PREVIEW OF KADESH

Kadesh takes place sixteen years after Mourningtide and eighteen years before Pharaoh's Son. Ramesses is King of Egypt. Hori, now Crown Prince, is serving as an acolyte at Opet (the great temple of Amun at Thebes). Ramesses is determined to show himself to be as great a King as his father. He will retake the city of Kadesh, the gateway to the lands along the northern boundary of the Mediterranean.

He is resolved. It only remains to set matters in motion.

THE TEMPLE OF PTAH, MEMPHIS
THE PYLON OF SETI I
Reign of Ramesses the Great, Year 4

Pharaoh stepped down from his chair and nodded to the servants. "Wait here," he said.

The pylon reared before him. He paused before it, his eyes moving over the two colossal statues of his late father that flanked the gateway. Carved and painted stone, and yet they caught his father's smile. He looked up at the wall of stone, gazing at the carvings, seeing the reality in the eyes of his mind...

> *Screams rise in the hot glare, a tangled tumble of bodies. The rising wind carries the metallic tang of blood. Thudding footsteps, screams of panic...*
>
> *The King's dark gaze moves across the plain, rising through the warring masses that run **before** him, hands raised in pleading as they tumble away toward the walls of the embattled citadel, towering above the plain surrounding it.*
>
> *He smiles.*
>
> *His horses strain at the reins, rearing and dancing sideways. He brings them back, the light chariot tilting as it runs a tangle of bodies. His hands open; the horses leap forward, their plumed headdresses nodding in the wind, foam spattering from their bits.*
>
> *A large chariot is before him, clumsy and awkward, drawn by a heavier term. The driver strains his gaze over his shoulder, eyes dilated with terror. His fear is mirrored by the mass of his soldiers fleeing headlong before him.*
>
> *The King overtakes the chieftain. Leaning forward to grip the man's sword arm, he gives the killing blow with his own curved sword. Wails of dismay-a rain of arrows cuts down the fugitives. The chieftain's body thuds upon the ground and vanishes beneath the chariot's wheels.*
>
> *The King raises his eyes to the citadel, commanding the Orontes River, the gateway to*

the south, now out of Egyptian control. "Not for long," he says.

The masses on the ramparts scream in terror as he approaches, his army behind him. Dead fall from the battlements, wounded throw their hands over their heads, defenders struggle to reach the safety of the walls.

The King folds his arms upon the chariot rail and looks up at the battlements with a grim smile.

"Take it," he says.

**   **   **

The sounds receded. The light wind, cooling in the afternoon, carried the faint scent of incense. The sun glinted from specks of mica in the limestone reliefs.

Pharaoh raised his head and gazed up at the King. His eyes traveled over the tangle of bodies to the carved ramparts of the city.

Kadesh... He said the name silently. The gateway to the north... He closed his eyes and saw the King once more, easily controlling his horses, turning his dark gaze on his son...

"I will take back the city, Father," Pharaoh said. He turned his back on the southeast pylon gateway of the great temple of Ptah at Memphis and strode to his waiting chair.

If all goes according to schedule, ***KADESH*** *will be released in 2022.*

[271]

A NOTE FROM THE AUTHOR

Thank you for reading *Mourningtide.* If you liked it, would you consider leaving a review?

My Website

For more information on *The Memphis Cycle* and my other books, you can visit my website, www.dianawilderauthor.com.

My Newsletter

If you wish to sign up for my newsletter, you can do so I on my websitr. I never share email addresses, and you can always unsubscribe by clicking the link at the bottom of the page.

My Other Books

I enjoy history. People will never bore you. I have written about other times and locations.

The Orphan's Tale

The Orphan's Tale is a trilogy set in Paris of 1834.

Autumn is beautiful in 1834 Paris. But to Chief Inspector Paul Malet, raised in a prison by the greatest master criminal in French history the season's splendor is overlaid by a sense of gathering danger: something is afoot.

When Malet learns that Victoria, England's young Heiress Apparent, will be traveling to Paris at Christmas for a state visit, all becomes clear. Her assassination on French soil would shatter the accord between France and England. And war can be a profitable business for those criminals daring enough to mold events to suit their own purposes.

Malet, familiar with the workings of evil, embarks on a hunt. The safety of everything he loves is at stake, and he intends to fight this battle on ground of his own choosing.

Intentions are not necessarily accomplishments. The foes Malet is fighting are formidable. Adding to his problems is the fact that he has succeeded in angering an urchin named Larouche, who is determined to bring him down or, at least, ruin his hat.

The final complication is that Malet has fallen in love with a lady.

It is proving to be a busy season.

The Safeguard
(Georgia, 1864)

Lavinia Wheeler had watched as her world had been torn apart over the past three years When the Civil War comes to her doorstep, her generosity in opening her house as a hospital brings a change in her life far beyond any blessing she could have dreamed of or asked for.

Between dealing with the Yankee-hating townsfolk, her former slaves, a passel of wounded Yankees, a government that takes a dim view of people who aid the enemy, and a group of raiders that is ravaging the countryside, Lavinia isn't sure that she has time to care for herself, much less fall in love

Cavalry Sergeant Asa Sheppard has been given the assignment to guard Miss Wheeler's treasures as a way to let him rest from the wound and exhaustion that had sapped his will to live Dealing with the peppery little woman and facing the dangers beside her not only cures his wounds; it brings him love again.

THE SAFEGUARD is a story of hardship, hope and joy in the midst of strife and suffering.

You can read more about The Safeguard on my website.

www.ingramcontent.com/pod-product-compliance
Lightning Source LLC
Chambersburg PA
CBHW071250250626
47163CB00002B/399